THE
TROUBLE
WITH
HENRY

THE TROUBLE WITH HENRY

A SY-FREI ADVENTURE

Shelton Keys Dunning

OLDEWOLFF PRINTS
Ramona, California

Oldewolff Prints: a subsidiary of Oldewolff Enterprises
326 Oak St
Ramona, CA 92065
www.oldewolffenterprises.com

Publisher's Note: This is a work of fiction. Names, characters, places, and incidents are a product of the author's imagination. Locales and public names are sometimes used for atmospheric purposes. All trademarks are owned by their respective companies and are denoted by the use of proper capitalization of the company and/or brand. Any resemblance to actual people, living or dead, or to businesses, companies, events, institutions, or locales is completely coincidental.

Book Layout ©2013 BookDesignTemplates.com & wrangled by OWP
Cover Design ©2013 HumbleNations.com

Ordering Information:
Quantity sales. Special discounts are available on quantity purchases by corporations, associations, and others. For details, contact the "Special Sales Department" at the address above.

The Trouble with Henry/ Shelton Keys Dunning. -- 1st ed.
ISBN 978-0-9896698-8-7

For My Parents
Who are my Lighthouse
Thank You
For keeping me Safe through Storms
For your ever-vigilant Guidance
For Giving me the tools I need
So that I might Navigate Successfully
The Most Dangerous of Coastlines
And find a Sheltering Anchorage
Where I can Come Ashore

THIS BOOK would not exist if not for the valuable support of my good friend and editor **S.T. Lynn**, my brilliant mentor author **Cameron D. Garriepy,** or the love of the bestest, most perfectest husband ever in the history of marriages, my better-half **Ioan Kendrick**
AND
The collaborative efforts of the staff at Oldewolff Prints, and the wonderful advice of Joel Friedlander, The Book Designer

—WORDS CANNOT EXPRESS

CHAPTER I

Unfamiliar Territory

S IMONE FREITAG WAS FURIOUS.

The tires of her Veyron chirped as she pulled into the well-lit parking lot. She was too angry to care about how she parked, and only noted that she used four spaces in the process. The Wint-Mart loomed before her, the 'n' of the marquis flickering in ominous fashion. Slamming the door shut and cursing as she chipped a fingernail, she marched towards the entrance.

She stepped into the store at 2:30 in the morning, feeling misplaced. Attempting to get her bearings, she took time reading the banners suspended from the ceiling that directed clientele to various departments with vague black arrows. She never set foot in a Wint-Mart before, and it was unfamiliar territory.

Automotive. The banner instructed her to turn left. The department was located at the back of the store.

She walked as steady as she could, forcing deep breaths with each footfall. As she passed the stationery aisle, two teen-aged boys stopped sniffing the permanent markers and stared at her, mouths ajar. A group of employees, chasing each other with foam swords and escalating violence, collided into an end display of slow-cookers

1

at the sight of her. She turned at the sporting goods and caught a wolf-whistle from one of three fishermen sorting through jigs and bobbers. Simone scowled, feeling conspicuous in her three piece designer suit and Italian leather kitten heels, and quickened her pace. The last thing she wanted was to be the center of attention. She was on a mission.

Affixed to a support pole next to the car batteries, a small sign instructed her to push a bright, red button for service, which she did. Twice. An announcement reverberated through the loud speaker system. "Associate to automotive," said a tinny, disembodied male voice. A minute passed. She pushed the button and held it there, not caring how redundant the action was.

When *Hello My Name Is Ted* arrived, she released the button. "Finally," she pointed to the cells on the shelves. "What is the strongest battery you have?"

The acne-scarred lad just out of his teens scratched his head, stirring a shock of ginger hair. "Hiya, I gotta ask. I love your accent. Where are you from, originally?"

"None of your business." Anger often betrayed her foreign origins, but she didn't want to get into it with a complete stranger right then. "Let's focus, shall we? Strongest battery?"

"Okay, woman of mystery. I get it." He nodded, eager and stupid. "What car do you need the battery for?"

She cast him a sharp look. "It's not for a vehicle; it's for the hot-tub."

Hello-My-Name-Is-Ted blinked. "I. Don't. Understand."

"What's there to understand? My curling iron didn't produce enough voltage and I need the bastard dead." Deep within the confines of her leather purse, a cell phone rang. She cut the melody short with a flick of the blue-buttoned device attached to her ear. "Henry? If you're still in the hot-tub, this is your last warning."

Hello-My-Name-Is-Ted was still blinking.

"No, I'm on my way..." A ski-masked man appeared at the end of the aisle and pointed a double-barreled shotgun at them. Hello-My-Name-Is-Ted fainted. Simone heard a sickening crack when the poor lad's head hit the floor. "That's going to hurt in the morning. Henry, I have to hang up. I'm in the middle of a...crime." Her finger flicked the button astride her ear, terminating the call.

The gunman was short for a male, but he had overdeveloped forearms Simone associated with laborers who hoisted pulleys or shoveled dirt for a living. His right forearm sported a multi-colored parrot tattoo, making him easy to identify if he stood in a line-up. He licked his lips as his gaze slithered over her. "Well, well, well..."

"That's a deep subject for a criminal mastermind," she meant to insult him; irritated that she was interrupted while she plotted her own caper.

The insult missed him. "You can pass over your jewelry and your cell phone."

She stood defiant. "No."

"But," he stopped. "But I've got a gun."

"Mmm, no, you don't." She wagged her finger at him. "What you have is something I suspect you swiped from the toy aisle. Did you break off the orange safety indicator or did you luck out and find one already broken?"

The ski mask concealed his features but it couldn't hide the fear widening his eyes or the color draining from his lips. She didn't give him an opportunity to recover. She kicked the toy from his hands and rammed the palm of her curled fist up his nose.

His nose ruptured, spewing blood through his raised fingers like lava from a volcano. He crumpled, a bridge in an eight-point earthquake, and panted on his knees as he held what was left of his broken nose to his face.

She wasn't done. While he knelt, she wrenched a battery free from the shelf and slammed it against his skull. He collapsed and lay unmoving, his arms curled beneath his torso in an unnatural contortion. She used his flannel shirt to wipe his blood off her hand, sidestepping the lake of plasma expanding across the floor.

She stood between bodies. She heaved a frustrated sigh and delivered a swift kick to Hello-My-Name-Is-Ted's thigh. "Oy, you alive?"

The acne-scarred youth groaned but did not stir. His radio popped and hissed with static and voices speaking in frantic tones. The conversation was muffled beneath the associate's body but she caught enough of it to comprehend that employees and customers alike were being rounded up by more gunmen and corralled at the front of the store.

She rolled her eyes. *What else could go wrong this evening?* Fate conspired against her personally. Her cell phone rang again. "Henry, I swear to high heaven and all the souls in purgatory-"

"Baby, please let me explain..."

"No," her anger was unrelenting. "You get rid of that good-for-nothing whore or I get rid of you." She disconnected the call and took a deep breath. "I'm on the veranda at the vineyard in Chardonnay," she said. Closing her eyes, she took another, measured breath. "The breeze is warm and sunny. I can smell the grapes ripening on the hillside."

Her mood improved and her breathing calmed. Hearing foot-
steps ghost across the linoleum floor, she opened her eyes. Another
gunman rounded the corner of the battery aisle. This one was different from the last, however.

He didn't wear a ski mask.

He held a real shotgun.

He lowered the barrel when they made eye contact.

Law enforcement. "Hello, Officer."

He shifted the shotgun to one hand and pulled a badge from his
pocket with the other. "Special Agent Kirby. You okay, Ma'am?"

No stereotyped suit graced his frame nor sunglasses his eyes, yet
his badge clearly identified him as FBI. She recognized the agent as
part of the fishing trio she passed earlier. He wasn't the one who
whistled. She took a moment to smooth a non-existent wrinkle of
her designer skirt. "No, not really. But in the sense that I took out a
gunman that wasn't really a gunman, I guess I'm fine."

She followed Agent Kirby's gaze to the crumpled body she had
bludgeoned with the car battery. "Nice work," he said, the casual sort
of remark one uses to describe a sculpture on display at an amateur
art gallery. He stooped and pried Hello-My-Name-Is-Ted's eyes
open. "He's out cold."

Her interest captured, she watched him work with a fascination
she couldn't explain. His build was in direct opposition of the long,
lean type she was attracted to in men. Agent Kirby came across as
swarthy and dangerous. A bit of stubble encompassed his square
chin, completing the rough-hewed facial structure. The muscular
definition of his broad shoulders could be seen beneath the dark,
long-sleeved tee he sported. He breathed, and she noticed.

He moved with militarily-trained confidence to check on her victim. Kirby tugged at the ski-mask; his fingers probed the gunman's exposed neck.

"Is he dead?" Her question was that of false concern. Simone was still trying to determine what is was about the agent that captivated her so. What could she possibly be feeling about him? It wasn't lust since he wasn't her type. She couldn't be rebounding from her failing marriage so soon. She didn't believe in love at first sight. She *somethinged* him.

"Not dead, but you did a real number on him." Kirby checked ac-accessible pockets. "No ID."

Simone caught sight of the eight-point star tattooed on the man's neck. The ink wasn't as clean as the parrot, lines bleeding together in amateurish purple. *Is that what prison ink looks like? Is he an ex-con?* Her imagination ran wild with the story of a man convicted of possession with intent to sell a regulated chemical substance. She pulled her thoughts back, realizing her mind was wandering, a symptom of dropping blood-sugar. She would get cranky soon.

"I'm concerned his blood hasn't coagulated yet. He could be a hemophiliac. He has a pulse but it's weak." The agent's expression was hard to read.

"Can hemophiliacs get tattoos? Could it be he's on blood thinners?"

"Sure, it's possible."

Voices drifted across the space. Without a sound, Agent Kirby tucked the shotgun into his shoulder and signaled her to follow him. She slipped out of her noisy heels, a reluctant decision, for a silent and hasty retreat.

She ducked the way he did around corners, very aware of the cold linoleum and hoping to catch a run in the heel of her stockings so she wouldn't be worried about slipping. As they passed the garden supplies, she grabbed a spray-can of insect repellent and pilfered a cloth laundry bag out of the display hamper when they went up the next aisle. They darted through the shoe department when she shoved her handbag and suit-jacket into the laundry bag with the insecticide. By the time they reached the sewing counter, quiet canvas deck-shoes adorned her feet. Using the counter as cover, they took a moment to catch their breath.

Kirby looked her over, noting the not-so-subtle changes to her attire. "You're resourceful."

She paused to listen to the echo of frightened voices before whispering, "I wish we'd passed the women's department. I would have picked up a change of clothes."

His expression stoic, his eyes narrowed. "Who are you?"

"Me? Call me Sy. Everyone does."

"Well, then, Sy," he coughed into his shoulder, "Do you happen to remember anything from the time you entered the store that could help me judge what we're up against?" His neutral voice gave no indication if the question was meant as a rhetorical one.

"Good question. I left my unfaithful husband and his lover as they lay in the hot-tub just after eleven-ish and I drove from Chicago until I could get my head clear."

"I meant something relevant."

"This is relevant because it's the only reason I stopped in this good-for-nothing town...where the hell are we anyway?" She didn't wait for an answer. "Well it doesn't matter where I am. This store was the only one I found open and I thought I could get a car battery and hook it up to an outlet using a copper cable, then I could drop the battery in the hot-tub and electrocute the both of them. So I walked through the automatic door at what, two-thirty, two-thirty-five?"

He whistled, soft and low. "You drove all the way to Sandusky from Chicago in three and a half hours? Were you driving a jet plane?"

"Is that where we are?" She shrugged. "I took the Bugatti Veyron. I kept the turns under a hundred fifty or I'd've been here sooner than that."

Envy colored his expression. "If we get through this alive, can I touch the Veyron?"

"If we get through this alive, I'll let you drive it. Help me kill my husband and I'll let you keep it." She was only half-joking.

An unexplained noise caused him to frown. The terrified cries of the hostages appeared to be grating on his nerves also. "Never mind the two-timers won't be there when you get back."

"Can't you let a girl dream?"

"I'm a federal agent for the United States government," his response was dry, deadpanned. "We don't allow dreams."

"You're a funny agent." She rolled her eyes. "All joking aside, when I walked in, the automatic doors didn't close as quickly as they should have. Someone might've slipped in behind me, I don't know. I followed the banners to automotive, passing a couple prepubescent dunderheads getting high, a mother with a newborn searching through milk cartons, and an employee stalking his coworkers with a bb gun."

"That might be why the gun case was unlocked when I requisitioned this shotgun. Idiots."

"That would make sense, I suppose." She remembered turning down the last aisle before the car batteries. "The floor polisher cast me a rather dirty look when I cut him off. I didn't pay him much mind, but I think it's odd that he wore all black while the other employees had standard blue vests."

"That could be odd. It could be nothing."

"I thought you wanted my opinion," she frowned, while another bullied exchange emanated through the store. *I wish they'd shut up.* She continued her tale, relating what she could from Hello-My-Name-Is-Ted's radio. "I don't think you're up against intelligent life forms. It might interest you to know that only four of the thirty-six security cameras I encountered in this store are operating because they're the only ones with the little red lights on."

"Color me impressed." He offered a handshake which she accepted. "Your observations are pretty detailed. Do you have a photographic memory?"

She flashed him a sly smile, "Only when I have film in the camera."

"I'm glad there were still some exposures left then." He twitched as someone's scream reverberated through the store. He rocked to his feet, preparing to bolt. "I need to get everyone out as safely as possible."

"Hold on Hercules," Sy gripped his arm, tugging him back to the floor. "You're outnumbered and outgunned. Shouldn't you be contacting the local LEOs?"

That comment earned her a sideways glance. "Did you just say LEOs, as in law enforcement officers?"

"Yeah. I know. I watch too many crime shows on television."

"LEOs would help, but I'm more concerned about the welfare of the hostages." He glanced about, as if seeking inspiration or looking for a way out. His heavy sigh spoke volumes of his burden. "I, uh, I could use some help, if you're up to it."

"The situation is unfortunate, but I don't know those people and I owe them nothing. I could care less about their survival and I don't see why I'd have to pretend I care. It would make more sense for us to just walk out of the emergency exit and into the parking lot. The alarm will sound, the authorities will come. I can get back to murdering my husband and you can go back to Langley." She caught his look of disgust. "Hey, at least I'm honest. Shouldn't that count for something?"

A minute stretched between them. She felt his irritation crackling like electricity in desert air. "Of all the times to leave my phone in the truck. I don't suppose you'd be willing to help your fellow man and give a call to 911?"

Guilt gripped her heart. He was right, of course, but she didn't have time to explain why and how she disabled the device. "I...can't...actually, not from this phone. The...GPS doesn't work."

"Fine." Unmasked venom flashed in his face. Anger, frustration, helplessness charged his thoughts so apparent in his body language. His knuckles were white with his grip on the shotgun. His jaw clenched. He was pissed, not only at the situation, but also at her.

She was cranky, too. She needed to eat something. She needed a shot of whiskey. She needed a fool-proof and final way of ending her marriage. Before she could control her mouth, spiteful words tumbled off her tongue. "I'm not your typical princess, okay? I have baggage like everyone else. I put on my pants one leg at a time, like everyone else. I certainly don't suffer the illusion that my shit doesn't stink. I just refuse to pretend to care about someone because society dictates that I should. I'd like to see anyone in this store actually stop and help a homeless man instead of throw a handful of pennies at him." She stopped mid-rant, realizing it wasn't helping accomplish anything constructive. She decided to part company here and made for the exit. "I'll see you at my husband's funeral when you come arrest me for his death."

"Shh." He pivoted, his gun at the ready.

"Shh, what?" she abandoned her idyllic getaway.

"SHH. Listen."

"I don't hear anything."

"That's just it. It's too quiet."

Together, they listened to the consuming silence while an unsettling eternity ticked by.

CHAPTER II

Winging It

"**D**O YOU THINK THEY RELEASED EVERYBODY?" Kirby leaned and glanced around the edge of their cover.

Sy listened a moment longer to the quiet before dismissing the idea. "I'll bet you dollars to dough-nuts that the bad guys duct-taped the hostages mouths shut. The newborn could be sleeping through it all."

"I wish I had a distraction. Then maybe..."

The speaker system popped alive. A disembodied voice echoed over the squeal of feedback. "Would the nice young woman in the suite and the man named Kirby please join your respective parties at the front counter? We're waiting for you."

"They know your name but they still don't know mine," Sy said. "Maybe that could help?"

"Maybe. Let's just hope that my friends didn't reveal I'm a federal agent. It could get complicated." Concern reflected in his expression as he stared at the shotgun in his hands.

Her headset clicked in her ears, starling her. *Shit!* Henry's ring-tone, though muffled, fought free from the laundry back. She took a breath before answering. "Now what!"

"Baby, please. Let's work things out. There's no need for a divorce-"

"No way. I haven't time for a divorce, you piece-of-shit. If you knew what was good for you, you'd take yourself out of my misery and spare me the trouble." She kept her voice as controlled as possible, but Kirby brought a finger to his lips to shush her anyway.

The overhead speaker system squawked to life again. The Voice seemed to teeter at the edge of violence. "Once again, Kirby, for everybody's sakes, I expect you to come forward. Don't make me start killing people at random. And Lady, if you want your shoes back, you'd better not mess around either."

"Henry," she said to the headset, "I can't talk to you and listen to a bunch of criminals bark orders at the same time. If you want to help, call 911 and send them to the Wint-Mart just outside of Sandusky. If you don't want to help, that's okay too, but please just stop calling me."

Sy yanked the device from her ear and thrust it into her acquired laundry sack, fighting tears. She didn't have the time or energy to deal with her marriage crisis.

With a heavy sigh, Agent Kirby placed the shotgun down and rose from the counter. Sy pulled him back down. "What do you think you're doing?"

"I'm handing myself over." His voice was too calm for her liking. "You said it yourself. I'm outnumbered and outgunned. I don't have more than two shots and I was banking on the idea that they didn't know of our existence. You got a better plan, I'm open to it." His cold eyes betrayed his fears. He wore his mortality on his shoulders like a badge of office. If he could save one life, he'd sacrifice his, no hesitation.

"I suppose I don't really, at least not one that didn't require a trebuchet and about four months to plan." She played with the hem of her skirt, defeated. "But if you're going to do something stupid, I'll support you. I promised you could drive my car which means you need to be alive to do it."

His eyes narrowed, suspicious. "Are you reading my mind?"

"Strange. Usually the question is 'can you read my mind?'"

The Voice interrupted them. "Say hello to your friend, Matt."

Another voice swelled over the system, "God, Brian? He's going to put a bullet in my eye."

Sy reached across the counter and latched onto the microphone. She flipped the toggle to the green circle and she could hear feedback through the speakers. "Mr. Kirby is otherwise engaged. I believe he's in the john."

"Ah is that our lovely woman missing a pair of Prada shoes?"

"They're Ferragamo, Genius, and if you have them then they're not missing, are they." Her blood pressure spiked high and she was spitting angry. The last thing she was going to allow this idiot to do was demean her fashion sense.

Kirby wrestled the mic from her hands. "Are you crazy? You're going to get people killed!"

"Oh I doubt that. If their intent was to kill people, they'd have done that the moment they strolled in here. It's easier to rob a store if everyone is dead or indisposed, don't you think? They're after something or they're rank amateurs. Right now, I think they're both."

He keyed the mic, but his words seemed directed at her and carried more weight in stereo. "This is Kirby. I'm coming forward. I'm unarmed." He returned the handset to the counter and turned to leave.

Sy grabbed his arm. "Wait. You still want a distraction?"

A muscle twitched in his cheek, "What are you planning?"

Her idea was still an infant, hiding in the shadows of her mind. "I'm not entirely sure. Just stall them for as long as you can. Maybe offer to trade me to let the hostages go. Tell them my ransom is worth millions."

"What are you going to do?"

"I don't know yet, but I'm almost there."

"Almost only counts in horseshoes and hand-grenades." His laugh was humorless, short-lived. "I don't suppose you've grenades in your purse."

"No, but that's an excellent idea. I'll pick some up from sporting goods."

He squeezed her shoulder, flashing a thin smile, and began his trek to the front with a slow, measured pace. She watched him until he was out of her line of sight. Picking up his shotgun and her laundry sack, she slipped out from behind the sewing counter and raced to the sporting goods department.

She crashed through the saloon door to the cash wrap, ready to pillage what she could. The keys to the gun display were still in the cabinet lock. *Thank God for forgetful employees.* Keys meant access to things without breaking locks or smashing glass. Taking the keys in hand, she looked around for inspiration.

I need a change of clothes. Crouching behind the register, she gave the go-back box a quick sift. Fortune provided a black velour lounging pantsuit. She stripped off her gray skirt and slid into the drawstring pants. The matching hoodie jacket engulfed her frame, but she gave the sleeves a quick roll and concentrated on her next steps.

An open box of flares caught her attention and she remanded them to her laundry sack with her skirt, as well as a used roll of duct tape and a flashlight. New noises echoed through the store and Sy could hear Kirby argue with his captors. She was running out of time.

She spied a light switch panel just under the counter tucked into a corner. She removed a few boxes to reach it. There were four toggles and a faded label indicating this was one of three emergency shut-off panels located in the store. Using the tip of the smallest key, she unscrewed the plate, exposing the guts of the box.

The front of the store was quiet again, but only for a moment. The familiar crackle of the overhead speakers snapped on. The Voice knew her name. "Sy is it? I'm a fair man. I'm willing to let everyone here go if you come without a fuss."

She fumbled for the mic. "Okay, give me a second to fix my hair and repair my fingernails. I'll be right up."

Her attention reverted to the switch box. The yellow toggle was labeled with a lightning bolt. She flipped the switch and the store plunged into darkness.

Sy took a moment to breathe. "I can smell the grapes in the nearby wine press. There are some cheeses and crackers and coffee on veranda table." Her heart calmed and her mind cleared.

Launching herself from the cash-wrap, she bolted up the camping aisle. She snagged a clear, plastic poncho, a telescoping marshmallow roaster, a cheap pair of binoculars, and a cigarette lighter. On the other side of the fishing poles and the pool chemicals, shelves of bath towels lined the edge of the home decor department. She opened her laundry sack and dumped an entire display of gel candles into it. Satisfied she was as prepared as she was going to be, she raced to the center of the store.

The dressing rooms were free-standing amid nightgowns and hospital scrubs. Atop them, a sturdy ledge served to support a few boxes of extra merchandise. Using the go-back counter to hoist herself up, she shimmied onto the ledge and into position.

Exhaustion swept over her as her blood-sugar plummeted. She wished she had passed through the candy aisle. The instant sugar rush of a candy bar would have been helpful. *Suck it up, it's not over yet.* Shaky, she ignored her complaining stomach and observed the situation at the cash registers.

Her vantage point afforded her a clear view of the front of the store. Hello-My-Name-Is-Ted, the other employees, and clientele were lined up facing the two-way mirror next to the cigarettes. There were two men wearing ski-masks that had rifles pointed in their general direction, displaying signs of fatigue. She compared the time a clock registered to her watch. It was 3:30.

Kirby knelt on the floor next to a ski-masked man who had the speaker mic at checkout two. The sudden darkness interrupted their operations better than she hoped, illustrating the criminals' inability to improvise. She felt she finally secured the upper hand.

If only she had given more thought as to how she was going to communicate with Agent Kirby. *So much for keeping that a secret.* She took a deep breath and closed her eyes. The veranda in France was still there and still smelled of grapes growing on the hillside. There was something wonderful cooking in the vineyard kitchens that wafted on the breeze. Opening her eyes, she peered out through and focused on the forehead of the federal agent. *Here goes nothing.*

CHAPTER III

Flaming Shrapnel

THE PAIN IN HIS KNEES from kneeling on the linoleum floor was the least of Brian Kirby's troubles. His spur-of-the-moment partner was running out of time and he had a 9mm pointed at his head.

He had worse days. He just couldn't remember when.

"Where the hell is she?" the Voice waved the handgun about like a loose cannon.

At least the safety was on. Still, an itchy trigger finger made Brian nervous. "I told you, I left her at the fabric counter. She's not exactly the sort of woman you can command to do anything."

The Voice's radio chirped into action. "Boss, she ain't back here. Toby's in the loading docks and he ain't seen her either."

"Just peachy. Keep looking." The Voice held his radio at his chin for a long while after he released the squelch.

Brian felt a tingling sensation at the base of his neck, no, *inside* the base of his neck. It spread through his brain, leaching thoughts like a damned tick. Then he *felt* her voice, smooth and thick as molasses, coating his mind.

Kirby, I need you to trust me on this. I'm sitting above the dressing rooms in the middle of the store. They need to release everyone unharmed. I won't come down until they do. Understand? Sy buzzed.

Was he dreaming? He shook his head to be free of her, but she held on. His crowded mind tried to fight her, to no avail. He searched and despite the distance and the dark, made eye-contact with her. "Hey Boss," Brian coughed. "I've found her."

The Voice barked, placing the gun-barrel against the bridge of Brian's nose. "What do you mean?"

Brian amended his statement with shrug. "I mean to say I know where she might be."

"I knew it! You were lying to me. So where is she?"

"Doesn't matter, she's not coming out until you've released everyone."

Tell him I've got a shotgun pointed at his head.

The buzzing hurt. He coughed again, tasting bile in the back of his throat.

Tell him!

Brian pushed back on the barrel, pain shooting up his legs. The buzzing in his mind affected his equilibrium. The ground began to spin under him. "She's got a shotgun pointed at you," he forced the words between his teeth.

"And how do you know that?" Boss said, looking around.

"She told me."

"When?"

"Just now." Brian shot a dirty look through the darkness and hoped Sy was close enough to see it. "Look I just know, all right?"

I mean it Kirby. If he doesn't start moving everyone out, I'm going to torch the place. He felt like a human radio station. Static. Her voice.

Static. Her voice. The buzzing. The tingling. *Kirby? Stay with me. You're not going crazy, I promise.*

Boss pulled the gun out of Brian's face and paced. Brian shifted his weight, which helped the pain in his knees, but didn't make it disappear. The squelch of the radio brought Brian back to the gunman. Whatever was said wasn't what Boss wanted to hear. "Well scan the store again, Red!"

The buzzing returned. *So that makes six people, doesn't it? They may have two more at least roaming the perimeter. This doesn't make sense. They don't strike me as being professionals. What could possibly be the reason for some small time thugs to act like big boys and hold up a Wint-Mart in the middle of the night? What is it they're hoping to accomplish?*

Stop it! His mind screamed and for a blissful moment, he thought it worked.

No, sorry, she broadcasted.

Radio silence wasn't happening on Boss's end either. Boss shouted orders into his handset, turning red and spitting. Brian decided not to fight it anymore, and the tingling subsided. Clarity shined through the fog and the buzzing no longer hurt.

That's it. Just relax. I promise not to make a habit of this.

Sy, you have to realize he has no intention of trading hostages for you.

I know. One step at a time though. I'm kinda making this up as I go along.

Boss jumped up on the check-stand's conveyor belt. "Sy! Come on out or I swear to God, I will put a bullet through your boyfriend's brain."

Without warning, the color drained from his lips and he dove from the conveyor belt. "What the FUCK!" Boss swatted at his head.

Brian smiled, recognizing the signs of invasion. His adversary blanched and groaned as if struck with something sinister and unexplainable. "What's wrong Boss? Did you just get raped by a ghost?"

"Shut up!" Boss boxed his own ears.

"Relax. It hurts less if you're not so wound up," Brian said.

Boss didn't heed the advice. He twisted his head from side to side, slugging his temples. "Shut up, shut up!"

"Boss? Boss!" Brian rocked to his feet. "Come on, I've told you she's prepared to torch the place. We'll burn alive in here. How 'bout you release the hostages, eh?"

The gun barrel was back in his face. Brian backed away, hands in the air, only to be stopped by the register behind him. Boss looked on the edge, a fiery glint reflected in wild eyes. "Where is she?" Boss spat. "Why can I hear her but I can't see her?"

"Who, Sy?"

"You hear her, don't you? That German bitch."

Brian grimaced. "No, Boss. I don't hear her. Let the hostages go."

Boss pulled the gun away again. "No, no she wouldn't hurt any of these people. Women never put anyone in harm's way."

"You're the boss, Boss. But ah, I wouldn't underestimate her. I happen to know she's a money-grubbing, selfish European-"

I heard that! Sy buzzed.

Brian ignored her, pushing beyond the tingling worming in his thoughts. "She couldn't care less about any of us, and you can bet your ass she's got a plan to get herself out. You think she's German? I think she's Swiss, or Benelux, and she's probably got some kind of diplomatic immunity. Her type usually does."

"How would you know?"

"You've pissed her off. She was plotting to kill her husband and you got in her way."

Boss paced, the 9mm shaking in his unsteady grip. "So, according to you, she's a certifiable nutcase with no remorse and we picked the wrong time to commence our little operation."

"That's the gist of it. And as entertaining as your situation is-" Reaching out, Brian snatched the gun from Boss's hand, a move drilled into him in training until it was second-nature. "-I should probably inform you that I'm an agent with the Federal Bureau of Investigation."

"Shit a fucking brick!" Boss retreated a few steps as Brian heard the two rifle men move into his blindside.

Brian held his ground, the 9mm secure in his hands. "You're in a world of hurt buddy. I'd suggest cooperating."

Oh, did I mention I have napalm and I'm not afraid to use it?

You ARE certifiably nuts! Sweat formed rivers at the base of his neck. "She's, uh, she's got napalm."

"No she doesn't." The riflemen joined Boss in hearty laughter. "Who carries that around?"

Frenzied screams erupted from a fireball in the middle of the women's clothing. A ski-masked man crashed through racks and shelves. He hit the water fountain at the front of the store, tore his mask from his face, and doused his eyes with water in awkward handfuls. Brian smelled pesticide.

Boss yelled into his radio, "Everyone front and center. If you see the woman, stand down and do not engage. Do you hear me? Do. Not. Engage."

A rifleman stepped from Brian's blind-spot, "Boss, we don't have time. It's almost four-"

"I know what time it is dingleberry!"

Agent Kirby, watch this!

A glowing orb soared through the air, like St. Elmo's Fire, and exploded upon impact with an umbrella display. Streams of orange fiery shrapnel coated sale items in a wall of flame. The ceiling fire suppression sprinklers sprang into action, but the raining water only spread the flames faster.

Sy stood on top of the dressing room ledge, wearing a plastic poncho, and hurled another bomb towards the back of the store. The rifleman raised his bolt-action her direction, but Brian disarmed him. In the chaos, gunmen and hostage alike abandoned all endeavors and ran for the exit.

"Sy! Come on!" Brian signaled her to move.

"I'm not done yet!" Another glowing orb sailed to the greeting cards, exploding on the last man standing. He burst into flames and a panicked run. "Bull's-eye!"

"Shit!" Brian grabbed the fire extinguisher from the nearest pillar and joined Sy as she dropped from her perch with an extinguisher of her own. Together, they doused the man rolling in vain on the floor. The heat from the rising fire was unbearable, but Brian wasn't going to quit. He pulled another fire extinguisher to use when his was exhausted. With the last of the suppressant dispensed, he couldn't help but think that the burn victim resembled a melting snowman. "Help me get him up."

"No."

Brian coughed, soot spewing from his lungs. He leaned to fetch up the man by his shoulders. "Fine. I'll do it myself."

Sy tapped him on the shoulder. "Let the professionals do it."

Stunned, Brian watched as the building erupted with fire-fighters. Three of the firemen rushed over and helped with the burn victim before Brian could recover from shock. He stumbled after them, coughing and spitting the whole way to the exit.

Outside in the cold, fresh air, the parking lot bustled with activity. Ski-masks were removed from the armed robbers as they were being handcuffed and stuffed into patrol cars. Emergency medical personnel treated the hostages. Brian wrung water from his shirt, grateful for his water-repelling hiking boots. After the whole ordeal, his feet were still dry.

It was more than he could say for the Wint-Mart. Orange tongues of destructive heat barreled through the entrance, like they too were happy for the fresh air.

"My father believes setting things on fire is good therapy." Her expression was hard to read and her words sounded so fragile, Brian had to move closer to understand her. "I think I agree with him. It's oddly liberating watching this place burn."

"That's how arsonists are born, or so I'm told." Brian shook water from his hair.

"Oh fear not. This was too much work to do on a daily basis."

Her response came dry like the heat. There was a malevolence to her demeanor, but he found himself drawn to her in spite of it. The hostages shared looks of fear or morbid curiosity, but Sy stood calm and quiet, as if she could walk through the middle of the fire and exit unscathed. "You are officially the creepiest person I've ever met."

"You say that like it's a bad thing."

He shed more water from his hair. "I'll have a ton of paperwork to do if I ever dry out. Next time you burn down a place, toss me a poncho too, or at least give me warning."

"Deal. Grr, this blasted soot is everywhere."

She wiped her eyes, the giant sparkle on her left hand catching his attention. Her wedding set sparked an envious knot in his chest. In what universe could he ever afford a ring like that?

"You were supposed to be on vacation, weren't you?" Her voice shook him from his thoughts. "You came to Lake Erie to do a little fishing with your two buddies."

"Are you reading my mind again?"

"No, I remember you from the fishing aisle."

"Yeah, well I guess I didn't expect my vacation to run smoothly anyway." He scanned the emergency crews looking for signs of his friends. "If our fishing gear hadn't disappeared from our campsite a few hours ago, we wouldn't have even been in that blasted store."

"I'm sorry if I'm intruding." Her cell phone rang and she rifled through her laundry sack to retrieve it.

"That Henry?"

"No, thank God, my lawyer." She touched the screen to answer. "Barry? So good to hear your voice..."

CHAPTER IV

A Breakfast Invitation

"ARE YOU OKAY?" Barry's bass voice rattled in her ear. "Henry called me, said you were a hostage in Sandusky."

"I'm fine but there's a man with a battery in his brain and another with serious burns over eighty percent of his body that might wish I wasn't." Sy added that she set fire to the Wint-Mart accidently on purpose. "I'm grateful you called. I might be neck deep in some legal trouble shortly."

"I'll put a call in to Drake and the other members of the board for Wint-Mart, and see what I can accomplish for you. In the meantime, be polite with the authorities and tell them nothing except your lawyer's on his way."

"Thanks Barry. You'll find the jet in the hanger. I'll see you soon."

Agent Kirby avoided making eye contact with her.

"Now what did I do?"

"I uh, you've got a jet." He shifted. "A Veyron, a jet, and a husband that bought that rock on your hand. I'm feeling out of my element here."

"Oh." He was soot-stained and dripping wet. It added to his somethingness. Sy wanted to say something witty, something to make him feel at ease. Instead, they stood for a long moment as a stream of police and firemen worked around them, before an EMT interrupted their silence.

"I'm fine," Sy waved him away, but the EMT was persistent. After she removed her plastic poncho, he checked her eyes and ears. He made her breathe in and out while he listened to her lungs. He checked her blood pressure. She was surprised it wasn't higher. Maybe she was in shock after all.

"Your name please?" the medical technician's left hand was poised to write on some forms attached to a clipboard.

"Simone Freitag."

"Marital Status."

"About to be widowed."

He looked up from his clipboard. "I'm sorry?"

"Never mind, yes, I'm married." Her head throbbed and the hollow feeling in her stomach returned. "Do you have a glucose tablet or something? My sugar is low."

He reached for his bag. You didn't tell me you were diabetic. That kind of information is important." He sounded cross.

"I'm not diabetic. Anybody's sugar would drop if they were fifteen pounds underweight. And they haven't eaten anything in the span of twenty hours. And wasted the last bit of energy they had in rescuing hostages from Wint-Mart." She felt snippy.

"Right. Here." He tossed a brown-wrapped candy bar at her, which she caught and ripped open without effort. "Contact information."

"Why don't I fill that part out? It would be quicker than asking, responding, repeating. Don't you think?" She said though a mouthful of chocolate peanuts as she reached for his clipboard.

"Okay, sure, but neatness counts." He passed the clip-board to her and turned to Kirby. "You next."

THE DARKNESS OF THE SMALL MORNING HOURS dissipated as the sun appeared along the eastern horizon. The fire was put out and vehicles trickled from the parking lot. Sy handed the clipboard back as the EMT repeated his routine with Kirby.

"You the woman they're calling Sy?" A local sheriff approached them. A caterpillar moustache hid his top lip and highlighted his deep-scored frown lines. Although he looked fit, he had a midsection that implied too many weekend beers. His receding hair line emphasized a widow's peak, making his appearance reminiscent of a taller grandfather from the *Munsters*.

"I am Sy, although I don't know which 'they' you might be referring to." Remembering her lawyer's instructions, she tried to keep her answers as non-specific as possible.

"You set fire to the building?"

"No."

"You're denying setting fire to the building when you're surrounded by all these witnesses?"

She measured her words, "Yes, I'm denying setting fire *intentionally* to the *building*."

"Well they say you did."

She closed her eyes. The vineyard was back and the sunny breeze stirred the muslin curtains in the master bedroom. Releasing her breath, she opened her eyes and forced a smile. "Sheriff, again, I don't know who you are referring to when you say 'they'."

Kirby stepped beside her. "Excuse me, Sheriff; is it your intent to arrest this woman?"

The sheriff shot Kirby a look. "It is my intent to ascertain the nature of her involvement."

Sy shrugged. "Well then, I will repeat. I did not intentionally set fire to the *building*. I only lit a few candles. Now, as my *lawyer* won't be present for another two hours, how about we meet you at your station around, oh I don't know, ten o'clock?"

"Don't worry Sheriff; I'll make sure she's there." Kirby pulled his I.D. badge from his back pocket to show the sheriff, who inspected it in turn with a degree of suspicion.

"She yours?" the lip caterpillar twitched.

"Negative, I'm on vacation. As far as I know there wasn't any federal investigation linked with this incident. I'm just offering our full cooperation." Fishing a business card from inside the flap of the wallet, he added, "It's a bit damp, but here's my card if you need to get a hold of us."

The sheriff nodded. "All right, if you're willing to keep her under surveillance until we can gather the evidence to arrest her, I'll take your word for it." After flashing them a severe look, he turned and walked towards the chaos remaining in the parking lot.

"Your buddies, where are they?" Sy searched the people milling about. "If you're planning on babysitting me until ten o'clock, I think perhaps you should tell them."

Kirby nodded; his posture stiff. "Just so you know, I'm sticking my neck out for you on this one. Do NOT screw me over."

Sy fluttered her eyelashes with a dramatic flair. "Now, Agent Kirby, after all we've been through, you don't trust me?"

"Honestly? No. I'd say you had a rather unfair advantage." He pointed to two men moving their direction. "Speaking of the devils. Here they come."

Sy noticed them enough in the store, but this time she took extra care to observe the two. Pangs of jealousy crept in as she knew that once the appointment at the police station was kept, her knight-in-something-armor would return to fishing and to the company of his friends. Sy wanted to know who she was losing him to, so she would know how to find him later if need be.

The taller man of the two was the wolf-whistler and wore camouflage like it was a fashion statement. *What could he possibly need desert cams on Lake Erie for?* Sandy curls of tangled hair jutted out from under a bright red beanie with Budweiser advertised in neon white across the front. His nose showed signs of a break that hadn't reset right. Other than his nose, his features were more or less average for a man in his thirties.

He handed Kirby a cell phone and leered at her. Judging by the look in his eyes, Budweiser had already mapped out what she looked like naked. He was happy to see her.

The other fellow was more on the nervous twitchy side. His slight build and small dark eyes reminded Sy of a scared rat. An abundance of gray hair in a number 2 buzz cut was indicative that he did not handle stress well. *Late twenties, perhaps?* A white stripe across his left ring finger announced his recent divorce. Sy figured Budweiser guilt-tripped Kirby into going fishing by stressing the need to take the Rat out to get his mind off of the bitch that took him to the cleaners.

"Thanks for grabbing my phone." Indicating Budweiser first, Kirby made introductions. "Tom Whitney and Matt Folsom, friends from the old neighborhood. This is Simone Freitag, arsonist extraordinaire."

"Alleged arsonist," Sy corrected as she shook hands with the friends. Tom's handshake was firm but sweaty, and Matt didn't have a grip at all.

"How did you get a hold of napalm?" Tom seemed eager, like he was shopping for Christmas presents.

"It's on sale right now, two for five, down the home decor aisle."

"Uh, guys, I gotta see to it that Mrs. Freitag gets to the station on time, so I'll have to meet you back at the lake." Kirby touched her elbow to escort her.

A Sy walked to her car, she heard Tom say, "If you don't tap her I will."

"He's so not in the ball-park."

Kirby groaned. "Sorry about that. I don't want Tom to know how easy it is to make napalm."

The teen-aged hostages were drooling over the Veyron and scattered as Sy and Kirby approached. The top was off of the jet black sports coup, exposing the black leather ergonomic sears inside. The machine was engineered with speed in mind. Only a handful would ever be seen in the United States, and there stood Kirby, speechless. "I realize this looks ostentatious, but it's not really my car. I grabbed Henry's keys in a rush to get away from Chicago." Sy tossed the keys at her new friend. "I promised you could drive it. You can drive a stick, yes?"

"My instructor says I'm promising."

"Well keep it under two hundred if you can. The fuel economy sucks." She allowed him some time to adjust the angle of the seat and the wheel, amused at the way he ran his fingers over the dash instruments and the center console.

"Thank you." She almost didn't hear him whisper. "If you weren't married, I'd probably make a pass at you."

She laughed a real, hearty, genuine laugh. It felt good. "How about I pass at you instead? We've two hours to kill, yes? I don't know about you but I'm famished. Breakfast?"

"Well, there's a diner up the street. They've got the best omelets this side of Denver."

"Sa mergem."

He cast her a cock-eyed look.

She realized the words she spoke weren't English. "Uh, lead on."

CHAPTER V

Patty's Diner

T HE RIDE TO PATTY'S DINER was comfortable, stable, like the air parted for the car before the Veyron touched it. Kirby drove the car like a professional, but if he had designs on opening the throttle to really see what the car could do, he showed remarkable restraint.

Sy tried to enjoy being the passenger, but her phone rang four times within the quarter hour trip. Twice from Henry, who still wasn't getting the fact that she wasn't coming home right then and even if she was, she was going to kill him; another call from her lawyer saying that he was boarding the jet and would be there soon, and the CFO of Wint-Mart, the insurance companies, and her accountant were all in agreement already as to the reparations of the damages. Her housekeeper was the last to call, passing along the message that the cheating whore was gone, which put Sy in a better mood.

When they reached the restaurant, Brian's knuckles were white from clutching the wheel as if he couldn't relax. She asked him why.

He rubbed his fingers. "New car anxiety. My real life vehicle is a Wrangler."

They looked like vagabonds when they emerged from the vehicle, disheveled and exhausted. Sy felt like a waif in hand-me-down velour and jewelry, still carting around her homeless laundry. A wooden sign at the entrance instructed newcomers to grab a menu and take a seat. They wandered through the packed tables and chose their own booth.

The smell of bacon and strawberries common to pancake houses woke up Sy's stomach and she was salivating like a ravenous wolf by the time the waitress found the path to their table. The woman was in her twenties and accustomed to hard work. Her hands weren't pampered and she had the pallor of someone who rarely saw time in the sun. Cheryl Lynn was written on her name badge, but she introduced herself as Silly and rattled off a list of the specials of the day. "What can I git y'all?"

"Coffee and the Firehouse Feast please," Kirby was quick with his order. "Can I substitute bacon for the sausage links and get egg whites only, scrambled then instead of sunny-side-up?"

"Of course ya can Darlin'. D'ya want toast or biscuit?"

"Extra pancakes possible?"

"Sure thing. Butter and maple syrup okay?"

"Unless you have molasses."

"We can do molasses instead of the syrup."

"Then molasses it is then, please and thank you." Kirby smiled as he handed her his menu. He unrolled the flatware from its paper napkin cocoon and waited.

The waitress focused on Sy. "An' for you dearie?"

Sy felt like a fish out of water. Hunger blocked her ability to think clearly and she wasn't accustomed to ordering from a menu. Henry discussed meal options with her and she'd agree to something and then he'd place the order. Without looking at the menu, she passed it along to the waitress. "Coffee yes, for the both of us, but as for food…"

"Ma'am?"

Sy layered her accent thick and heavy for affect. "Sorry, Silly, I'm truly not accustomed to ordering off the menu, so may I beg a favor?"

"Uh…sure hun, whatchya need?"

She struggled with her conscience for a moment, knowing what she was about to ask was borderline inappropriate. She needed comfort food and from her experience, diners like these didn't have crepes on the menu. It was unlikely that the line cooks knew what a crepe was, let alone understand how to make one properly. "Do you mind if I cook?"

She squirmed under Kirby's harsh look. Sy knew he wouldn't understand. Silly, however, seemed to take it in stride. "Give me a sec hun and I'll ask my manager." She turned and walked away through the maze of crowded tables.

Kirby's whisper was forced and embittered. "What are you thinking? Are you really that pompous?"

She took a deep breath. France tickled the edge of her mind, ready to be called into active duty. If only she wasn't so hungry. "Yes, I guess I am."

"You couldn't just order something, anything, like a normal person could you?"

Yielding to her crankiness, she tapped a finger on the table. "You tell me what the difference is between what you just asked her to do and what I am proposing to do for myself?"

Kirby blinked. His expression cycled through a few seasons. "What are you talking about? I ordered off the menu."

"No you ordered a meal off the menu and then proceeded to change everything about what made it a Firehouse Feast. I counted no less than four specific things you asked to be different. Bacon instead of sausage. Egg whites and scrambled instead of yolks and sunny-side-up..."

"The menu says substitutions are allowed." His argument was weak.

"Hmm, yes, so the line cooks back there will have to decipher exactly what it is you want regardless of the giant FF written on the ticket? I at least am not going to request savory crepes and expect them to work outside of their comfort zone."

If Kirby had a retort, they were interrupted before he could say it. The manager stepped up to their table and introduced herself. "I'm the Patty of Patty's Diner. I understand you have an unusual request?"

Sy relied upon her strong accent again. "I'm a stranger to your country and I have trouble reading the English. I can't tell what the food is from the pictures. I think it would just be easiest for me to cook the meal myself yes?"

"Ah." Patty looked as unsure as her words. "I don't know..."

"You can, how is it you say, charge? You can charge what you like? I pay."

Greed won the day. Patty explained the health department could come in and write her up for allowing personnel in the kitchen who didn't belong, and she thought maybe twenty-five dollars would be adequate for the privilege. Sy promised to keep out of the way of the line-cooks, told Kirby to stay put, and she followed the owner to the kitchen. Within twenty minutes, she juggled her own creative work of art, and his Firehouse Feast complete with exceptions, returning to their table upbeat and happy.

They wasted no time making a dent in their food. While their voices were silent, their forks clanked against plates. It was an efficient dance to a symphony of food. At one point the waitress topped off their coffee cups and deposited their check. "No hurry on that you two. Take all the time you need." And she was gone again to see to her other customers.

Sy offered Kirby some more cream, which he refused after gagging the color of the coffee in his cup. "So Agent Kirby," she placed the stainless steel creamer back down on the glass topped table, "do you have a first name or is Agent your first name?"

His eyes focused on her from far away. "Well, you did allow me to drive your car I suppose. It's Brian. But you can call me Agent if you want to. I don't mind."

She hid her smile behind her mug. "Brian Kirby. That's a solid Irish name you have there."

"And I even work in the family business. Grandfather used to say that we were descended from the man who arrested Cain. Of course, Grandmother says that there are just as many of us behind bars as in front of them." He chuckled, punning. "Or in them. My family is pretty stereotypical. Quick to anger, stubborn as all hell, heavy drinkers the lot of us. But we do know how to throw a wake."

"Sounds nice. I'm envious. Do you have a large family?" She sipped her coffee, savoring the liquid bitterness as well as the warmth of the conversation.

"Larger than most, even for Catholics here in the States. I'm the oldest of five brothers and two sisters. I have thirty-one first cousins from my father's side alone. Family reunions are very chaotic..." His eyes wandered into the distance again, focusing on nothing in particular.

"Did I just intrude where I shouldn't have? I'm sorry."

After a beat, he shrugged. "No need to be. I just haven't seen the folks in a while and the first vacation I get, I avoid them and spend the time fishing with friends."

"Don't forget rescuing damsels in distress."

"Hardly," he shot her a knowing look. "I seem to recall you didn't need much help. I think I actually got in your way."

"No I wouldn't say that. You kept me grounded when I was absorbed in my own little struggle." Guilt rapped on the door of her feelings, seeking entrance. She refused to entertain it, but she knew it was there.

Brian leaned forward, focused on his coffee. She sensed him struggling with something. "Can I ask you a personal question?"

She raised an eyebrow. "You may ask me whatever you wish. It's my choice whether I answer or not, truthfully or not."

"This particular...talent...of yours. How did you come by it?"

Sy sighed. The truth, although deserving, was complicated. She understood so little of the past that haunted her nightmares. She needed answers as much as he did. "I have no idea how or why. It's just something I've always been able to do."

"Always?"

"It terrified me, as a child. I spent some time in a psychiatric hospital until my father put a stop to it. I don't know what strings he pulled or how much it cost him, but it's not even mentioned in my medical history now."

"You're family has always been influential then? Ah, don't answer that. That didn't sound as rude in my head."

Eager to make light of the situation and put behind the ghost of her youth, she flashed a quick grin. "Always. I'm the last in a long line of people so important, governments covet us."

He rolled his eyes and clicked his teeth. "Ask as stupid question…"

"Seriously though, we're lucky people and we know it. We've always had money, even during depressions and communist governments. My grandfather never once lost a bet at the tables. He broke the bank once at a casino in Monte Carlo and was banned from setting foot in Monaco ever again. Both my uncle and my father have the same sort of luck."

"You do as well, I take it. Remind me to take you to Vegas."

"I don't gamble. I have more money than God but that doesn't mean I need to throw it away unnecessarily."

He motioned towards the front of the restaurant. "You don't think that Veyron is overkill?"

"I told you the Veyron isn't really mine. That's Henry's little rebellion against the world going green or something." She placed her coffee cup back on the table. "I'm a firm believer in you get what you pay for. I'm lucky enough that I can afford to be picky, but even I think that machine is a waste of petrol."

"Fair enough." Brian checked his watch and reached for the tab.

She stayed his hand. "Please, let me pay for the bill. I was difficult in my request and…"

His hand flipped to hold hers. He gave it a gentle squeeze. "No, you were absolutely correct. My order was no less complicated than yours and I didn't bother to cook mine." His thumb traced the diamond band on her ring finger. It felt so comfortable, so natural, that Sy wished beyond hope that Brian *somethinged* her as well. All too soon, the moment between them vanished as reality and their food began to digest in their systems.

CHAPTER VI

The Interrogation

THE STERILE INTERROGATION ROOM was cold and lacked definition. It could have been an interrogation room for any station anywhere. The large two-way mirror so often depicted in movies was real. It forced the suspect to look at his own reflection, knowing that the observation room was right on the other side. A couple of standard government-issue chairs lined up against the steel table bolted to the concrete floor. The florescent light kept the dark at bay by flooding the room with an emotionless glare. Silent, the stark walls fed off the misery and despair of those who entered the room, and would remain unsatisfied in their thirst for more secrets to trap and keep stored forever.

Sy thought that a vase of daisies might do the trick. At least the room would appear less dreary. Perhaps a window treatment across the mirror, and a bamboo plant in the corner also would add to brighten the room, along with a fresh coat of pale powder blue paint. She realized that the decor was minimal for the officer's protection, but surely the department could splurge for an aromatherapy plug for the vented air-conditioner, with a nice calming scent of vanilla or lavender.

Barry Fletcher sat in as her legal representation. He was a life-long friend of her father's and watched over her like a hawk. The lawyer was the only man she ever met who had multi-tasking down to a precise science. His eye for detail in the most mundane of paperwork made him positively brilliant at finding loopholes and forcing the laws and regulations to bend to his every whim. Barry was also six-foot-nine and looked like a biker regardless of the Versace suit and Rolex watch, with his strong, barrel chest and long hair pulled back into a pony tail. Facial hair varied every time she saw him. Today, he sported a pencil thin mustache and a goatee.

They spoke in Romanian. It was Barry's idea of buying time and maintaining privacy. It was highly unlikely that anyone employed in the station would know Romanian fluently enough for them to interpret in the observation deck behind the mirror. "While they might have a case against you for intentional property damage and arson, the cost to prosecute outweighs the danger you pose to the general populace, and it's likely that a judge would toss it out during the pretrial motions simply due to the situation." His accent could use a little help, but his fluency in the language made up for it.

"And what about the scumbags pressing charges against me for assault and attempted murder?" Her question came from curiosity more than fear. Barry always won. Always.

He laughed. "That wouldn't stick to a fly if it was flypaper." He opened his briefcase and pulled out his laptop. "Besides, popular opinion of the natives around here paints you as something of a hero. Even the hostages who were scared of burning alive were grateful you showed up and are organizing a rally in case you need their show of support."

"Then I should be able to walk away from this without having to call the cavalry?"

"Yes, this one is easy. Honestly Sy, if you want to stump me, you'll have to do better than this."

"How about getting me off the hook for murder?"

He looked puzzled. "Do you mean the hemophiliac you allegedly killed with a car battery?"

"No, that one I'm not worried about. That was a case of self-defense. And I'm still not convinced he was a hemo anyway, because he had tattoos. No, I mean the murder of my husband."

"You killed him?" His fingertips drummed the table.

"Not yet. But I caught him stepping out on me, Barry. In our flat in Chicago. In the hot-tub." Tears waited in the corner of her eyes as the full weight of her failing marriage came down around her. "Ten years. Am I really that blind?"

He took her hand and gave it a squeeze. "Murder isn't the answer Sy, you know this. I'll draw up the divorce papers."

"Divorce is a sin." She was grateful she took the opportunity to wash her face in the ladies' room after breakfast. Mascara saturating her tears would have stained her cheeks otherwise.

"And murder isn't?" His laughter echoed in the small space. "Sy your logic never ceases to amaze me. Besides, divorce isn't a sin when there's been infidelity."

And just like that her heart was lifted. "I'd forgotten that loop-hole."

The door opened. Two officers entered. Neither one was the sheriff from earlier. Both wore suits. "Guilty people get lawyers, Ms. Freetag."

Replying in English, Barry parried. "Smart people always have legal representation when speaking with law enforcement. Any other defamatory accusations you wish to direct at my client?"

He tried a counter-attack. "Rich people have legal representation more often."

"According to the most recent tax laws established by your Internal Revenue Department, the definition of rich is any unmarried person making over fifty-five thousand per annum in the Great State of Ohio, and any married couple with a combined annual income of over eighty thousand. Tell me Officer," Barry turned away from his laptop and leaned forward, placing his interlocked hands on the table, "which category would you fall into?"

"We are not here to discuss my financial situation. We're here to have a polite conversation with your client."

"Whom you've already drawn a conclusion about. While you might call it deductive reasoning, outside of these four walls, the interpretation of that standard operating procedure is called profiling, and is deemed prejudicial. Are you positive you wish to continue with this current argument?"

The officer looked defeated. It was obvious he hadn't prepared for a battle of wits with a lawyer of Barry's caliber. "Not particularly. Your point has been made. Shall we start over?"

"My name is Barry Fletcher, and I'm representing Ms. Simone *Fry*-tag in a legal capacity."

The quiet man introduced his partner as they sat across from Sy. "This is Officer Brown. I'm Detective Mercy."

"Our pleasure." Barry smiled.

Officer Brown lost all trace of superiority in his baritone voice. "Interesting incident just happened. Our station received a call from the governor who implied very heavily that we were to provide for your client every courtesy available at our disposal. Any reason you can think of that the governor might wish to extend that courtesy to you?"

"None." Sy never met the Ohio governor. She would've remembered that. "But I'll have to include him in our Christmas card list."

The officer looked constipated. His face squished up so his wrinkles scored deep and red. His partner however, seemed to want to make the best of a difficult situation. Mercy's next words were rehearsed but light. "We thought we should tell you that you aren't in any legal trouble, Ms. Freitag, regardless of our friendly reminder from the governor. We've already been in contact with the insurance companies handling the claims regarding the fire and such, and everything is being handled in a business appropriate manner."

"Thank you Detective." Barry picked up his laptop and placed it back in the briefcase. "Then, as your forty-five minutes are up, and you have no intention of charging my client with anything, we will waste your time no further."

Officer Brown held up his hand. "Wait a second, please. We were going to ask you if you wouldn't mind giving us an official statement about the incident."

Sy shrugged when Barry shot her an inquiring look. She was willing to cooperate as long as she wasn't going to jail. "Very well, we'll assist you in any way we can." He pulled a legal pad from the briefcase and a silver-toned pen.

"I need to tell you that we are tape recording the inter-view."

"As we expect. I'll let you know when you've over-stepped a boundary." Barry began to scribble in shorthand, an ability that always impressed Sy. She liked the times when he was old-school.

She told her tale for them, starting from the time she drove into the parking lot. Her interrogators interrupted her from time to time, asking if she knew where people were standing in the store, taking notes of their own. She'd give a quick update on the others and return to her story. It took less than a half-hour to get to the end. "That's when the firemen showed. You have the other details from there, I'm assuming."

"You mentioned the perp with the parrot tattoo. You claim he pointed a shotgun at you?" Mercy looked up from his notepad, as Officer Brown excused himself from the party and left the interrogation room.

"Yes, that's when the employee passed out. I reacted out of fear and grabbed the nearest thing I could to defend myself." There's no need for them to know that I knew it was a toy gun.

"And that's when Agent Kirby found you?"

"Yes, as I told you already, he came around the corner just as I was trying to get my breathing under control. I was still a bit shaky."

Officer Brown returned and showed a clipboard of documents to the detective. After a brief sidebar, Mercy returned to his questioning. "But you never met the perp before?"

I wonder what he's getting at. "Never, at least that I'm aware of."

"And the ringleader, a Mr. Anthony Pacelli, had you ever seen him before this morning?"

"Are you referring to the idiot with the microphone?"

"Affirmative."

"No, I've never seen him. Again, at least, that I'm aware of. Although I must say I really didn't get a good look at him in the store either. All I could see from the ledge was his ski-mask."

"Did he strike you as acting crazy at any time?"

She frowned. "You mean other than holding up a Wint-Mart in a one-horse-town in the dead small hours of the morning? No, but I think he suffers from headaches or something. At one point I swear I saw him grab at his head like one swatting at flies."

Mercy put down the clipboard. "Here's the thing. Mr. Pacelli claims that you put your thoughts in his brain."

Her transgression was coming back to haunt her. She should've had better control of her anger. She rolled her eyes for effect. "How? I'd love to know."

"We've got him under psychiatric evaluation. Trouble is; that's just about the only part of the polygraph he did pass."

CHAPTER VII

The Suite

B RIAN SHOT A CURIOUS GLANCE down the hallway. Sy was held up in one of the interrogation rooms. He wondered how she was handling the situation. As a federal officer, he was extended the courtesy to be interviewed by Officer Mueller at his desk.

"In your opinion, did Ms. Freitag and Mr. Pacelli have any prior knowledge of each other?" Mueller asked simultaneously with recording the conversation in his computer.

"Negative, as far as I could tell. I know very little of Ms. Freitag myself, but I understand she's from Chicago. It doesn't seem likely to me that a woman of her peerage would have cause or opportunity to have an association with Mr. Pacelli."

"So it is your belief that Ms. Freitag was not a part of the criminal circle that executed this crisis."

"Affirmative."

"Thank you, Agent Kirby. Your cooperation has been most welcome. It's a rare thing." The printer on Mueller's desk jumped into magic action, presumably responding to the computer's command.

Brian leaned back in his seat, uncomfortable though it was. "How so?"

The officer leaned to take the statement off the printer. "You federal types are generally too high'n'mighty when dealin' with us beat cops."

"I apologize on behalf of the Bureau then." Brian gave a private chuckle. If pressed, he'd have to agree with Mueller.

The officer handed Brian a pen. "Your John Hancock please, if the statement looks in order."

Brian scanned the document, looking for discrepancies and finding none. He drew chevrons through the blank spaces to deter fraudulent amendments out of habit, and finished with his signature at the bottom of the last page. It wasn't much of a signature. His mother often joked that he should have become a doctor.

Sy was accompanied by a tall man in an expensive suit when she emerged from the hallway. She looked tired, but none the worse for wear. Brian rose and shook hands with Mueller before joining the couple. He withdrew her keychain from his pocket. "Here you are. And thank you, for allowing me to drive it."

Their eyes met as their fingertips touched and the keys transferred hands. "No, thank you. I was useless until I had food in my stomach. I'd've probably driven us into a tree. Special Agent Brian Kirby, I'd like you to meet Barry Fletcher, my lawyer and good friend."

Barry's handshake was efficient and firm. His demeanor exuded confidence. Brian couldn't help but like him.

Sy bounced the keys in her hand. "So, do you need a ride back to your fishing buddies? Or you could come to my hotel room and get cleaned up first, if you'd like."

It was a tempting proposal, one that he might've turned down if not for the hopeful expression on her face. He didn't want to become further embroiled in her personal drama, but he couldn't resist making her smile. "A shower sounds good; if you're sure it's not too much trouble."

"Come on then," she beamed. "Barry booked us a suite overlooking the water."

AN HOUR LATER, BRIAN STEPPED OUT of a shower and into the most luxurious bathrobe he ever felt. His idea of normal life was suspended, although he felt out of his element. The bathroom space was larger than his first two apartments in Bethesda combined. The suite alone occupied enough acreage that it needed its own zip code, housing two stately master bedrooms, each with a full-sized bath en suite. The adjoining sitting room featured a generous kitchenette and a wet bar that any man-cave would be envious of.

Barry apologized for the hovel. Some rock-star booked the preferred penthouse, but the view of Lake Erie from their suite was adequate and should soften the blow. He said this was roughing it. Two days ago, Brian would've sneered at the idea. Money was never something he had an excess of.

Wiping the fog away from a section of the gold-framed mirror, he stared long and hard at the grizzled face before him. The man in the reflection had gray peppering his temples. Brian resembled his father more and more each day.

Sy was kind enough to order a toiletries case through room service. He grinned as he pulled out its contents. She had read his mind again, for the items were his usual brands. There was an unexpected surprise in a bottle of cologne. Brian gave the cologne a hesitant sniff. *Expensive. Beyond-my-budget-ever expensive.* He debated using it after shaving, knowing the result would earn him a razzing from his friends when he showed back up at camp smelling pretty. *Oh what the hell. After all, it's a gift.*

Another surprise awaited him as he emerged from the steamy bathroom. Laid out on the bed were a brand new pair of jeans and his style of plain, long-sleeved t-shirt. He dressed; everything fit like a glove. Sy overlooked nothing.

He wandered into the sitting room, where Sy and Barry discussed the details of her coming divorce. "I want the vineyard in Chardonnay. As often as I use it to keep my blood-pressure under control, I believe I'm entitled."

"Agreed." Barry made notes on his legal pad. "I know Henry doesn't appreciate the history behind those vines anyway."

Sy continued. "He can keep the villa in the Virgin Islands instead. And I keep all the holdings I had before entering into this miserable union. Who knew I'd've needed a prenup?"

"We did, remember? Your father and I insisted and you snapped like a gator."

"Grr, I know!" She ran a hand through her hair. "You can get all that for me though, can't you? I'm not sure what I'm entitled to as a Swiss national."

"Well if we were going up against me I'd say your chances were thin, but since we're not." He winked. "What about the Da Vincis?"

She squished her nose. "He can keep them. He's the one obsessed with still-life. And that damned car...Brian, you want the car or not?"

He raised an eyebrow. "The Veyron you offered in payment if I helped you kill your husband? I'd have to say no again."

"Well I'm not murdering him anymore. Barry ruined all the fun for me. Do you want the car anyway?"

He could just see it, being on a high-speed pursuit of a criminal only to run out of gas in the first sixteen seconds. The Bureau wouldn't approve. "Ah, uh, no. No thank you. I, uh, I can't afford the gas."

Sy turned back to her lawyer. "Let Henry keep the Veyron while you're at it. It goes so well with his mid-life crisis."

"I need to advise you to keep the life insurance policies on him, as well as the kidnapping/ransom insurance policy."

"I don't need it, and I don't care if he gets kidnapped."

"You can donate the funds to charity if you want after he's gone. He's still a target for any enemies you have or obtain."

"True." She wore the indignant look of a woman scorned. Brian would hate to be in Henry's shoes.

The break in conversation provided an opportunity for Brian to speak. "Thank you by the way, for the goodies. How much do I owe you?" He wasn't sure he was prepared to hear the room-service tab generated on his behalf, but he wasn't going to take advantage of the situation either.

She tsked him. "Don't be silly, Kirby, it's a gift. I'm apologizing for the inconvenience."

Brian glanced around him. There were marble and gilded furnishings, and a bottle of fifty-year old Scotch on the granite wet-bar counter-top. He was having a difficult time feeling like a victim of circumstance. "Thank you for your generosity then."

"Hell, I tried to give you a Bugatti." She shrugged. "To each his own."

Barry held up his hand to silence them as he unmuted the television by remote. "You're on the news."

Sure enough, a reporter with a fake tan and a California attitude relayed the few facts that were leaked to the public about the Wint-Mart incident. "While local law enforcement is silent about the reason behind this morning's attack, an interview with one witness described the situation as equivocally the most terrifying event of his life. The coroner's office released a statement that the one casualty was one of the masked gunmen and appeared to have been crushed by debris that had become dislodged in the fire. He bled to death before officials could reach him."

The scene changed from the sterile newsroom with studio lights to a field reporter standing next to the news van in front of the yellow caution tape that marked the perimeter of the parking lot. The damage to the building looked extensive, but that didn't keep the reporter from bemoaning the fact fire crews didn't allow pictures of the inside of the building. "What all the hostages are saying about this incident was that one woman, who they know only as Sy, single-handedly brought this operation to a fiery end, sacrificing merchandise but saving lives in the process."

A recorded interview with Hello-My-Name-Is-Ted was on next, while onlookers made faces at the camera. "She was hot, man. You know, smokin'."

The reporter pressed on with inane questions like a Pulitzer Prize was on the line. "And how did you feel when all this went down?"

"Dude, I was like, scared man. But then this lady, man, she was like, all Kung-Fu and sh-stuff. And then she released the napalm and everyone scattered. She's a hero, man. Like Wonder Woman."

The scene changed back to the field reporter stuck at the scene of the building clean-up. "So what I've been able to ascertain is that this

mystery woman made several calls just after the hostages were rescued, and ensured that although the store would be closed during the
reconstruction, all hours and salaries are expected to be honored for
the duration, which clean-up crews estimate will take less than a
month to complete." The reporter identified the station and signed
off with a serious "Back to you, Liz."

Sy clapped. "Barry, you've already managed damage control! I'm
so glad you like me. I'd hate to be on your bad side."

He winked again, muting the television as Brian's cell phone
rang. Brian excused himself to answer it, stepping out through the
sliding glass door and onto the balcony. "Yeah, what's up Rosalie?"

"Sorry to bother you Brian," the familiar voice of his department's administrative assistant crackled in his ears. "I know this is
your first vacation in months."

"Years, but who's counting." Brian adjusted his stance and
blocked the ambient sound from his other ear with his free hand. "I
assuming since you're calling that the witness cooperated?"

"Finally, yeah. When are you coming back?"

Brian glanced through the glass door to Sy and her lawyer, feeling wistful. Sy was a unique woman. If they had met under other
circumstances...who was he fooling? Where would they have met
under different circumstances? He rubbed his forehead. "Unless another Wint-Mart blows up, I'll be back on Monday."

"Thanks for the warning." The phone disengaged.

Brian took a moment to soak in the view. Lake Erie looked calm
and her boats drifted back and forth to their own purpose. The sun
was warm, but askew above them so he was standing partially in
shadow. His perspective on the world changed over the last twenty-
four hours. He didn't believe in paranormal things, and yet what

explanation was there for the telepath in the sitting room? What other imaginary creatures existed in this universe? He half expected South Bay Bessie to rise up from the lake and stick her tongue out at him.

"Do you need that ride back?" Sy poked her head through the door. Her eyes were puffy and her nose pink. She'd been crying.

Brian noticed for the first time that her eyes were two different colors, both sapphire-blue and chocolate-brown, with golden flecks that danced in the light. He'd seen that pigment defect only once before. In his first years at the Bureau he saw a four-year-old too afraid to talk. It was like a small blue thumbprint was left across her iris. The department shrink said it happened in rare cases as a result of severe trauma.

What trauma could a rich girl have faced that changed the pigmentation in her eyes so much?

Could that trauma have anything to do with her telepathic ability?

He realized he was staring. "Yeah, I guess I'm ready when you are."

FORTY MINUTES LATER, HE APPROACHED the campground, hiking from the main road so the Veyron didn't have to go off-road. The campsite was crowded with tourists' tents and trailers. Passing some vacant-looking pop-ups and the small playground, he walked past the fish cleaning station and straight up the hill. He was surprised to see his friends were at camp, figuring they would've ditched him long ago for the water.

"Ooh, don't you stink purty," Tom goaded Brian for details. "So how far d'jya get?"

"Cedar Point," Brian answered, ignoring the sexual inference. He had practice as the butt of Tom's jokes since childhood. Back in the day, it was Tom who was the chick-magnet. Brian never understood why girls flocked around the jackass when he treated them so badly. Mike was always fortunate to pick up one of the others.

But the girls all took one look at Brian and let him be.

That was fine by Brian, truth be told. Tom and Mike told him to loosen up a bit, but Brian rarely found anyone he wanted to waste his time on. Tom was the sort of person who never understood that.

"Seriously man, don't hold out on us. How was it?" Tom persisted while Matt hid his interest by rummaging through a duffel bag.

Brian fought the urge to punch his friend's nose. "Seriously, she's nice enough, but she's high maintenance, she's expensive to keep, and she's *married*. We had breakfast, we went to give statements to the LEOs, I took a shower at her hotel room while she plotted her divorce with her lawyer, and then she deposited me here with you two idiots. Now if you don't mind, I'm tired."

He crawled into his tent, leaving his friends staring at each other. Sleep fast overtook him and he dreamed of flying first class to the Cote d'Azure. Beside him on the plane was a crazy, brunette princess with odd-colored eyes sipping a glass of champagne and speaking in a foreign language to the flight attendants.

It wasn't real, he knew this. They were from two different worlds and with her prospects it wasn't likely that she'd view him as a potential candidate for her affection anyway. Still, there was something about her that captivated him, threatening to make dating even more difficult for him. Not only were his hours at work not conducive to a stable relationship, but he would now forever be comparing his date to Simone. And if this dream was any indicator, they would never live up to her example.

CHAPTER VIII

Homecoming

S Y STOOD BEFORE THE ELEVATOR from the parking garage of the condominiums for a long time before she pushed the up button.

She really didn't want to be home. She didn't want to see her husband. It had to be done though. Sy wasted enough time before returning to Chicago. After dropping off her knight-in-something-armor, she spent a restless night at the hotel. She opted to drive to Pennsylvania the next day, explaining to Barry that she wanted to find an Amish quilt.

Excuses are not becoming.

The up button lit up at her touch and the familiar ding of the opening door was almost instantaneous. The car was empty, so there was no one to see her cry.

Not that she was going to cry. She refused to cry. Crying was for the weak and Simone Freitag was not weak. A tear escaped and paved a trail down her cheek, and was soon joined by others. She surrendered to her emotion. "Damn."

Their penthouse condominium occupied the top floor of a historic ten-story building on the edge of the Chicago Arts Center. The two condos on the ninth floor had been vacant and on the market for some time. Before she discovered Henry's infidelity, they had discussed purchasing both units; with the goal to remodel the spaces so they would become one giant living space. Sy made a mental note to disagree with the purchases prior to the divorce. If Henry still wanted to remodel, he could do it on his own.

Sy fumbled for her key as the elevator doors opened to reveal the door to her condo was slightly ajar. Curious, she poked her head inside and called for Henry. Then she realized no one was going to answer her. Henry lay on the floor in front of the door in a pool of blood and brain matter, his half-dressed mistress lying in similar fashion across from the foyer. The housekeeper was nowhere to be found.

Henry's wide eyes were unmoving, void of the sparkle of life. The man she wanted to murder had become the victim of a murder. She didn't know whether to laugh or cry. She stood for a long while, focusing on the blood spatter patterns that were reminiscent of the Rorschach tests she had to endure as a child.

"What do you see?" a taciturn man with square-rimmed glasses asked her on occasion.

"An ink blot."

He flipped to a different card. "What about now?"

"Another ink blot."

"And now?" as yet another card was flashed before her.

"Oh my God! It's an ink blot!"

Her ear-piece clicked as her phone rang, shaking her from her recollection just as she wondered what Doctor Hammerschmidt would have thought if she responded to the test with 'a blood blot'. Back in the future, she answered the call with automation. "Barry, I need your help. Notify the authorities and have them come with the coroner to the penthouse."

"Sy, I told you divorce would be cleaner." She could hear his land-line phone bleeping 911 in the background.

"I didn't do it Barry, I swear! I just found them like this. I got out of the elevator and the door was open..."

"Stay put and don't touch anything. I'll be there in a minute."

The phones disengaged. Sy leaned against the door-jamb for support. Her legs felt too weak to support her meager weight and she fought the urge to vomit. Once she stabilized herself, she headed her lawyer's advice and inched back out to sit on the bench in the landing. She had seen enough true-crime dramas on television to realize her entire home was now a crime scene.

The smell of blood finally penetrated her senses. A hint of sulfur mingled in the salty sweetness that coated her mouth. She closed her eyes against the flavor and arrived in Chardonnay again, with the sunlight on the western horizon. Paper lanterns lit the veranda as twilight fell and somewhere nearby, her father played the viola. "Simon," he said. He always called her Simon; that was how she got her nickname.

Alas the viola was the sirens of approaching emergency vehicles and no one was calling her name. A few minutes later, the elevator dinged as its doors opened, and officials spilled onto the landing.

A uniformed officer introduced himself as Giordano. He asked her some questions; was she okay, could she tell them what happened. Someone else said the coroner was on his way and most of the medical emergency team returned to the elevator. A three-ring-circus erupted on her landing, complete with uniformed clowns. "I don't know," she managed to respond, "I just got home. Someone called me. I told them to call you. I sat down here. I waited for you..."

Giordano came into focus; his dark eyebrows were knit together with concern. "Do you know the victims?"

She nodded. "The man in there is Henry Freitag. I'm his wife, Simone."

"The woman?"

"Henry's...I don't know her name."

"Does your husband have any enemies?"

"He should, all things considered. He wasn't exactly the world's most honest businessman," she shrugged. She was beginning to feel like herself again. The questions helped, somehow. "But everyone loved him. Everyone. I'd say he might only have a handful of viable enemies that could do this to him, me included."

Giordano gave her a half-smile and wrote something down in his notepad. "We'll need that list of names, if you don't mind."

"Sure."

"Tell me this, why do you include yourself on this list?"

Like a scientist would speak of a series of Petri dishes, Sy answered. "Are you kidding me? I know how this works you know. Of course I'm suspect number one. Not only am I his widow, but less than seventy-six hours ago I caught my husband in our hot-tub with that whore in there doing naughty things that married men should only do with their wives. Not to mention I already tried to kill him...sort of. I mean, in a fit of anger, I threw my curling iron in the water but it didn't work. Who knew it had to be plugged in to kill anyone? So I took the keys to the car and stormed out. I drove and drove and drove. And a few hours later I found myself in a Sandusky

Wint-Mart. There were some armed robbers, and some hostages, and I had napalm and an off-duty FBI agent."

"What time was that?" He scribbled some more notes. "I mean when you found them in the hot-tub."

Did he just completely ignore the Wint-Mart story? "Oh, um, last Thursday. My jet landed at O'Hare an hour late because some president or other was getting a haircut in Air Force One. Well I say it was an hour late, even though I left a few days earlier than anticipated. I collected my bags, I'd say around 9:30, and grabbed a taxi home. Yellow Cab Company number five-twelve, if you're interested. Traffic was brutal because of the ball park. Cubs lost by the way, in case you didn't know. The stop light at Baker, you know there under the L, was on the fritz."

"What flight were you on?"

"You'll have to check with my pilot for the flight number." She fumbled through her wallet to fish out a business card for the officer. "Andre DuPont. We parked at the private hanger as usual. He'll have the flight charts and approvals. We were in Madrid."

Giordano rolled his eyes. "Money," he muttered with a snort.

He pissed her off. She was being cooperative so she didn't understand the attitude. Taking a deep breath, she smelled the grapes of Chardonnay and continued. "So I arrived home around 10:30. There were rose petals all over the floor and I thought Henry must've found out I was coming home early and was trying to do something romantic. He did those sorts of things often you understand. Like one summer, he kidnapped me from my photo shoot and he flew me to the South Pacific and we spent the whole week lying on a beach like we were the only ones left in the world and, well, effectively completed our fourth honeymoon."

"So you saw the roses and thought nothing was wrong."

"Correct."

"But the petals weren't there for you?"

"No, they weren't. I went through to the bedroom and I didn't see him, but the sheets were turned down. I used the bathroom and I noticed my curling iron was left out on the counter, something I never do. So I took it with me, don't ask why. I may have meant to ask Henry about it. I went to the kitchen and there was still nobody around. That's when I heard music from the patio and as I made my way through the sitting room, I heard her giggle."

"And then what happened?" he raised an eyebrow.

Her muscles tensed up. "What happened? I went out to the hottub and there they were, a couple humpback whales grunting and splashing like it was their last day on earth. I shrieked. She screamed that it wasn't what it looked like. Henry yelled at her that I wasn't stupid. I thanked him for defending my intelligence but then said to prepare to meet his maker and I threw the curling iron in the water. I felt silly that it didn't work. I told them I'd be back with a better plan and I grabbed the keys and ran."

"And how long were you gone?"

Ding went the elevator and Barry stepped out. Clean-shaven and his hair pulled back into his standard pony-tail, he was a giant in the small landing space.

Giordano jumped back. "Hang on Buddy; this is an active crime scene investigation."

"Yes it is and I'm representing Ms. Freitag in a legal capacity. Barry Fletcher."

"Officer Giordano. Ms. Freitag did not mention you were on your way."

"I was the one who phoned her as she made the unfortunate discover. She asked me to call you all down here. She was in shock."

"Thank you Barry," Sy blurted. "I've been honest with them so far, but I've been a bit blubbery and I think they have more information than they'll ever need about my last few hours in this place." she relaxed again. Mr. Fix-it was there to fix-it and make everything all better.

It occurred to her that not only was she in hot water now, but so was Special Agent Kirby. The Federal Bureau of Investigation had a whole unit devoted to murder-for-hire. If Kirby mentioned that she offered him a car in return for his assistance in Henry's demise...She shivered. She didn't want to think about going to jail, or worse, getting deported. Speaking in Romanian, she asked Barry about the consequences.

He replied in the same language not to worry. "It's obvious he didn't take you seriously or he would've arrested you in Sandusky."

Returning to Giordano's unanswered question, she continued, "I was gone almost three days, just returning home tonight. I had been in constant contact with Henry for at least the first day of that. He called me incessantly. It annoyed me."

The pencil made another series of scratches in Giordano's notepad. "And can someone vouch for your whereabouts over the last twenty-four hours?"

"Barry can for the time the Sandusky police department can't. I'm sure if you showed a picture of my car, anyone anywhere I drove could identify it."

"It sticks out?"

"Bugatti Veyrons tend to."

The elevator doors dinged open, announcing the arrival of the housekeeper. Annika Christensen dropped her shopping bag, visibly startled at the sight of the officers. "What ees it zat ees happenick heer? Ms. Freitack?" Fear darted back and forth in the housekeeper's eyes.

"Officer Giordano, this is Annika Christensen, my housekeeper."

"I come to kleen." Her wide eyes were glued to the condo doorway and the pool of blood that seeped into the landing. "Whar ees 'Enry?"

Giordano cleared his throat. "Ma'am, I'm sorry..."

The door to the condo chose that precise moment to swing a little further inward revealing Henry's hand. Annika screeched, curdling blood, and fainted, collapsing onto Giordano, throwing him off balance. For a moment, it appeared as if he, too, might go crashing down like a chain of dominoes, but he regained his footing and eased the woman down to the floor.

Sy suppressed an inappropriate giggle, concentrating on her chipped nail to avoid eye contact with the officer. A name flashed in her mind. "I bet that whore in there is Sandy Petrusky. That's the name of his most recent arts dealer. I wondered why he bought that butt-ugly Picasso knock off. That rotten, good-for-nothing, son-of-a..." She put her feelings in check. As exquisite as it would be to call him foul names, Henry was dead and he couldn't defend his honor now any more than he could when he was alive. Alive, he could at least respond in kind.

A crime scene investigator with the name Scofield stitched above his flak-jacket pocket, approached Giordano with a handbag. "Hey Jard, I think we just ideed the second vic. Found a small purse with a California driver's license in it."

Giordano took a peek at the license. "Well I suppose it could be her, if her face was still intact. We'll have to compare her fingerprints to the DMV record. The vic is blond. Name says Jasmine Colby according to this, ring any bells?"

Sy shook her head. The face on the driver's license was definitely the blond in the hot-tub, but in the picture she had black hair. There was a post office box in Huntington Beach listed as the mailing address. Date of birth was October 23, 1982. She was five-foot-five with blue eyes. If the whore in the condo was Jasmine, then who was Sandy Petrusky? The officer handed the license back to the investigator.

Annika looked pensive as Barry helped her onto the bench next to Sy. "I's sorry Ms. Freitack. I remember tellink 'Enry he should pack his belongkinks and how you say...heet zee road Jack. He escorts her out. She take her back. He ees comink back een, 'n' he say to me to call you to let you know he keeck her out an' he leeve her no more."

Trying to follow any conversation with Annika in English was difficult so Sy switched to Dutch for her. "He said he was leaving her or no longer living here?"

"Leaving her." Annika was much more comfortable speaking in her native language. "He said he was going to leave all of them, if you ever came home."

Barry groaned. Bile threatened Sy's stomach.

"What was that all about?" Giordano asked.

Barry rubbed his chin and translated. "There's more than one mistress, apparently."

Sy stood up and before anyone could catch her, she stepped through the condo doorway. She then proceeded to kick Henry's lifeless form with everything she had. It took Officer Giordano and Barry both to pull her off of him. Taking several deep breaths, Sy turned to the officer and spat, "You can post that I'm offering one million United States dollars to the first person who can bring us to the killer. And you can tell the killer when you catch them that I insist on paying for their lawyer as a thank-you present."

CHAPTER IX

The War Room

BRIAN ARRIVED AT HIS OFFICE on Monday morning, heading straight for the coffee pot in the break-room. He poured the thick, dark liquid into a Styrofoam cup, his thoughts drifting back to his fishing trip, and Sy. Her half-blue, half-brown eyes haunted him almost as much as the peculiar telepathic capability she possessed. He wondered where she was at that moment and whether she served papers on her husband yet.

He and Sy had parted ways without exchanging contact information, much to the disappointment of his friends and his own irritation. Leaning up against the break-room cabinet, he stirred powdered creamer into his java while he toyed with the idea of calling her lawyer. If he did, would he need to invent an excuse to call or would 'I'd like to talk to Sy' be enough?

His supervisor, Robert Jericho, entered the break-room, interrupting. "Hey, you awake yet? What'chya got on your plate?"

When Jericho stepped out of his office, it was never good news. Brian adjusted to reality. "Uh, I'm meeting up to interview someone this afternoon to discuss the Andersonville case, remember? Why? What's up?"

Jericho nodded, "Send Carter out instead. We're going to need your help on a different investigation."

Frustration leached into his veins. "Sir, all due respect, but do you know how long it took before this witness would even step forward? I've been trying to pull this case together for months. Abandoning her at this stage of the game is not just rude, it's unethical."

"Objection noted. Send Carter instead. Grab your coffee and join me in the war-room for a quick debriefing."

Crap, what's gonna happen now? He poured a splash more of the department's miserable excuse for coffee into his cup with another unhealthy dose of creamer, and followed Jericho's wake towards the war-room. Catching Carter in the hallway, Brian told him the Andersonville case was sitting on his desk and thanked him for being flexible enough to take over.

"Don't mention it, bud." Carter clapped Brian's shoulder. "Anything in particular you need me to cover that you can think of right off hand?"

"Affirmative. It's her son that's the alleged writer. She's bringing in some of his old school notebooks so we can compare styles."

"Got it. And no worries Kirby, I'll be on my best behavior."

THE WAR-ROOM GOT ITS NICKNAME from the red tint to the brick that lined the outside wall. There were only a couple people present, whom Brian recognized as being from the violent crimes team. Jericho motioned him to the empty seat next to his as Special Agent Weller stood to address the room. Her voice and general appearance was that of tired determination. "Good morning, ladies and gentlemen. I realize this is a sudden meeting, so I'll keep this as brief as possible.

"We've received a tip regarding a possible hit-for-hire in Chicago which calls for a certain degree of subtlety. Those of you who have seen the news this morning will note that Henry Freitag was found in his Chicago condo by his wife late last night. He had been shot to death, along with an-other victim, a woman, a Miss Jasmine Colby."

Brian set his jaw. He didn't like surprises and his boss had just thrown him to the wolves. "Is the vic's widow Simone?"

Weller flipped a few pages in the file in front of her then regarded him with a raised eyebrow. "Er, yes. Simone Freitag. She's a Swiss national in the country on a permanent visa. Jericho says you're acquainted somehow with the family?"

Brian winced as some quiet chuckles escaped the meeting attendees. "All right, everyone, I know you've all heard the story about the Wint-Mart in Sandusky. The woman who assisted me with the hostages was Simone."

Weller tucked an errant strand of hair behind her ear. "Well she's lawyered up and our federal government is receiving pressure from the Swiss for some reason. This lady is apparently one very important cookie and this case needs special handling."

Brian groaned. "Let me guess. You're about to ask if I can show up as a friend of the widow, poke my nose in her affairs for a week or two, and give you a run down on how she could or could not have hired someone to pull the trigger."

Jericho clapped him on the shoulder. "Well, apart from the asking bit, that's it in a nut shell. We don't want her jumping the country without seeing that some form of justice is carried out."

Knowing he wasn't responsible for telling the Bureau about Sy's proposition of murder, Brian wondered who was. "Who gave us the tip?"

Weller looked uncomfortable. "It was the heist man from your botched robbery."

Brian rolled his eyes. "Seriously? We're taking this thug's word for it like it's the real deal?"

"We're sure he's trying to get the district attorney's office to cut him a deal. We investigate this tip; we'll keep both the prosecution and the defense happy." Weller folded her arms and sneered. "Somehow, Sandusky officials got the impression that we cooperate happily and that we would do anything to help them with their investigation. Does that have anything to do with the goodwill they experienced while you were their guest?"

Sam, one of Weller's team, leaned forward and interrupted. "Weller, I don't like this case, one, and two, if we are taking this case, why are we just handing it off to a different unit, no offense Kirby."

"None taken, Sam. I happen to agree with you." Brian rubbed his forehead. He felt warm under his collar. "Anyway, the Chicago office can't handle this? It's in their neck of the woods after all."

Weller's voice pitched higher. "Did I mention that we have the political roster of who's who leaning on us? Embassies are calling us non-stop? It's not just Switzerland either. And it's not that they're worried about a possible international incident as much as they're worried about pissing off this woman. I think the only government we haven't heard from since this news broke is North Korea, but the day's still young." She cleared her throat, "Kirby, you happen to be the only one of any federal or state department that already as open dialog with her."

Sam shook his head again. "Well it sounds like the CIA or the NSA ought to be involved then, since it's a case of such national importance. Or where are the Secret Service guys? Why aren't they barking at our door?"

She tapped the table. "Who said they weren't? They're chomping at the bit to delve into this. No matter how far-fetched this possibility might be, we have to be the ones to act on it and get our ducks in a row. It just doesn't fall under their jurisdictions. Hell, it barely falls under ours."

Brian released a measured breath. He wasn't in the mood. "It's not going to work you know. She'll know why I'm showing up."

"Only if you tell her." Jericho leaned back in his seat. His voice dripped with greed. "The Bureau's giving us carte blanche on this one. You don't have to take a team in if you don't want to; we'll let you make the call. Tell her whatever story you want."

"That's just it, boys and girls; I don't think you truly understand how perceptive she is." Brian's leg jackhammered under the table. "I may have established a small rapport with her during my vacation, but she's not going to allow me to just drop into her life after that. She's got money and status, and she knows I don't. I don't travel in her circles. She watches enough crime-shows on TV that she'll guess the reason I'm there before she even sees me." *Not to mention she can read my mind like an open book.*

Jericho continued. "Listen, I'm clearing you book of all your cases. Your only concern right now is Simone Freitag. And after you're done, we'll pay for your next vacation to wherever you want to go and for however long."

"Oh and that makes spying on her okay?" Brian knew he was fighting a losing battle. "You're pushing way too many perks on me for this to be clean, especially since I can tell you right now she didn't do it. I was sitting in her hotel room listening to the divorce stipulations."

Mentioning the hotel room produced another round of snickers. Jericho waved a hand to dispel the outburst. "She might've decided murder was cleaner, especially if someone did it for her."

"Not a chance. Her lawyer is superman. I've done the research. Barry Fletcher said divorce would be cleaner and that man says nothing he can't deliver on," Brian said. "And if she had managed to do it, I have a feeling the signed confession would have been at the local police station seconds after she pulled the trigger and we'd be deporting her to Switzerland. This is wrong and everyone here knows it."

The table was quiet for a moment. Weller smirked. "That being said, we pooled our resources and with a little assistance from our Agency partners, we have every scrap of information that is available on Simone Freitag."

Brian tried not to sound interested. "And?"

She tossed him the manila file folder. Brian flipped through it as casual as possible, although it was hard to do. The file was only a half-inch thick and focused mostly on the recent usage of her Swiss passport. More than three-fourths of the papers were redacted. There was a random cell phone bill and a bank statement that had figures in the millions, and a copy of a filed 1099 from several years earlier that implied the United Nations contracted her for translation services. The only photo apart from her passport was taken as if she was a hundred miles away from the camera, but she was looking right at it like she knew it was there.

Weller added, "We have the fact that her father is a former citizen of communist Romania before his family defected to Switzerland, and his file is even thinner than hers. Her family just doesn't exist on paper."

"That doesn't mean anything in the scheme of things." Brian knew there was a special level of hell reserved for him as he skimmed the pages of redacted intelligence. This was not how he wanted to intrude into her personal affairs, researching the astringent, black-and-white narrative of her known particulars. He would've preferred dinner, a glass of wine maybe.

He laughed to himself when he found that they listed her eye-color as "not applicable" in one description. Blue-brown apparently wasn't an option.

Jericho pleaded with him. "You're the only one who got close enough to her to have any form of conversation that didn't end with the words get stuffed. Every official down the pipeline wants to be you right now, thinking it'll get them a shiny gold star and a sizable raise."

Brian flipped the file back to Weller, nervous about the implications. "So why are we doing this again? Is it because the CIA wants us to, or the CIA is telling us to? Do they view her as some sort of threat? Espionage is not my expertise, for Christ's sake; I deal with copyrights."

"Eh, I don't think they even know. They can't link her to anything or anyone. She travels all over the world but she never goes anywhere that's considered questionable. Most of her trips are divided between Canada, Switzerland, and the States, but as frequently as she travels, there are Wall Street suite types that travel more often and to more American-unfriendly places."

"So it's a fishing expedition then. Perfect."

Weller examined her fingernails and sighed, "Listen. I like this even less than you do, truly, but of all the people here, you're the only one who can pull this out of the cesspool pissing match that it's in and make the department look good at the same time."

"Oh there's no pressure there..." Brian crossed his arms. He wanted to be anywhere but there. "I suppose you're going to have me report to a handler?"

Jericho shook his head. "Negative. We've made it clear to those goons that this is our case, our rules, our jurisdiction. Trust me. Meeting with them at five o'clock this morning was a farce. They were coming up with every cover in the books, with tech gadgets and the like..." He threw his hands up, defeated.

"Heavy hardware for a domestic dispute?" Sam knit his eyebrows together. "That would signal to my three-year-old daughter that something was amiss."

Jericho agreed. "For a company that runs covert ops all the time, I would think they'd understand the need for subtlety."

Weller opened the file again. She looked lost. "Look Brian, we want you there to look into the hit-for-hire. The CIA wants someone there who can make an unobtrusive observation that will help them rule her out or in. A little collaboration will go a long way. If she questions why you're there, tell that it's just a precautionary measure. We know that Henry had some art dealings. Tell her you're following up on a tip about some art fraud and you want to make sure she isn't a victim."

"Art? Craptastic." *What do I know about art?* Brian exchanged hard looks with everyone in the room. "After this, do we leave her alone? Or is the Bureau going to expect me to belittle myself even further?"

Jericho was quick to respond. "We leave her alone, which will cross us off the inter-companies Christmas party list, but I think we can handle it."

Weller's expression softened. She almost sounded human. "We're giving you complete control over this one you know. It's just a murder. You clear it up, you come home. The Bureau looks benevolent instead of selfish, and everyone is happy."

"Fine." Brian didn't trust any of them not to leave him stranded if there was trouble. "But I go in alone. No team. But I'll need full and immediate administrative on-call support."

"Done." Jericho started to rise.

"Oh, no you don't. I'm not done yet, not by a long shot. I'll need a sufficient spend account. The woman travels in some pretty pricey circles, remember? I'll try to keep the spending minimal but I don't want to be stuck in a roach motel and have to keep up appearances."

Weller and Jericho made eye contact. "That's reasonable." She sounded like it was going to come from her personal account.

"And," Brian took a deep breath. "In addition to the vacation you promised, I need a stand-by life-line extraction in case things go sideways, like any other undercover agent."

"You got it," she wrote something on a sticky-note and handed it to her assistant. "That it?"

"That's it, but if I think of something, I don't want to get the shaft. In the meantime, give me the file you've collected on her late husband, since we have nothing on our prime suspect, and I'll see what I can do. Be prepared for the President himself to call though. The woman has connections."

Weller turned green and Jericho cleared his throat. "Kirby, I believe he already has."

BRIAN LEFT THE ROOM after the briefing concluded an hour later, feeling dirty. Spying on the woman he had developed a small crush on felt like stalking. The fact that it was government sanctioned made it worse somehow. She would be able to see right through any flimsy excuse of an undercover story. Brian decided that honesty would be the best policy. Perhaps in this case the truth would set them free.

Back at his desk, he poured over the Henry Freitag file. On paper, the victim was a clean-cut individual despite being a part of the Hollywood party elite. He was a movie and sometimes stage producer, his works appearing often at the film festival in Cannes. The Academy gave him several nods during his career, with his most recent endeavor earned him his third win. There were no scandals related to a casting couch or for overselling a project, or fixing numbers. His finances were above board. His stocks adviser on Wall Street was squeaky clean too, so there weren't any hidden pitfalls financially. Absolutely nothing stood out that anyone would be threatening him for any reason.

So, except for Simone, who would want to kill Henry Freitag?

In spite of his misgivings, however, Brian was looking forward to seeing her again. He booked a flight from Kennedy to Chicago O'Hare leaving the next day. That gave him a full night to study the particulars of Henry's life. Grateful that he still had Fletcher's business card in his wallet, he pulled it out and dialed his phone. He didn't need to worry about inventing an excuse now.

CHAPTER X

Breaking The Ice

BRIAN COLLECTED HIS BACKPACK, paid his taxi-driver, and met with Barry on the front steps of the hotel. "Thanks again for agreeing to this. How is she holding up?"

Barry looked grim as he motioned Brian towards the hotel lobby. "Sy's doing a decent job of fooling everyone, except me."

"I hope I'm not going to be an imposition."

"I wouldn't worry about it." The elevator opened as Barry pushed the arrow up. Before the doors closed, he pushed the twelfth floor button. "She's going to be happy to see you."

Brian's heart felt tight in his chest and some butterflies hatched in his stomach. "You didn't tell her I was coming?"

"No, I didn't want to ruin the surprise." The lawyer checked his black, ceramic watch, then looked at Brian through the reflection in the elevator doors. "Try not to look so guilty, Mr. Kirby. I'm truly glad you're here. My schedule is pretty hectic and I'm afraid I can't devote time to sitting with her. We really don't want her to be alone if possible."

"We?"

"Yes, I've counseled with her father several times. He's doing his best to wrap up his business in Greece. He's grateful she has a friend."

"I'm ah, honored if she thinks I'm her friend...that didn't come out right."

"I know what you meant."

They exited when the elevator doors opened and Brian followed Barry down a few corridors. At the last door down the hallway, Barry knocked. "Sy, you up for company?"

A familiar, feathery voice drifted through the core of the door. "Sure. Why not?"

Barry turned and left Brian standing alone in the hallway. He straightened his back and heard a distinct squeal. The door wrenched open. "I can come back another time...if you'd prefer," he offered.

Sy didn't look as put together the last time he saw her. Her face was void of makeup, her nose pink and her eyes puffy from emotion. Or scotch. Her brown hair was pulled back into a simple ponytail and she wore the velour pantsuit she'd liberated from Wint-Mart.

She dragged him inside. "I don't care that you're here because the FBI told you to be. I'm just glad you're here. Care for a scotch'n'soda?"

Brian moved like a cat in unfamiliar territory, setting his backpack against the wall beside the door. "Uh, sure. Three fingers, hold the soda."

"I'm giving you five fingers, Agent," she poured a rich, amber liquid from a crystal decanter at the mini bar. "My fingers are small and this one is worth it."

He accepted the glass. "Brian, please. I need to say this before I get sidetracked. I don't want to spy on you, Sy. I'm truly sorry for your loss."

She shrugged. "My loss, your gain. This should be an easy case for you. I didn't kill Henry, and I didn't hire whoever it was who did. Unless..." Sy cast him a wayward glance. "You didn't do it, did you?"

"That's a negative."

"Good. I wouldn't turn you in, mind, but I couldn't give you the Veyron because I offered it to the charity raffle for his art of the pageant masters show." She tossed herself on the hotel-room sofa. "They should be able to release it shouldn't they? I mean the cops, in time for the raffle? It's not supposed to happen for another three months."

He sat down at the opposite end of the couch, draping his arm across the back. "The LEOs confiscated your car to process for evidence?"

She nodded. "I don't know what it is they expect to find, but I'm sure the car is the highlight of the evidence garage at the moment."

Brian popped tension loose from his neck and took a long sip of the scotch. Its buttery warmth coated his throat, carrying notes of sherry and oak, and a smoke of peat. She was right. It was worth it. "I'll bet."

She sniffed, furrowing her brow. "Hell, I might let them keep it. I'm not sure Henry's worth the hassle. They can keep his corpse, too, for all I care. Let his mistresses bury him."

"Speaking of...well, this case. I should let you know that this assignment...How do I say this?"

To Brian's surprise, she laughed. "I already know what's going on."

"You do?"

"Sure. MI5 is probably leaning on the CIA, and the CIA has placed the FBI under thumb as a result. Oh, don't look so guilty," her lips curled down in a mocking pout. "I'm a big girl with elusive habits, several foreign bank accounts, a private jet, and the expensive giant-sized passport because every year I run out of pages. My father is even more elusive. So, I expect to be spied on, lied to, and harassed by governments. It goes with the territory. America isn't the only dog sniffing either. Have you ever been followed by a Peruvian ambassador?"

"Peruvian? I can't say that I have, at least that I'm aware of." He let go the breath he was holding.

"Why are you acting so freaked out over this? I honestly don't care, Brian."

"I don't know. I just didn't want to be the reason you took offense I guess."

"Well, don't you worry. I'm not an operative, covert or otherwise. I'm simply misunderstood."

"I'll say. They gave me the combined agencies file on you."

"Oh?" her eyes twinkled. "What did it say?"

"Nothing much. You might be interested to know the CIA has no idea how to classify your eye color."

She giggled, "Most don't."

They shared a long silence, easing into the comfort of companionship. Brian took another sip of his scotch for liquid courage. "Are you up to telling me what happened?"

Her mood darkened as the clouds rolled in, threatening to rain again. She chewed on her lower lip. "I dropped you off at the campsite and spent the night in the suite. I made a wrong turn on the way home and ended up in Pennsylvania. I figured, what the hell? Try to find an Amish quilt. Killed almost twenty-four hours that way. Especially since, with the Veyron's fuel economy, I had to stop for petrol every five minutes or so. To be honest with you though, it was just because I wasn't ready to come home."

"When did you get home?"

"I pulled into the parking garage at eight o'clock on the nose according to the Fifth Avenue Cathedral church bells. I took the elevator up, stepped onto the landing, and saw the door to the flat was open. Thankfully, Barry called when he did and handled everything else. I might still be standing in the middle of it all, wondering what to do next."

"Was the other vic the whore from the hot-tub?"

"Oh thank you for calling her a whore. You made my day, again." Her smile shined. "According to the driver's license they found in her purse, her name was Jasmine Colby. I thought she might have been Sandy Petrusky. I've never met the woman, but I thought she was the arts dealer Henry was stupid for. That bloody Picasso knock-off he bought was more expensive than it should have been."

"Is it possible Henry may have been involved in or the victim of some sort of art fraud?"

"If he was I doubt it was on purpose. Don't get me wrong, the man was brilliant when it came to fund-raising for a project and ensuring key people were employed for the appointed film, but he was an idiot when it came to still life."

Brian took another drink, finishing his scotch, and set the glass down on the coffee table. "You said he was working on some art project here in Chicago?"

Standing up and crossing the room, Sy opened the briefcase on the dining table. She withdrew a portfolio of papers and pictures and passed the items on to Brian. "The Breathing Gallery. Someone approached Henry with the idea a while back and he ran with it. Basically, the idea is to use performers from the Chicago Opera House and recreate a living scene based on famous paintings."

Brian inspected the collection of photos. "Sooo...Actors become the painting, and the painting becomes...a play?"

"Exactly. Part of the draw is that the pictures aren't just random. They're carefully chosen to a plot. There's going to be a full three acts, with up to four different endings that could possibly be on any particular night." She shuffled the sketches around for him. "It's truly a brilliant concept if you ask me. I was trying to finish up my obligations so I could devote some time to help with the fund-raising events. It was the whole reason I returned early from Madrid."

Silence found them as he flipped through the compilation, reviewing the obscure and random notes scribbled across magazine clippings and concept art. She shifted beside him and he realized then how close they were. Feeling heat build in the space between them, Brian was self-conscious. He needed an excuse to move.

Scotch.

He rose and placed the folder on the coffee table, picking up his scotch glass, and walked to the decanter to pour another drink. "So who do you think killed him?"

"No one. Anyone. The doorman, the wife, the house-keeper, the hired agent..." Her eyelashes fluttered.

Brian smirked.

Her smile faded. "Henry should have had a ton of enemies, as loose as he played with the truth. But he was so charming, I mean really charming and fun to be around. Everyone loved him, especially when he lied to them."

"Is that how someone like you ended up with someone like him to begin with?" Brian restoppered the decanter.

"Someone like me?" The smile returned. "Are you flirting?"

He shifted, laughing. "You're intelligent, funny...beautiful." He cleared his throat. "He's an ass."

She stood. "You are flirting!"

Guilty, he took a look at his glass and decided more scotch was in order. He poured another quick splash. "That doesn't change the question. Wouldn't your talent see through that crap?"

She collected the folder and returned it to the briefcase. "It's a fair question I suppose. You have to understand, I have no idea why I can read minds or what affects my ability to do so. Maybe it has something to do with a mutual desire to communicate, or maybe my own psyche wouldn't allow me to see the obvious in order to spare me pain."

He brought the decanter and an empty glass as he returned to the couch. "Your eyes. I gather that was caused by trauma. When you were little, something happened to you or you witnessed something."

There was pain behind her expression. Tears shined in her eyes. "The worst part is I remember nothing, except random flashes of lab coats and experiments."

He smacked the seat next to him and then poured her a drink. "I'm sorry, I shouldn't have said anything."

"No, it's okay." She accepted the drink and cocooned herself on the opposite end of the couch. It was a long moment before she spoke again. "You know, Henry was a brick wall to me most days, except when I wore red. Then I could see his thoughts more clearly than I could see my own."

"And you married…" He asked with equal parts jealousy and curiosity and hoped she didn't notice.

She stared into the swirls of amber of her drink. Her voice sounded far away, like it was crossing from a neglected memory. "I met him in Singapore." A tear appeared on her cheek. She explained the circumstances of their chance meeting in Kula Lumpur, where a police offer asked Henry questions and she offered to help bridge the language gap in passing. "As it turned out, the officer thought he was speaking with Tom Cruise and he just wanted an autograph. We laughed about it later."

"You speak Malay?"

"Mandarin, but not fluently. And I know the film industry, so I was able to translate."

"You speak Chinese. Barry says you speak Romanian and Dutch. How many languages can you speak?"

"I've lost track actually. I grew up the equivalent of an embassy brat, we traveled so much. You tend to pick up languages quickly that way."

"Well I'm a bit envious, having completely butchered Spanish in high school," he admitted. "Henry's file picture didn't do him justice if the officer thought he was Tom Cruise."

"People thought that because of his smile. Henry was taller than Tommy though. After the policeman left him alone, he charmed me right into a cab and out to dinner."

"And then…"

She squished her nose and shrugged. "A year of dates here and there, depending on where we were in the world with respect to one another. Then I happened to be in Nice when he asked me to attend the movie festival in Cannes. We took a side trip to Monaco and he proposed to me on the palace grounds."

"Smooth."

"Yeah, well," she sniffed. "Looking back on it now, he probably only proposed because I was the only one he couldn't seduce right out of the starting gate. My father didn't like him, which should have been an alarm to me. Called him a used-car salesman, you know the type. Henry, well he could steal the ice from an Eskimo's igloo and sell it back to him as ice cream, and at five-times the going rate."

"How is it Henry didn't have enemies by the thousands?"

She knocked the remainder of her scotch back and coughed. "You'd think he should right? A few of his projects'd go south, some of his regulars would feel slighted at the loss of their investments, or they didn't like that they thought they were investing in something they weren't. But I can't stress this enough, Brian, everyone and I do mean everyone, worshiped the ground he walked on. So most enemies he had or the disagreements that developed were short lived."

"And no one in particular springs to mind?"

Her eyes rolled up, conferring with the ceiling. "No, no one stands out, at least to me. He almost lost his shirt over the Casablanca Project so the culprit theoretically could be found among that list of people I suppose. I think if they were going to try something though, they wouldn't have waited five years to do it."

"Casablanca? *The* Casablanca?"

"He was pushing to get Cage to reprise the role of Rick and Depardieu for Captain Renault. I forget what the snag was over that. I remember telling him to drop the idea and let someone else lose face. He eventually agreed with me. After all, why mess with perfection?"

"How do you figure into the Hollywood crowd? Is it just by association with Henry?"

"I scout locations for film and photo shoots, freelance. I have such an affinity for the movies, with my travel experience; it just seemed like a natural career choice."

"Okay, last question. Why movies?"

Her response wrenched his heart. "In a movie theater, or even watching videos, I can never read an actor's thought. Not even accidentally. The story is a complete surprise to me the first time through. You have no idea how refreshing that is."

The sun was close to rising when they agreed that they should try to get some sleep, although she wouldn't let him leave. While the two room suite she was booked in wasn't as large as the one in Cedar Point had been, Sy insisted he take the vacant room. "No need to pay full price for something you're only going to use for three hours," she offered. "Especially since this room is already paid for, and it's empty."

"I appreciate it, but the Bureau-"

"Don't make me beg you." She looked fragile then, a wounded sparrow. "Please, I really don't want to be alone right now."

And Brian stayed.

CHAPTER XI

Lazy Morning

THE LAZY MORNING FOUND THEM still in bed when house-keeping knocked on the door. Sy woke to the alarm and emerged from her room to explain housekeeping would not be needed that day. "Just leave us some extra towels." She withdrew money from her wallet to tip the girl.

It was 11:30 according to the clock, and she decided to order a small brunch from room service. A quick shower later, she dressed and sat down at her laptop to answer a few emails before the food arrived.

Barry called her cell phone as room service knocked at the door. "I've released your statement to the press," he said. "I assumed you didn't want to be on the news just yet. I imagine the paparazzi have made themselves pests. Fortunately for you, I know someone that can call them off and I gave him a jingle already."

"Thank you, Barry. You're a prince."

"My bill is in the mail."

She laughed, "So's the check."

"You sound like you're doing better. I take it Special Agent Kirby was a welcome sight then."

"Oh you have no idea. I needed him like the desert needs rain. Hey, since you brought him up," She tipped the wait-staff as they left and dropped her voice to a whisper. "What do you think of him? Do you think Papa will like him?"

"Sy, do you honestly think I would have dropped him off if I didn't like him?"

"And Papa?"

There was a long pause from his end of the line. Sy could swear she heard him smiling. "Goodbye, Sy."

"Cheers," She ended the call, took a deep breath, then knocked on Brian's door.

Moments later, Brian emerged and thanked her as she handed him a mug of coffee. He stood next to the mini-spread of fruit and crepes, sausage and scrambled egg whites. "This can't be for just the two of us. Where's everyone else?"

"I don't know about you, but I'm ravenous. I haven't eaten anything since before you arrived yesterday."

"I've gotta go to confession on Sunday. Evil, evil gluttony." Brian heaped food on his plate and settled in at the dining table.

Sy joined him with her own plate. She wondered why time flew by in his presence. Had it ever been that easy with Henry? There was something so comfortable about Brian, like the universe knew what it was doing when it threw them together. She sipped her coffee, watched him eat, ignored her stomach pains, and enjoyed the view.

Brian caught on that he was being watched. "Aren't you going to eat? I thought you were starving."

She expressed a giggle. "Sorry, I just got side-tracked."

A HALF-HOUR LATER when their appetites were sated, Sy asked what he had planned for the day. "I know you're here to investigate me, ultimately. I was just wondering if that means I get to tag along or if I have to let you alone for the sake of your cover."

"Well, it's my case so it's my call. I see no reason you can't tag along. I need to check out the art gallery anyway, where this Sandy or Jasmine is from." He looked embarrassed. "I could use some help in that department."

"Let me guess, you're a number-cruncher, not an art critic."

"I won't mislead you. I couldn't tell you the difference between an oil or an acrylic."

"So the art you know consists solely around dogs playing poker?" She teased him, poking his shoulder.

"Well, I don't know about that. I like Remington's works well enough."

She raised an eyebrow. "Sculpture or firearm?"

His eyes sparkled. "Aren't they the same?"

Sy laughed. "I love both, to be honest, so that's some-thing we have in common. However, I prefer the things that go boom."

He squinted at her, head cocked to one side, as if he was trying to figure her out. "I didn't know you were a pistol-packer underneath all that designer fluff."

"Give me a Sig and a box of ammunition and I can turn anything into a pile of smoking goo."

"Hey, don't tease the animals. You're not joking are you?"

She crossed her heart and held up her right hand as if to take an oath. "If the crime scene investigators ever release my condo, I'll be happy to show you my qualifying certificates."

"Qualifying? Were you a cop in your past life?"

"Not a cop," she shook her head. "I'm a Swiss patriot, Brian. I joined the militia voluntarily at nineteen. I went through some pretty rigorous training too. I wasn't going to join up for a desk job, you see. I could get that in the private sector."

"You were in the military?"

"Yes, for two years." She rubbed her shoulder at the ghost of the physical aches of boot camp. "It was a fun time for me. Got to do all sorts of things, including fly a helicopter. It was hard to leave when my enlistment expired, to be honest. But Papa needed some help with his business, and I was ready to do something else."

"So you have experience with firearms."

She nodded. "My favorite thing to shoot was the Browning .50cal."

His jaw dropped. "No way, you fired the Ma Deuce?"

"Jealous?"

He whistled low. "And surprised. You weigh what, a hundred pounds dripping wet?"

She laughed. Knowing she impressed him made her something him even more. Sy wanted to share experiences with him. She wanted to show him all the places she's been.

She wanted him to take her home and introduce her to his family. He made her feel like walking away from her world and finding a corner of his to settle down in. And all he had to do to make her feel that way was smile.

Not once did she ever feel that way with Henry. Not that intense. Never.

"You speak a dozen languages, you know how to find napalm in home goods, and you know how to handle a firearm." He shook his head. "Is there anything you can't do?"

"I can't tune a piano."

"Ha! Serves me right, asking a silly question. If I'm going to hang around you any longer, I'm going have to confess to more sins than just gluttony." He rose from the table and stretched. "If you give me a moment, I'll grab my wallet, then we can head out if you're ready?"

"Sure."

He disappeared through his bedroom door, leaving Sy alone with her thoughts. She stacked up the buffet plates onto the cart and wheeled it out into the hall, humming a nameless but cheerful song the whole while. She was happy.

The best thing Henry ever did for her was get himself murdered. Maybe she'd claim his body and bury him after all.

CHAPTER XII

Wilcox & Sherry

BRIAN OPENED THE DOOR FOR SY and the indiscreet ring of the door alarm announced their presence as they stepped through. The art gallery, Wilcox and Sherry, was industrial in decor and structure, housed as it was in a converted warehouse. Sy explained that the building was once a receiving point for liquor during Prohibition. The cellar was raided often, until the gangsters got wise and shipped their goods through a different locale. The revenue agents didn't learn though, and carried out several fruitless raids on the place before the ratification of the Twenty-First Amendment.

Free-standing walls in the front of the gallery had varied framed works hanging from them. Tall bronze statues of half-naked men and woman scattered the floor and some statuary of whales and other sea-life were displayed in cherry-wood hutches. An easel in the center of the room sported a framed canvas that had the details of a monthly featured artist. That month it was Native American artist Jasper White Horse.

"I know that name from somewhere," Brian said, surprise lacing his tone.

"You might know Mr. White Horse better as an actor. He played Magua in the remake of Last of the Mohicans."

"Ah, yes. I do remember. He played a voice in Tonto's Field as well, didn't he?"

As she nodded, a well-dressed man in his late forties stepped out from the front office to greet them. He had the pallor of an old-western undertaker and looked out of place without the Victorian top hat. His mannerisms were effeminate, but it was his condescending attitude that was off putting. "Do you have an appointment?"

Sy glared down her nose at him. This sort of person she was used to working with, the prima-donna directors and the busybody producers who would interfere with her ability to do her job. She never backed down from the pecking order fight when it presented itself. "Save your act for the peasants," she crooned, her accent as thick as she could make it, working the foreign mystique to her fullest advantage. "I need no appointment." Her t's carried extra emphasis.

The undertaker doubled his efforts, filling more space by straightening his back and squaring off his shoulders. That action only made him less imposing as he took on the appearance of a stuffed goose. "And might I inquire as to who you believe yourself to be?"

Sy sensed Brian reaching for his badge. *Don't, I got this,* she broadcasted. She made a point of inspecting her fingernails. "Your impertinence has not gone unnoticed, little man. Do run along and fetch your mistress. I refuse to converse with the help."

The man had no alternative but to slink back to his office like a battered dog. *He's creepy.* Brian seemed to be getting used to her in his mind. He didn't fight it as much. *So, bets on if he's actually getting her or do you think he just decided to leave Earth without a forwarding address?*

Sy rolled her eyes. *With any luck, he'll do both.*

Soon thereafter, a woman emerged at the top of the staircase and glided down as if on rollers. Her makeup was refined but overdone for a small gallery. "My name is Harmony. I'm the art director for this facility. Stephen implied that you wished to speak to me."

Sy narrowed her eyes. This woman was not Sandy Petrusky either. She was in her fifties, overweight in the midsection as menopausal women get, but put together well and carried an air of sophistication. Accent still strong, Sy spoke as if the director was more than whale slime, but still less than human. "And I dislike waiting. I want you to know I found your employee in my hot-tub with my husband. So far, I am unimpressed with the service of your gallery."

The director's refined, mature exterior melted away to a mousy remnant of its former glory as the woman took an unexpected step back. "Madame," she croaked, "surely a scene would be beneath you. Shall we step into my office? I'll be happy to address your concerns there/"

"Oh very well. Sa margem." *Okay, Brian, let's see how far we can push her.*

Brian nodded.

The three climbed the sterile metal staircase to the row of loft offices occupying the partial second floor. On the landing, the manager turned left and rounded passed two small cubicles and through an even smaller break area. Harmony then ushered Sy and Brian into a corner office with rich mahogany furnishings and subtle Victorian decor. Sy noticed the chair behind the desk was raised higher than the chairs in front and the blinds were adjusted so the sun would be shining directly into clients' eyes. Picking up on her unspoken cue, Brian headed straight for the blinds, while Sy slid into the chair behind the desk.

"I, uh, if you don't mind," Harmony pulled out a client chair with emphasis.

"Actually, I do mind," she read the name plate. "Ms. Sidle, I never sit with my back to the door."

The woman was now at the disadvantage that she tried to put her clients in. She stood motionless for a moment, gripping the back of the chair, her knuckles turning white from the effort.

Sy slammed her hand on the desk. "Sit!"

The director took a seat, banging into the desk with her haste to obey. Sy pushed the laptop towards her as one might a secretary, hearing Brian chuckle under his breath as he peered through the blinds and out the window.

Sy leaned forward in her seat. "Now then, pet, what can you tell me of Jasmine Colby? How is it that I found her in flagrante delecto doing naughty things with my husband? Is that the policy of this gallery?"

Harmony squirmed, adjusting her posture. "No, no of course not. If Jasmine was there, it was on her own time."

"So you encourage fraternization with your clients?"

"No that sort of relationship is strictly against company policy." Harmony's eyes darted to Brian, who had moved from the window and began perusing the books and knick-knacks on the shelves.

"So you hire individuals that break company policy on a regular basis?"

"No ma'am."

"Well," Sy allowed her voice to drift up an octave, "Either she was there because she was supposed to be or she was encouraged to be. Which is it?"

"Please, I must ask you to calm down. Let's look at this situation as rational adults..."

"Rational! Adults! Honestly, woman, your lack of urgency in this affair is unsettling to say the very least. What was that woman doing in my home?"

"I d-don't know. She's n-not allowed to d-do deliveries."

"No?" Sy tapped the laptop. "Pull up her schedule on your little computer screen and prove it."

Harmony fumbled with the laptop latch and bringing up the program. She tossed nervous glances at Brian as her fingers stuttered across her keyboard. "This is her schedule here and you see that, um, well...That's odd."

"What is odd?"

"Someone scheduled her to handle a few evening deliveries during the last month. Maybe, is your husband one of them?" She turned the screen back to show Sy.

"Yes, Freitag, and a total of five nights. Did Henry Freitag buy five nights worth of art?"

"I-I can't d-discuss-"

Sy reared back to spit fire. "He is my husband you miserable wretch of a manager. If I want to know what he purchased, you will tell me!"

The screech of a metal drawer drew Harmony's attention to Brian as he invaded a file cabinet. She half-rose from her seat. "Sir, that information is sensitive-"

Brian tsked her, but didn't shut the drawer. "You don't say? You should look into locking these things up then."

Sy lifted the telephone receiver from its cradle. "Listen you little pimple, in one phone call I can own your pathetic excuse for an art gallery. So you will do exactly what I want you to do without your mundane, stupid, little questions, capiche?"

Fear flashed across the woman's face as images of the Godfather flooded the broadcast-space of her mind. Sy smiled as Harmony imagined waking up next to a horse's head. She sat down. "Y-yes of course. I, please don't hurt me," she hiccupped her words as she typed a serious of commands on her keyboard. 'It was Freitag right? He purchased three portraits from a local artist: *The Gray, Wind,* and *Red River Valley.*"

"I have never heard of these titles. Who is the artist?"

"William McKealy. His style is like if you mixed Picasso with Rembrandt."

"Five nights to deliver three portraits? Did Miss Colby fail maths in school?"

"I don't know why there were five nights...perhaps she delivered the wrong pictures or the wrong frames? I'll ask her when she reports for her shift on Tuesday. She's currently out on vacation."

"And how much did it cost me for my husband to have an affair with this employee of yours?"

"Ah the portraits were all originals you must know and McKealy is a very prominent artist with a great deal of notoriety already..."

"How much!" Sy shook the receiver in Harmony's face.

"Roughly four thousand. Each."

"My husband purchased your employee's body for a mere twelve thousand?" She slammed the receiver back into its cradle. The director jumped. "You may yet hear from my attorney, Ms. Harmony Sidle, if you do not accept those pictures on return. I will expect repayment in full."

"Of course," Harmony looked relieved. "Bring in the pictures and we will happily wave the restocking fees and return every cent of the purchase."

"Come, I am sick of this place," Sy wiggled her finger at Brian and he followed her out and down the stairs. Once outside in the chilly afternoon air, he whistled down a taxi and they settled into the back seat.

"Thank you for playing along," Sy said after giving instructions to the cab driver. "She thought I was Italian Mafia."

"It was entertaining watching you intimidate someone again," Brian said. "Either she's unaware of the untimely death of her employee or she's a brilliant actress."

"After what I put her through, she doesn't know, trust me. What puzzles me is why she didn't mention the fourth painting. I'm sure Henry purchased *Girl in Hammock* from that studio. Sandy Petrusky must have sold it to him, and he decided he wanted more McKealys, and found Jasmine...I'll tell you one thing though. I don't like that assistant of hers. I know I put on airs but you would think he had a corner on the market with his attitude."

Brian agreed. "He was definitely intense."

The cab stopped at the next intersection. Sy watched pedestrian traffic for a moment. "Why did you get into her files? It helped with the whole mafia charade but isn't it a big no-no without a warrant?"

Brian draped his arm across the back of the seat. "Ordinarily, yes. But, it's been my experience that persons in her position only have the file cabinets to look important. I was testing a theory."

"And?"

His smile was wicked. "She's got nothing in there but printer paper and take-out menus, and several packets of instant soup. I'll bet she wasn't as incensed as she was embarrassed by my poking around in there. I didn't even have to break the lock, which, if it had held sensitive information, it would be a big no-no on her part."

They didn't speak for the remainder of the drive back to the hotel. While Brian appeared lost in his own thoughts, Sy found it difficult to concentrate on anything other than the vacant, dead stare of Henry's eyes. The smell of his blood still lingered in her memory, driving the smell of his favorite cologne into the further recesses of her mind. There was something about the odor that night she couldn't place, however, and his dead eyes weren't helping. Of course, there was also the mistress half-dressed in the foyer, a woman no-one seemed to know was dead yet. She sighed as the cab turned onto the hotel parking lot.

She wondered if she'd ever be free of Henry's haunting.

As THEY APPROACHED THE HOTEL SUITE, Sy turned to Brian, pouting. "I hate to ask this of you..."

"What's on your mind?"

"We're friends, right? It's just, I mean...Well..." They stood in the hallway and she was about to fall apart.

He took the keycard from her hand and swiped it through the door lock, ushering her through to the common room. Once inside, with the door closed, he turned to her with his arms outstretched. She smiled, her lip trembling, then burst into tears and buried herself in his arms.

His hold was gentle. "Shh, it's okay." His voice echoed through his chest.

She sobbed until the steady rhythm of his heart beat chased away her tears. She felt dampness trickle into her nasal canal and she withdrew, begging the need to find a tissue. She went to her bedroom and dabbed her nose, and took an extra moment to repair her makeup and run a brush through her hair.

Composed, Sy returned to the room. Brian hung up the hotel phone. "There was a red flashing light so I took the liberty of calling the courtesy desk for your message. Your condo is being released tomorrow afternoon. I guess they're wrapping up the processing of the crime scene. We can call them in the morning if you want, and make an appointment for after lunch?"

Sy nodded. She still felt out of focus.

Brian waved a hand in her field of vision, drawing her back to reality. "Do you want to grab a bite to eat? It's on the Bureau's dime."

Food! "How about McClouds? It's Irish, you're Irish. They have three types of cider on tap and twenty-seven whiskeys available to sample."

He chuckled. "Sold."

CHAPTER XIII

The Crime Scene

BRIAN ESCORTED SY through the door to her condo the next afternoon with a small degree of trepidation. The last time he was at the scene of a violent crime was in his early years with the Bureau before he transferred to the copyrights division. He warned her before they left the hotel to expect to find items out of place or missing, preparing her the best he could for the complete lack of cleanup. Bloodstains were still visible in the carpet and on the wall-paper in the foyer, although it didn't seem to bother her as much as the sight of the dried remains of rose-petals littering the hallway. She muttered something about grapes and sunshine, and turned away from the sight with obvious derision.

He watched her, preparing himself to deal with an emotional af-termath. She threw a quick smile his way, but it lacked the bright-ness of the previous hours. She turned her attention to the missing parts of her home. A piece of carpet had been removed for evidence from two separate places on the floor, exposing the cold sub-floor. Sy looked over the detective's itemized list and pointed out that a crystal vase from the hall table had been remanded to the evidence locker as well. "Henry got it as a birthday present from his mother one year. She had the worst taste. It's a hideous, vulgar thing. I caught him trying to throw it in the trash the next day and I told him she'd blame me. He put it on the stand there and ignored it after that."

Inspecting the empty space, Brian was distracted by something shiny underneath the stand. A few splintery shards of crystal were embedded in the carpet and there was evidence shot had pierced the wall behind it. "I think maybe the gunman didn't like the vase either."

She laughed. "Well, I guess that's two favors I owe the gunman. Well, three. The third being the demise of the mistress." She turned back to the hallway.

"I know someone who can handle the hazardous waste cleanup, if you're interested. He's not local, but he's trustworthy."

She nodded. Her focus was on the blank wall space on the wall next to the hallway. She flipped through the pages of the evidence list, shaking her head. "That butt-ugly Picasso knock-off is supposed to be there. It was there when I followed the rose petals down the hall. Henry was so damned proud of the purchase. I told him it was poorly constructed and way over-priced, but he wasn't having any of it."

"The investigators didn't take it?" He peered over her shoulder at the documents.

"I don't see it listed anywhere. I don't see any of the pictures listed actually."

Brian rubbed his chin, "Do you think he took your advice and returned it when he thought you were leaving him?"

She squished her nose. "I would think not. Knowing him, he'd wait until I returned and hacked it to pieces with a pair of scissors and then try to guilt-trip me over it later. Besides, that Sidle woman would've said something if he had."

Brian raised an eyebrow. "Henry could guilt-trip you? I find that extremely difficult to believe. I thought you didn't have a conscience."

She slugged his arm. "Chivalry is so dead."

He made a hasty grab for her hand and kissed it, "Me thinks you doth protest too much."

He thought he caught the hint of a blush color her cheek as she snatched her hand back. "No, Henry couldn't guilt-trip me, but that didn't stop him trying. You know something though? I've been thinking about who Sandy Petrusky might be. I've never met her, and Henry was all impressed at her knowledge of artwork. She was supposedly one of the first people he spoke to about his art production, and she encouraged him to use the Chicago Opera House. At least that's what I remember Henry saying when I spoke to him about it."

"So the question truly is: who is Sandy Petrusky, and where is this Picasso knock-off now?"

"And does it have anything to do with Henry's death?"

A THOROUGH SEARCH OF THE CONDO REVEALED another puzzle. The other three paintings Henry purchased from the art gallery and that were allegedly delivered were also nowhere to be found. "I need caffeine if I'm going to work on puzzles," Sy said. "Want some?"

"Sure." Sy went to make some coffee and Brian placed two calls. The first was to his clean-up crew so he could set an appointment for next morning. The second was to his office.

"Kirby? How's life in the style of the rich and famous?" Rosalie asked from the other end of the line.

"Too rich for my tastes I'm afraid. Listen I need some help with my cover. I'm supposed to be down here to inquire after possible art fraud, and I'm way out of my element. I'm meeting up with someone tomorrow," he lied. "So I need everything the Bureau has on William McKealy. He's supposedly local to the Chicago area."

"I'll see what I can pull together for you, and I can overnight it I suppose." Her tone was teasing and nasal.

"Can you get a courier out? I need some time to study the material before I show up at the gallery." She didn't need to know that he had already been there.

He could hear some computer keys clicking away in the background. "I suppose, but it'll cost you."

Brian groaned. He was afraid she'd say that. "Come on Rosalie."

"No, I mean it Brian. I want some appreciation."

"Fine," he sighed out of frustration. "Get the info down here by ten o'clock tonight, and you'll have payment in the morning."

"Deal," she ended their call.

Sy brought a mug of coffee to Brian, the color and consistency he liked. "What payment?" she asked.

Brian groaned again, "Rosalie is a beautiful, capable person, but she's lazy and needs constant attention. She likes getting flowers and chocolates and other crap so anytime I ask her...what?"

She raised an eyebrow. "It sounds to me like she just likes getting flowers from you."

Brian thought back, but couldn't think of any evidence to support her theory. "No, I'm sure she does that to everyone. We're coworkers after all."

Sy shrugged, "De-Nile is not just a river in Egypt you know. Has she ever invited you out after work for a quick bite to eat or a quick drink with a group of people?"

"Yeah, but it's with her usual crowd. I've never had the time or inclination to take her up on it."

"Next time, accept her offer, and I'll bet you another Veyron and a year's worth of petrol that she says everyone canceled on her so it's just the two of you."

He paused to sip his coffee. He wasn't convinced but his sister often teased him about how oblivious he was to attention focused his direction. "I think not. If what you say is true, I'd best not encourage her. Anyway, it's not like she's going to do all the work. She's going to call the Chicago branch and have the guys in archives do the legwork for her."

"Stop sending her chocolates then, and start sending her sausages. I'll bet she stops charging you for favors."

"That's horrible, sausage?" He grinned. "Can you actually send sausage?"

She rolled her eyes, "Honey, I have received every type of gift that can come through the mail or be shipped as a thank you. My sister-in-law sent me a party parrot once…but there's a different story altogether."

Sy's cell phone interrupted them. Her face lit up as she answered, "Buna ziua?" After a brief conversation that Brian guessed was in Romanian, she hung up the phone and announced. "My father just landed at O'Hare. I need to find something to make for dinner."

Brian followed her back into the kitchen and once again felt pangs of jealousy. The eight-burner Viking range alone was worth the price of admission. Part of the kitchen island was a dedicated pastry board, made of white marble, with a selection of black ceramic knives on a nearby stand. Eight barstools wrapped around three sides of the island to facilitate dining or conversation space. Two double-paned glass doors led to a walk-in freezer and refrigerator. The kitchen was large enough to host its own show on television and yet still retained an atmosphere suggesting grandmothers could bake cookies with their twenty grandchildren in comfort.

His family gatherings would be comfortable in a kitchen like this. They'd all actually fit.

Sy was a magician. The room was soon filled with spiced aromas as she moved to and fro. A large pot was placed on the stove and filled with water from the flexible faucet on the side. Flour and eggs were whisked together and then drawn through a pasta extruder. She instructed Brian to lay the pasta over the stand to dry a bit before it could be used. Ripe tomatoes were sorted through and thrown into an industrial wattage blender, along with some balsamic vinegar and red wine, and a handful of dried basil and parsley. A pepper mill dispersed finely ground pepper into the mixture which was then poured into a sauce pan while some Italian-style sausage was browned in a skillet.

THE WATER WAS WELL INTO A ROLLING BOIL when the doorbell rang. Sy squealed and told Brian to add the meat to the sauce as she rushed out to answer the door. A heavily accented voice boomed through the condo, conjuring an image of a Transylvanian James Earl Jones in Brian's mind. Romanian infused conversation drifted through the kitchen archway before Sy did, dragging her father behind her.

Brian felt intimidated at first. He was reminded of his prom night, meeting his date's dad at the door and coming face-to-face with a loaded shotgun. Sy's father was smaller than Barry, but not by much, and carried the same sort of build and taste in expensive suits. A roman nose betrayed an eastern European ancestry and was marred as most of his face was by several scars that crossed from the hairline on the left side of his forehead down to his neck on the opposite side. They shook hands as Sy introduced them.

"Papa," she said, switching mid-sentence to English, "I'm sure Barry's given you the run down already, but this is Brian Kirby. Brian, Viktor Tomas."

"Kirby, it is Irish, yes?" Viktor asked.

"Affirmative, although both sides of my family have been stateside for centuries." He tried not to stare at the scars.

He tried not to squirm under Viktor's intense scrutiny.

"I would like to express gratitude. You have been good friend to my daughter, and this has importance."

"The pleasure, so far, has been mine."

"Coffee?" Sy offered a mug to her father and he accepted. "I've placed you in the master, Papa. I hope you don't mind. I can't bring myself to be in there quite yet."

"Is okay Simon. If you wish, I have place torched. I have connections."

She laughed, "No, Papa. A girl's got to learn to do these things for herself."

Sy finished preparing supper while Brian and Viktor sat on the barstools at the island. Their conversation centered on the weather in Greece and the fishing in the Aegean Sea. Sy excused herself then, and disappeared down the hall after instructing Brian to watch the sauce.

"May I ask you question? I am curious, no?"

Brian moved from the barstool to peer into the saucepan on the stove. "What about?"

"Simon, she say you are federal agent. You investigating her?"

"Yes and no." He gave the sauce a stir. "The Bureau received a tip that she may have hired someone to kill Henry, and they felt I was in a position to investigate without angering influential politicians in high places. If you're asking me if I believe she did it? No, I don't."

"So tell me, Mr. Kirby, how is investigation going?"

"Call me Brian, please. Mr. Kirby is my father. Now, to be honest, I'm out of my element. Art and murder are not part of my usual purview at the Bureau. I investigate copyright infringement."

"Ah. This is big problem, yes?"

"I never have downtime." Brian still found it difficult not to stare at the disfigurement.

Sy returned with a bottle of wine, which she decanted after shooing Brian back to his seat. Before long a large pasta bowl of goodness was placed on the counter along with the decanter of petite syrah. After fetching utensils and china, Sy acquired the corner stool between her father and Brian and they proceeded to eat in the kitchen.

A small conversation in Romanian took place between Sy and Viktor, which she apologized to Brian for being rude. "It's just business, I promise."

"No worries, I was enjoying the sound. Romanian is rare in the Midwest." Shifting a bit in his seat, Brian summoned up courage to ask the next question of Viktor. "My turn to be curious and ask you a personal question, if I may?"

"Of course. About my scars, yes? Shall we say I had disagreement with alligator and leave it there?"

"I didn't mean to pry," Brian frowned. It was hard to gage the tone in the man's voice.

"No, you mistake my..." Viktor looked to Sy.

"Papa gets that question all the time. He isn't bothered by it," she interjected on her father's behalf. "He just sounds menacing because his accent is Romanian. What he doesn't like saying is what the disagreement was about. It's not as interesting as the actual scars are."

Brian caught a mischievous look in her eyes and relaxed again. "Oh?"

After getting an approving nod from her father, Sy related the story. "First, you need to understand that Papa volunteers time and money to the World Society for the Protection and Preservation of Alligators. He has on many occasions, helped with the transportation of the creatures from zoos, testing clinics, Florida swamplands, and the like. Now, about the time I was born, Papa was called upon to help clear a nest of sickly alligators from an abandoned piece of property that the United States IRS had confiscated. He slipped, and landed face first in the jaws of a doped alligator. By the time they got the jaws unlocked, the damage had been done."

Viktor pushed his plate away to lean against the counter. "I prefer to say I was on safari in Africa or hiking through Himalayas. Is more exciting that way, no?"

"The Society was scared they'd lose their largest financial supporter, but Papa believes in the cause. He doesn't back down simply because of a tiny mishap. He just wears more appropriate shoes in the Everglades now." Sy began to clear the dishes and shot Brian a dirty look when he got up to help. Brian sat back down.

"Enough of alligator scars and copyrights," Viktor poured Brian another glass of wine. "Now you have another drink. This time, enjoy flavor. Let wine roll around tongue and truly taste it."

Brian grinned before following the instructions. "I told you I was out of my element."

"Is okay. I take you under wing. By tomorrow, you be expert, yes?"

"I'll give it the old college try."

CHAPTER XIV

After Dinner

THEY RETIRED TO THE SITTING ROOM. Brian decided he liked the decor. What wasn't a genuine antique was a high-end reproduction. The room was warmed by shades of green and gold. Although the two sofas were inviting, he got the impression no one ever put their feet up on the upholstery, or the coffee table for that matter. He sat in a harmless-looking wing-back chair and was surprised when Sy pulled the concealed button on its side and it turned into a recliner.

Viktor strolled over to a roll-top desk in the corner with a laptop bag fetched from the foyer. As he set his workstation up, Sy poured herself another glass of wine and sat down on the sofa across from Brian. "He likes you," she whispered.

"How can you tell?"

"He hasn't threatened to feed you to the alligators."

Brian studied her for a moment. "I see you get your violent streak from your father, not your mother."

Viktor spoke, "You would not say that if you knew her mother. Now," he turned from his computer screen, "let us suppose for a moment killer is someone you know, Simon. Who would it be?"

"I'd lay even money on the widow. She was just all over the Midwest threatening to kill the victim, and even tried to bribe an FBI agent to do it."

Her father's voice was quiet, but stern, and sent a cold chill up Brian's spine. "Be serious, a mea vrabie."

"Honestly, Papa, I have no idea. The widow is certainly capable."

"It isn't the widow," Brian stated. "She's got an iron-clad alibi. All anyone has to do is trace her phone records and voila, no proof of a hit-for-hire either."

"Too bad Henry insisted on keeping the security cameras on our floor disabled. He liked his privacy and didn't want starlets stalking him, or at least that was the excuse. I didn't want to argue with him over it."

Viktor folded his hands, tapping his fingers together. "We can assume then footage politie has is rahat, no?"

"How would you do it, Papa? How would you smuggle in a shotgun, fire it without drawing suspicion, and then vacate the premises before the wife comes home?"

"You assume killer believe you were not home. What if intent was to kill you also?" Viktor's expression was steel. "Even if you have few enemies, I have enemies enough for both of us."

Sy frowned, her eyebrows knitting together. "I hadn't thought of that."

Brian tensed up. If the murderer intended to take Sy out of the picture, she could still be in a great deal of danger. "Didn't you say you arrived home earlier from Spain than you expected to?"

She nodded. "By three days."

"And then you were so upset you jumped in the car and drove to Sandusky?" Brian popped the footrest back into place and leaned forward in his seat.

A strange look crossed her face as the color drained from her already pale skin. "Had I not deviated from my original flight plans, I would have arrived home the same day I got back from the Wint-Mart heist, only I would've been here a good three hours earlier."

"And according to your description of the crime scene, I'd say that was about when Henry and Jasmine met their untimely deaths." He didn't like where this conversation went. He exchanged a worried glance with Viktor.

She flashed a humorless smile, "Oh I can take care of myself. There's no need to worry about me."

"Is too late for that." Viktor dialed a number on his cell phone. He spoke to whoever answered in what Brian assumed was Romanian. Sy started to protest something she heard but Viktor silenced her with a sharp look.

"Who's he talking to?" Brian asked.

"One of his security teams." She swallowed a hearty drink of wine, wiping her mouth with a shaky hand. "He's asking about threat assessments and how soon a detail can be in Chicago."

"His security teams? Is he a dictator of a small country somewhere?"

"No, but some of his clientele are." Her voice cracked.

It was the first time he saw real fear in her eyes. "Hey, I'm not going anywhere. I promise I'll help you through this."

"But what if I'm putting you in harm's way?"

"Let's get this straight, right here and now. Yes, the Bureau sent me here, but I want to be here. You can't put me in harm's way if I'm already there...That didn't come out right."

She reached out to grab his hand and squeezed it tight. "No it came out perfect. I'm glad you're here."

"Good, so...until we know what's going on, I'm going to close the drapes, eh?"

She nodded. Brian set his glass down and crossed to the window, careful to minimize exposure. Once the heavy drapes were secured, Viktor ended his call. "No threats on scope. Sebastian is to research for me."

Brian returned to his seat, "Let me know if you need my resources. I might be able to secure a channel with the CIA community."

Viktor shook his head. "Nu. I understand your intent, but CIA have vulnerabilities. I promise you, my people will know what is happening before CIA."

So what does Viktor Tomas do for a living? The alligator scars seemed more sinister now. Brian wondered if there was more to the story.

Sy released a noisy sigh. "Enough, both of you. I can't function like this. You're turning me into a frightened sparrow."

The land-line telephone rang then, startling all three of them with its shrill alarm. Meeting Brian's gaze, Sy tiptoed at the edge of his consciousness. *Would you be willing to answer it for me? I don't think I'm up to just yet.*

Brian twitched, uncomfortable with her brief, unexpected invasion. *As you wish.* He crossed the room to the sideboard and the buzzing subsided. She was out of his thoughts again. Lifting the receiver, he answered in an even tone. "Freitag residence."

"I, oh, who is this?" The contralto was female.

"You've got this backwards don't you? I get to ask you first." Brian's suspicion alarms went off in his mind.

There was a long pause. "Is Simone around? She's not answering her cell phone. I was starting to get worried."

"No. First your name and what business you have with Ms. Freitag."

"Well, my business...look is she around or not?"

"You have five seconds to comply."

Silence.

Brian began the countdown. "Four...three...two...one. Time's up. Have a good night."

"No-no wait. Just wait. My n-name is..."

"I'm waiting, jackass."

Her answer made him set his jaw. "My name is Sandy Petrusky. I'm Henry's fiancé."

CHAPTER XV

An Artist's Life

S Y GRIPPED THE TELEPHONE HANDSET so tight her knuckles hurt. Her blood pounded in her ears.

"First off you need to understand I had no idea he was married," the whore said.

She struggled to keep her composure. "And how is it then that you have my cell number, one, and two, even know who I am?"

"I uh, fair questions. But, can we meet? I need to discuss something with you, and I don't feel comfortable over the phone."

"Oh sure, let's meet. That's a good idea." Cynical Sy surfaced. She wanted more than anything to be able to reach through the phone-line and choke the ever-loving shit out of the woman. "Why don't we go down to the police station and we can kill two birds with one stone?"

"No please, I-I already talked to them. I think they think I killed him."

"No, I'm pretty sure they think I killed him. You weren't the only one he stooped and I have a better motive."

"Listen, I'll be at the opera house tomorrow at around two o'clock. Can you be there too? I-I have something I think belongs to you and I want to return it. Oh, crap, I gotta run. Please just come to the opera house tomorrow. I'll explain everything then."

Sy listened to the dial tone for a moment, wondering if she was going to the vineyard or just going to pass out. She decided neither action would help the situation and she returned the handset to the cradle. Her father walked over and squeezed her shoulders, giving her emotional support, before asking if she wouldn't mind if he lay down for a moment. "It was long flight, and you know I never sleep on airplane."

"Of course, Papa. Brian is here. I'm okay." Viktor walked from the room, leaving her alone once again with her knight-in-something-armor. She discussed the phone call with Brian. "What's the plan?"

"I have no idea." He shrugged. "What do you want to do?"

"I want to bury her alive, under six feet of pig manure."

"For her taste in art or her taste in men?"

Sy shot him a look and exploded into giggles. "I can't really fault her taste in men, can I?"

Brian smirked. "I wouldn't say that. You were conned by a professional and that doesn't mean you're stupid. Just perhaps a bit naive."

"You think Henry conned me?"

"I do. It seems to me this Henry spent his whole life conning people out of money or out of their pants. True, it might be all above board and legal, but I think he was a confidence man nonetheless. Chalk it up to my FBI intuition if you want. You at least demanded more of an investment from him before he exposed his true nature. You can be proud of that, I think."

She beamed. She could have kissed him then. He managed to find the one thing to say that made her feel better about the whole situation. Sy held onto that moment for a long while, basking in its warmth. "I'm glad I stopped to get a car battery."

"Even if I got you involved in a hostage crisis?"

"I suppose it was hardly fair to them. After all, I did have the advantage. Hey wait; do you remember something odd about that night?"

"Before or after I got to drive a Bugatti Veyron?"

"There was something supposed to be dropped off there. Don't you remember? One of them said 'it's almost four' like they were on a time crunch. They were expecting a delivery maybe. They weren't there to rob the store. They were there to hijack a tractor rig!"

Brian leaned forward in the armchair. "Why pull a heist in the store then? They could have just as easily dealt with the dock hands and took the rig without the chance of exposure."

"Distraction? Misdirection?" She paced around a sofa. "We know they were amateurs. Hell the one idiot I took out used a plastic gun he'd requisitioned from the toy department."

"True."

"So then the question is: did the rig just not show up? Or did someone hire them as decoys so they would get caught intentionally?"

"Intentionally?"

"Yeah, so they could, I don't know, hold up a diamond exchange on the other side of town."

Brian reached in his pocket for his cell phone. "Whatever their employer told them, Pacelli and his crew believed they were doing an actual heist. The LEOs are still looking into it. I'll talk to Todd when he calls back and see if they considered that angle at all." He punched out a text message.

Sy nodded. The hostage situation hadn't settled well with her, but she had to push it to the back of her mind. She needed to focus on her own little struggle and let Sandusky's finest do its job.

WHAT DOCUMENTS ROSALIE MANAGED to source for Brian arrived by courier minutes later. Sy went to make some more coffee, leaving Brian to set up shop at the dining table. While the machine brewed, she decided a change of clothes was in order. She slipped into her stolen velour pantsuit and a pair of no-slip socks before returning to the coffee. Went the brewing was done, she brought two mugs of steaming caffeine into the dining room. "Two creams, right?"

Brian looked up from a series of articles, smiling. "Affirmative. You've really become attached to that pantsuit."

"I finally got the smoke smell out of it, and it's surprisingly comfortable," she said, handing his coffee over. "Your FBI boys are fast."

"Yeah, proof positive that you're special." Brian pointed at his layout. "I've attempted to put things in chronological order. There's still half a box left to do."

"Wow, that's a lot of info for a local artist." She picked up a photograph of one of his paintings. "No wonder Ms. Sidle thought McKealy was a cross between Picasso and Rembrandt."

Brian picked up McKealy's license picture. "Is there a resemblance between the three?"

"I'm not speaking physically." She waved at the still life represented. "I'm talking about his landscapes. Picasso was more abstract than realistic in his art pieces, but he had moods. There was a blue phase, a red phase, and you can tell McKealy has done the same thing."

"Ah, I see now. There's a lot of yellow in his first works. And blue here."

"And he's been partial to red in his mature works."

"So, where's the nod to Rembrandt?"

Sy scrutinized a blue mood picture. "Well, he's not as talented as Rembrandt was, but I think McKealy suffers from stereo blindness the way Rembrandt did."

"Stereo blindness?"

"Normal human beings use both of their eyes at the same time to see. It gives us the natural 3D view of our world. Stereo blindness causes a man to use one eye at a time when looking at something. While it's a curse to non-artist folk, it helps a painter because his depth perception is skewed."

"Meaning he can take what he sees and immediately translate it to a two-dimensional picture."

"And Brian receives a top mark on his art paper and is promoted to the head of the class," she teased. "You're doing fine. Soon, you won't need me anymore."

"Maybe, but I won't need you any less either...That sounded better in my head."

She chuckled. "I know what you meant."

CHAPTER XVI

Lucretia

BRIAN AND SY PERUSED the mundane details of the artist's life. McKealy was born in Chicago in July of '69 to a loan broker and a waitress, who divorced in the fall of '75. He remained single the whole of his life, at least, there were no records of a wife on file. McKealy had no offspring, and no siblings. His only trip outside the country was in '89 when he went to Madrid, Paris, Amsterdam, and Berlin with his art class from Lake Forest College. He dropped out of college the semester before he was scheduled to graduate, citing financial difficulties in his exit interview. While working three jobs to help pay off his student loans and his mother's medical bills, he picked up a few commissioned art jobs and continued to supplement his income from the occasional sales of his paintings.

"What were the titles on the ones Henry purchased?" Brian asked just after midnight and his third cup of coffee.

"Ms. Sidle said *Wind*, *The Gray*, and *Red River Valley*. I know the one Henry hung in the hallway was titled *Girl in Hammock*. Yes, this is the one." She fished one of the earlier works in bright toned yellows out of its place and handed it to Brian.

There was no mistaking the hammock in the middle of the picture. Even the sky was yellow, indicating an early morning setting. The grass was covered with bright yellow poppies and dandelions. The yellow and white striped hammock was suspended between two yellow tinted trees. All that was visible of the supposed girl was a long slender leg draping barefoot over the side.

Brian shook his head. He didn't get the attraction. There wasn't a single dog playing poker or a cowboy roping cattle.

"I think I found *Wind*," Sy handed Brian another photo from the yellow spectrum. Leaves in various shades of amber and gold almost drifted across the canvas.

"I can almost appreciate this one. The leaves are highly detailed."

"Does the file mention the others at all? I can't seem to find them."

Brian flipped through the file to the last page. "Not that I can tell. They could be new pieces or maybe he commissioned them specific, intent on keeping them a part of a private collection. Those types of pieces don't make it as timely into these sorts of files."

Sy stretched like a cat, arms reaching across the table before she arched her back, shifting from sitting to standing. "I think I'm done for the night. Are you going to stay up?"

He stifled a yawn and rubbed his forehead. "Just a little while longer. I need to find some sausage to deliver to Rosalie in the morning."

"If you need a laugh, go to party parrot dot com. Trust me." She said goodnight and vanished down the dark hall towards the spare bedrooms.

HE SHOULD HAVE FOLLOWED, as tired as he felt. It had been a long day, and he was finding it difficult to concentrate. As his mind wandered down paths of a vineyard in Chardonnay he'd never seen, Brian packed up the pieces of William McKealy and put his life box in the hall closet on the top shelf.

He turned off the light in the foyer and stood for a moment in the darkness, trying to decide if he wanted to send Rosalie anything at all. He didn't want to encourage a crush in the workplace. Until Sy had mentioned the condition, Brian was blissfully ignorant of Rosalie's intentions.

He decided to go to bed and deal with the aftermath of a Rosalie scorned later. As he turned, he heard the elevator ding, announcing the arrival of the carriage to their floor. He reached for an umbrella from the closet and moved to look out the door's peephole. He spied an older woman fussing through her pockets and then extracting a set of keys. When the lock slid open, she reached in and turned on the light.

She screamed at the sight of him.

Brian tried to hush her, tossing the umbrella back in the closet. She only screamed louder. Sy flew down the hallway in a silk nightgown, brandishing a Sig P226 which she lowered at the sight of the screaming woman. "Annika, it's all right. Shush." Sy shoved the 9mm in Brian's hands. "Annika, He's okay. He belongs here. He's not going to hurt you."

Brian held the handgun behind his back and pulled his badge out of his pocket. "I'm a federal agent."

Sy continued to talk the woman down, in a language sounding more Germanic than the Romanian Brian was becoming used to. As Annika responded, taking deep breaths, Viktor appeared from nowhere in pajamas and a bathrobe with a glass of whiskey. His deep booming voice bellowed through the foyer. "Annika, there is no need to be scared, no? We are all here, in one piece, and having party."

Annika hiccupped but accepted the whiskey and knocked it back in one gulp. "I try geet heer soonar," she said. "I geet heer late and I try to be the quiet."

Sy held on to the woman's shoulders, "it's all right. We're all of us still a little shaken up about Henry."

The scared look on Annika's face was replaced by one of spitting anger. "I tell heem he ees een varken and he ess to geet zee horse oot af zee house or Ik zal hem doden."

"I know, I told him the same thing," Sy laughed. "I think we still have some coffee if you'd like some."

"Wie is die man?" Annika pointed to Brian.

"Brian Kirby, a friend, and a federal agent. Brian this is my housekeeper, Annika Christensen."

Brian let Annika take his badge to give it a closer inspection. "Ah zees ees ze efbee eye aygeent, yah?" The whiskey seemed to be working. "Het is leuk je te ontmoetn."

Before anyone could interpret for him, Brian understood the gist. "It's nice to meet you too."

"Come, a mea vrabie," Viktor offered his hand. "Let us see about coffee." The housekeeper returned the badge and followed Viktor, rattling on in her native tongue.

Sy breathed as Brian slipped his wallet back in his pocket. "I'm so sorry. I forgot to tell you she was coming back home tonight."

Brian focused on the gun in his hand to keep from fixating on Sy's nightgown. "I nearly brained her with the umbrella."

"Thank you, for trying to protect me. I rather enjoy being the damsel in distress around you."

He coughed, uncomfortable. "Yes, well, I think your housekeeper hates me." The silk nightgown moved closer to him. A cold sweat slid down his neck.

She stretched out her hand. "May I have Lucretia back please?"

He forgot for a moment about the nightgown. "You named your Sig Lucretia?"

She nodded. "She's named for Lucretia Borgia, for her lethal beauty."

He handed Lucretia back to her small, delicate hand and sighed. "I have to go to confession. Tomorrow. Or I am bound for the special hell."

Sy frowned, casting a look toward the kitchen. "Why? For scaring a housekeeper?"

He let loose the most wicked laugh he could conjure. "Honey, if you could read my mind right now, you'd be scared of me, too."

CHAPTER XVII

Past Evils

T HE SMELL OF BACON AND COFFEE drifted under the door and roused Brian from a dead sleep. He dressed while his stomach growled, ran a comb through his hair, and followed the scent of breakfast to the dining room. Viktor sat at the table with a plate of eggs and toast, reading the newspaper. They exchanged good mornings, and as Brian attempted to fetch some breakfast from the kitchen, he was ousted by the housekeeper.

"I breeng eet too you." She threatened him with a spatula. "I make you egg white scramble and baycon and aebleskivers. You go seet down an I breeng eet to you."

A carafe of coffee sat on the table next to a pitcher of cream, and as Brian returned to claim a seat, Viktor poured him a cup. "How you take it?"

"A little cream, that's perfect. Thank you."

Viktor eyed him then put the pitcher down. "What are your intentions towards my daughter?"

Brian swallowed hard; the sip of coffee burned a new tunnel down his throat. Thirty-six years old and he was still intimidated by fathers. He remembered the shotgun from his prom night in vivid color. "I have no intentions at this time. I am content with leaving things the way they are."

"That is, how it is said, horse manure."

"Sir?" Brian wondered if anyone tried to date Sy in high school and succeeded.

Viktor gestured, a motion that appeared weary and dismissive, as if directed at the rainfall for the fortieth day in a row. "Not sir, you call me Viktor. I am not your enemy. Henry, I was his enemy. I tell him when they marry I kill him if he even thinks about thinking about hurting her."

"The more I learn of him, the less I like him." He was feeling less threatened now. Even the scars were less unsettling. Being on first name basis with the date's father meant the shotgun would be left on the wall above the mantle. "In spite of the fact Sy insists that everyone loved him, I'm starting to get the impression that to really know Henry is to want to kill Henry."

"Love is blind, that is what is said, no?" he sighed, appearing lost in thought. "I want only to say this to you. She not as strong as she make herself out to be, eh? Inside her shell is still frightened little girl I found in mental hospital. She will need you, before this is over."

Brian wondered if he was allowed to ask about that. Sy only hinted at her past in their conversations, but he knew there was a great deal of pain that would never heal. "You say you *found* her?"

"Da. Her mother take her when she was just baby and they disappear like magician. It take me two years to track her down, and only Simon I found. They had her drugged and confined. It make me sick to see."

Annika set a plate of food before Brian and left before he could say thank you. "Sy says she doesn't remember much about those years. Some tests, faces of psychiatrists, but nothing else really. That could be a blessing in disguise."

Viktor chuckled as he picked his paper up, "And yet she has good memory for everything else, no?"

Sy waltzed in the dining room, dressed to the nines in a black leather skirt and red cashmere cap-sleeve sweater. Her hair and makeup looked flawless again. Her jewelry was of simple design, but consisted of an entire matched set of rubies. Knee-high black leather boots with a low heal finished her look. Her wedding ring was absent. "I only have a good memory when there's film in the camera, remember Papa?"

Brian dropped his fork and tried to cover it up by rising from the table until she sat down. He was not prepared for being so breathless at the sight of her. "We were just discussing..."

Her odd-colored eyes looked though him. "My stay at Zarnesti? Papa says I was traumatized by the conditions there, but I honestly don't remember. I didn't have film then, I guess. Buna dimineata, Papa." She leaned over to kiss his cheek.

"Where is Zar..." Brian already forgot how to pronounce the word.

"Zarnesti? It's in Transylvania. The mental hospital there was where officials sent the undesirables to be poked and prodded at by a group of white laboratory coats." Her voice was clinical, detached. "Orphans, elderly, Alzheimer's victims housed right alongside the actual nutcases; some violent, some just ate their checkers. It was extremely difficult, even dangerous for Papa to extract me from the hospital and then smuggle me back home to Switzerland. The Romanian revolution didn't happen until 1989."

"Why Romania?" Brian asked between aebleskivers.

Viktor shifted in his seat as if approaching a delicate conversation. "Why her mother bring her there, I do not understand even now. Her mother was American, and should not have been allowed to travel freely though Romania, let alone abandon our daughter there."

"Aren't you from there?"

Viktor nodded. "I was born there, yes. My father was lucky man in communist country. Government left him alone, so my brother and I were raised with underground privilege until we defect to Switzerland."

"That must have been rough," Brian empathized, feeling a new appreciation for his American freedoms. "I can't begin to imagine really."

"Is okay. It was long time ago and we did not have it so bad as others." He turned to Sy. "What is plan for today, a mea vrabie?"

"I suppose we need to meet the whore at the opera today. Brian, you wanted to meet with the gallery director again didn't you?"

"That was the original plan, but I think I'd better swing by the police station and see if I can get a little intradepartmental collaboration. I'm curious to see what the cameras picked up, if anything."

The housekeeper brought a plate of food to Simone. "You'll have more success without my presence I think. Danke, Annika."

Brian caught Annika's attention before she disappeared into the kitchen again. "You were the last person alive who might know. Do you know when Henry took the hammock picture down from the hall?"

Annika responded in rapid Dutch, pointing towards the hallway.

Sy frowned, "But it was there when I came home that night, when I caught them in the hot-tub."

Annika shook her head, "He took eet down aftat you leave and he geeve it to zat art vrouw."

"Jasmine? The hot-tub whore?" Brian asked.

"Nee, het vas de andere, Sandy. Tat's when he say he leeve them and he tell me to call you and tell you she vas gone."

Brian heard Sy mutter something about Chardonnay and Viktor threw his paper down. They both looked disgusted. The housekeeper scurried from the room as if to avoid the wake. Brian wondered how long the housekeeper knew of the affairs and why she didn't tell Sy about them.

He felt a familiar buzz. *Let her be, Brian. She's fearful by nature.*

Still, he replied, *it speaks to her character. I wouldn't let you be ignorant of any husband's transgression.*

The clock on the wall chimed ten o'clock. If they were going to meet up at the opera house, they had better get their day started.

CHAPTER XVIII

Gunny

S Y WAS SILENT IN THE ELEVATOR RIDE down to the lobby. She
seemed lost in thought, almost nervous about the day. Brian
tried not to telegraph the concern he felt. She didn't need the aggra-
vation.

The elevator doors opened as if curtains for a stage and Sy's demeanor transformed in an instant. She stepped from the carriage
and into the lobby as a queen might to make an appearance with her
adoring public. She belonged here; even as she professed her condo
was only transitory. The marble tiles and rich mahogany furnishings
paled in comparison to the nobility she exuded. Brian wasn't sure if
he was impressed with the building, or simply the way Sy conducted
herself as she crossed the threshold to the security desk.

The guard was an older man, with a wizened face that spoke of
decades of hardship and sacrifice. He was built like a bull dog and
wore the uniform as if he had been born with it. Creases were military crisp and the standard issue, long-sleeved dress shirt was still
fresh-from-the-package white. His face brightened as he made eye
contact with his queen.

141

"It's good to have you back, Sy. The place hasn't been the same without you," the grizzled war-dog said.

"Buna ziua, Gunny. I'm glad to be home as well, although I'm sorry to say I'll probably move as soon as they give me clearance to roam about the cabin freely."

"I'm sorry for your loss."

"I'm not. The bastard had it coming. I'm just sorry I wasn't the one to do it. You remember my father, don't you?" She gestured to Viktor.

"Good to see you again, sir." Gunny snapped to attention.

Viktor took his sunglasses from his sport coat pocket. "How is family Gunny? Your daughter still at Harvard or she is finished?"

"Graduated two years ago. She's working for an oil company in Texas now, and has discovered that she detests country music and American football." The war-dog turned his eyes to Brian. "Who's the cop?"

Sy touched Brian's shoulder. "Brian Kirby, I'd like to introduce you to Robert Monroe. Gunny, you'll like this one. He's a fed."

Brian shared a firm handshake with Gunny. "I'm nothing special, just a paper-pusher," Brian said. "You were once a Gunnery Sergeant?"

"Retired Marine Gunner, Chief Warrant Officer. She calls me Gunny because she likes to."

"Thank you for your service," Brian said.

The war-dog winked at Sy. "You're right, I do like this one. No one else around here gives a damn. Did she tell you she served her country too?"

Brian nodded, grinning. "Along with a rather frightening description as to how she could turn anything into a sticky paste with the appropriate firearm."

Gunny laughed in response. "That's my girl!"

"You'll have to come up for dinner tonight, Gunny," Sy insisted. "We've got a story for you involving a car battery and a bunch of gel candles."

Gunny sobered. "Napalm? But what was the car battery for?"

"The hot-tub."

The elevator dinged and opened up to reveal a tall blond, wearing a pink dress that barely covered her anorexic frame. The dress would have been better suited for a fifteen-year-old ballerina, suspending the air of reality around the woman who appeared to be pushing thirty. "Oh Ms. Freitag," she stumbled towards them, slurring her speech. "I'm ssorry about your hussband."

Brian knew from the look on Sy's face she was standing in a vineyard in Chardonnay. Her subtle accent was thick again, like she just stepped from the airplane. "Thank you, Miss Tanner."

"Ooh, who'ss your new friend?" she ignored Viktor and stretched her arm out to Brian for a handshake. "My name is Tori. Tori Tanner."

Brian observed her eyes. They quivered, as if trapped in a REM cycle of sleep, and her pupils were dilated. Perspiration formed across her forehead. She wasn't letting go of his hand. "Brian Kirby."

"Mmm, you're yummy. I could jusst eat you up." She cozied up next to him.

Sy interrupted, her odd-colored eyes narrowed with concentration. "Miss Tanner, you are late for something?"

"Oh crap!" She let go of Brian's hand to smack her own forehead. "I forgot. Where was I going?"

Sy folded her arms, disbelief registering across her features. "You have a...job...interview?"

"I do?" the pink pixie scratched the base of her head. "Oh right, the bank. That'ss where they keep money, right? I'll catch you later, Mr. Yummy." She stumbled towards the elevator.

"Miss Tanner," Sy pointed, "the door is over there."

"Oopss." It hurt to watch Tori navigate the U-turn and list to the door.

"High as a kite," Brian watched her struggle with the glass round-a-bout security door.

Sy's accent returned to feather subtlety. "She raves often. Ecstasy maybe?"

Brian shuddered. "With any luck she'll forget she met me. That was scary. I should call it in if she's going to drive."

Gunny shook his head. "No need. She rolled her Rolls last year and the judge refused to give her license back, ever. Her daddy kept her out of prison, but he wasn't pleased and refused to buy her a new car. He's placed a real tight grip on her money."

"Who's her father that he managed to keep her out of prison?" Brian asked.

"He's a judge also, in a different district. You met Barry? Barry's had dealings with him before. He's a good man, charismatic. She shames him daily, I think." Gunny took a pen from the desk and made a notation on a clipboard.

Sy tapped the desk. "Don't forget, you're coming up for dinner at the end of your shift."

"Yes ma'am." Gunny saluted.

"Well, we'll be off then. Papa and I need to see a man about an alligator. Please don't forget to come to the opera house this afternoon Brian. The life you save just may be hers." She linked arms with her father and the strolled to the door. Brian watched them hail a cab through the glass and then they were gone.

"So are you some sort of spook?" Gunny's grizzled voice brought Brian back to the lobby.

"Negative. I'm with the Bureau, not the Agency."

Suspicion didn't fade from the man's eyes. "Well, I'll accept that for now. She's had a few agency types poking their noses in her affairs from time to time."

"Wonder why." She had creepy connections with influential political people, but Brian was unsure how much of that influence was because of her father.

Gunny shrugged. "Don't know. It's not as if she's a threat to America or Americans in any way. She's Swiss for Christ's sake. When was the last time you heard of a Swiss operation that didn't directly involve the pope? They're only famous for knives and chocolate."

"Don't forget watches." Brian wondered if the Swiss government knew of her telepathic ability. Perhaps they were doing everything possible to keep her secret. After all, no spy could be more dangerous than the one who could read the minds of foreign diplomats. "She travels the world as a free-lance location scout, served for a time in the Swiss military, and she's got some sort of official sanction somewhere in her connections. The Agency is bound to get involved in her affairs. They're a suspicious lot."

"You think Simone's a spy? Bullshit. I'd believe it more of Henry. He was the one always acting suspicious and paranoid."

"Did you know Henry disabled the security cameras on their floor?"

"Yeah, he never made it a big secret. The homeowner's association used to give him grief for it, but that's all they would do. Once in a while some eager young maintenance man would come along and fix them, but that would only last for a week or two at the most."

"And the affairs. Did Henry flaunt them about whenever Sy was out or did he at least make the attempt to be discreet?"

"That's the real question isn't it?" Gunny heaved a sigh and tossed the pen to the desk. "Henry was a genuine piece of work. He could spin a smile so warm you'd forget it was winter in Chicago, and everyone would fall for whatever line of bullshit he was feeding them. He even caught me receptive on occasion." There was distaste in his voice. "I noticed there were several lady-folk who were regular visitors, but in the stream of all the others he entertained on a constant basis, well, I lost track and without tangible proof, there wasn't much I could do."

"Were you working the day she found them in the hot-tub?"

"No, but I was working the day of the shooting. The building itself was quiet. I left after my shift was over at four."

"I know you probably gave a statement to the police, but did anything strike you as unusual about that day? Maybe even something you might not have mentioned because you didn't think it noteworthy at the time?"

"Nah, just your regular comings and goings," he waved his hand dismissively. "But since you're not from around here, you might not know about the wind. They don't call her the Windy City for nothing. The wind ripped through town pretty bad the whole weekend, so there had been fluctuating power outages. Not this building, but some nearby. And on the day of the shooting, two transformers blew"

"Loud?" Brian asked. In New York, the noise level would depend several factors: the transformer's location, if nearby neighbors were partying too hard, if there were enough buildings nearby that could amplify and echo the sound. When Brian lived in Bethesda, he noticed the dynamic of the land and buildings caused different patterns to emerge.

"Yeah, I was here during the first explosion. Jefferson said there was another one that blew during his shift that night. It might be how no one noticed the gunfire. I would've, but then I've got a military background."

"Okay thanks. Look, I should probably get going. If you wouldn't mind doing me a big favor though," Brian checked for eavesdropping passersby passing by, "I think there's a slim chance the perp may have been after Sy, and was disappointed. Maybe he's waiting for the murder to be hanged on her or maybe he'll try again."

"Sure, I'll keep my eye out for you and let you know if I come across anything suspicious."

"Appreciate it."

CHAPTER XIX

Missing Footage

B RIAN MET WITH RESISTANCE when he arrived at the police precinct, but he was prepared for it. Municipal forces often reacted to Bureau presence with overt derision, and not without good reason. Arguments over jurisdiction perpetuated cycles of prideful distrust between local law enforcement and federal agents. Sometimes the rivalries ran hot.

"I'm not here to seize control of your case, Detective," Brian said, signing the visitor's log. "I don't want to step on any toes, trust me."

"Then why are you here?" Detective Shelby slipped his hands into the pockets of his slacks. He was a mountain on two legs and his voice fit his gruff manner. His eyes were hallmarked with tired circles and he looked in desperate need of a scotch-and-soda. "What's the Bureau of Idiocy's interest?"

Brian laughed, "Our interest is purely idiotic, I assure you."

A dry smile emerged, "Well, you're the first I've met with a sense of humor."

"Do you have time now to discuss the case with me? I really appreciate it."

"A fed with manners? You are a rare species." His eyebrows tipped in question.

"Could be why they usually keep me behind a desk. They have their reputation to maintain after all."

"Say, what's retirement like at your level? I'm getting nowhere rapidly here."

"Depends. Your pension here might actually be worth more in the long run, what with the government cutbacks and all. At least you have the union to protect you."

Shelby snorted. "Only if it suits them. They owe me eight weeks of vacation on top of my regular five. Someday, I'm going to cash it out and bankrupt them."

They entered the crime lab located on the second floor. The cold glare of fluorescent lights common to business structures seemed all the more garish here, as a grouping of whirring machines beeped and chortled in their corners. Brian caught the whiff of rubbing alcohol coming from somewhere, which made the additional smells of instant coffee and dough-nuts seem rancid. Individuals with safety goggles and latex gloves wandered about with purpose between rooms and desks with choreographed synchronization. Shelby led Brian to the viewing room, where the surveillance feed was supposed to be waiting for them to examine.

Monitors cast a blue light into the dark room. A computer tech sat at the ready to enhance and print frames of security footage at their direction. Her name badge read Mandy Hines underneath the mug-shot of a young woman with pitch black hair in a Betty Paige cut. The live version looked too young for the horn-rimmed glasses perched on the bridge of her tiny nose. Silken scarlet swirled like strawberry-topped chocolate ice cream in the cone of her French twist. She smiled at Brian's introduction and kicked the conversation off. "You're looking at six screens here. The first is of the landing at the vic's condo. You'll notice it's blank the entire time."

Brian explained Henry's security habits. "As much as the victim was in the public eye, he sure hated to be on camera."

Detective Shelby smirked, "Probably because he didn't want to have to explain his mistresses, who are coming out of the woodwork like roaches in a housing project."

The tech continued, "The one next to that is of the subterranean parking lot elevator, the next two are of the lobby, and the next two floors up."

"Why are there only six screens then? There are ten floors in that building," Shelby folded his arms.

Seriousness lined her face, "There's the question. Allow me to show you. If you'll take a gander at the screen over here," she pointed out the next cluster of screens with one hand and typed a few keystrokes at her keyboard with the other.

Flickering white snow in the screens acted like strobe lights. Brian blinked to stay off the feeling of uneasiness.

"Static and rot," Shelby grumbled. "Are they all like that?"

She nodded. "Most of them, yes."

"What caused them to get like that? Are they just old?" Brian turned away from the television winter.

"Well these aren't exactly the top-of-the-line cameras." She typed at her keyboard and the strobe disappeared. "Now, these are at least digital recordings, so we're not dealing with tape, but the downloaded information could have been retrieved after some form of corruption in the memory. An electromagnet, a mouse, a kid swiping parts to build his own video camera, refurbished rubbish from the factory, any number of things could cause this."

"So we only have the second and third floors?" Brian turned back to the screens. "What about the fire escapes? Anything on those external staircases?"

She stared at her computer screen as she toggled back and forth between files. "Mmm, now you mention it, looks like we have all of them, appearing now on my left."

"Okay then let's start from the time dispatch received the 911 call and work our way backwards." The screens showed all target feed on a slow rewind until Brian caught sight of Sy backing out of the elevator in the parking lot. "There's the widow," he pointed.

"That's a good spot then. We have a ton of ambiguous footage and it would be nice if we could narrow frames down without sifting through every little boring detail." Mandy seemed pleased.

FOR OVER TWO HOURS, Brian worked with the tech and detective, perusing through raw footage, dismissing people as they were accounted for by cross-referencing their testimonies. The only happening truly noteworthy was a small power flux about three hours before Sy returned home, which caused some of the cameras to go blue screen for a few seconds. "We had random power outages that day due to winds. To be expected I suppose," the detective said.

Brian shook his head. "There's no way the perp could have known that was going to happen unless he could control the weather."

"Maybe he saw his chance and decided it was now or never?"

"Even still, that security guard is on his game. He's greeting everyone in the lobby, stopping those he doesn't know and harassing some of the ones he does. I'm thinking the killer either lives in the building or came up by the fire escape or parking structure." Brian rubbed his stiff neck. "Another thing, I didn't see when the female vic arrived that day. Maybe she spent the night?"

Detective Shelby whistled low, "Lucky dick. Imagine; he virtually had everyone he wanted."

Brian fought the distaste of his rising hatred from his mouth. Henry was a bastard in the third degree. "I wouldn't call it luck as much as greed. I think the vic is the prime example of how people with every privilege inevitably want more." Glancing at his watch, he thanked the detective and tech for their hospitality. "I need to get going. If I come across anything in my investigation of the artwork, I'll let you know."

"Let me know if you want to take another peek at the footage." Mandy said as if through a dream. "I practically live here. I can grab us some stale coffee and cold Chinese food and we can have another go."

"Sounds good." Brian fished business cards out from behind his bureau I.D. for the both of them. "In the meantime, give me a buzz if you come across something that wouldn't be hampering your investigation to let me know about."

Brian left smiling Mandy as Shelby escorted him out to the main lobby.

At the door to the street, Shelby stopped him. "Hey, what's your take on this widow?"

Brian's chest tightened and his stomach clenched. He could say the wrong thing if he wasn't careful and blow any chance of maintaining the open dialog with the investigators on this case. "My take?

154 | S.K. DUNNING

She's eccentric, certifiably nuts, and she's got questionable taste in men."

"Well her alibi checks out, so she's not really on my radar anymore. And you don't think she hired someone to do this, do you?"

"No, I think despite the manicured fingernails, she's a hands-on sort of girl. If she had done it, she wouldn't lie about it. She'd sign the confession without hesitation and have the gall to insist upon thousand-thread-count sheets for her cot in prison."

"Yup, that's the impression I got as well. Listen, I don't like Bureau dogs sniffing around my precinct, but I like you. You stick with the art angle and keep your nose outta my murder, and you and I will continue to get along just fine, eh?"

"Fair enough. I've enough on my plate without having to steal work from Chicago's Finest. And I've got deeper resources for the art."

"Just so we're on the same page."

BRIAN CAUGHT A CAB from the precinct and glanced at his watch again. If he was going to save Sandy Petrusky's life, he was cutting it awfully close. Traffic crawled along the Magnificent Mile as people left work for the start of their weekend. Busy shoppers and law types in expensive suits with their gourmet coffee house cups walked the crowded sidewalks, sometimes moving faster than the cars on the road. While New York City desensitized him to heavy traffic, Brian felt his patience with humanity wearing thin. He was a long, long way from his Blue Ridge roots.

The yellow taxi turned onto Wacker Drive and pulled up in front of the opera house with less than two minutes left to spare before Brian's appointment. He tipped the driver and turned. Standing before the opera house, he wondered where he should try to enter. The box office was closed, but a sign at the will call window indicated the main office was located around the back of the building. A dismal alleyway channeled him to the side door, which was propped open with an old, cement brick.

The house manager met him at the door. "Are you Kirby? If you are, your party is waiting for you in the orchestra pit." She pointed towards a double-door at the far end of the aisle.

The empty theater rows reminded Brian of a cemetery, each velvet-upholstered seat a tombstone standing silent against the march of time. Stage hands built and painted flats on stage. Other than Sy and her father in the pit, the audience comprised of a few studious types lingered about in the balcony taking notes, no doubt to fulfill a class requirement.

The doors slammed behind him, the sound echoing in the cavernous house. Sy turned and waved him over. Brian inched the narrow walk in the row just in front of theirs. "I'm starting to believe she's going to be a no-show," Sy said as he took his seat.

He turned, his arm draped across the back of the seat. "Well, we can leave whenever you want. Just because she wants to meet you doesn't mean you have to meet her."

"Thanks, but this is one puzzle I have to solve or it's going to bother me the rest of my life. How did the collaboration with the police go?"

"I think that precinct actually passed sharing in kindergarten. They've got some partial images from the fire escape cameras they might be able to enhance, but there's little else. It's safe to say you're no longer suspect number one though. I believe they've already ruled you out."

"What?" Brian wasn't prepared for her irritated response. "How dare they take me off the suspect list? I could have done it. I'm capable."

Viktor squeezed her shoulder. "I do not believe is supposed to be insult. You should not take offense, yes?"

Her scowl darkened her expression, "I suppose you're right, but how rude."

"How did the man with the alligator go?" Brian felt a change of topic would be welcome.

Sy scowled deeper, "Ask Mr. Security."

Viktor's eyes rolled towards the vaulted ceiling. "Simon dislikes that I have concern for her well-being." He turned his scolding tone to his daughter. "It is father's prerogative. You will accept this. It is not negotiable."

"I...shouldn't have said anything. Sorry." Brian ran a hand through his hair.

Viktor's piercing gaze carried the weight of fatherhood. "No, is okay. Perhaps she will listen to you. She ignore her father as if he is tampit, how is said, idiot."

The darkness melted from Sy's expression as she heaved a defeated sigh. "No, Papa, I don't think you're stupid. I'm sorry. I'm hurt and angry, and I'm taking it out on everyone..."

"So what happened?" Brian asked.

"Papa pulled a security detail off of their mission and he's reassigning them to me."

Brian nodded, catching up. "The man with the alligator."

"I still think it's unnecessary, but I can't say I wouldn't do the same if the roles were reversed." She leaned over and kissed her father's cheek. "Imi pare rau, Papa."

Viktor pulled Sy close, tucking her under his arm in a protective hug. "Is okay, a mea vrabie."

Brian decided then he could handle whatever wrath a scorned Sy could unleash, but crossing Viktor was suicide.

CHAPTER XX

Girl in Hammock

A FEW MINUTES BECAME A HALF-HOUR. Sy was ready to abandon the theater when a disheveled woman stepped out on stage with a clipboard, placing a framed oil painting on an easel. She barked instructions at the laboring stage hands. "I realize this is for concept work, but if it doesn't look right, this idea won't sell. If it doesn't sell, we'll lose our shirts and none of you will get paid. Are we clear? Get that color adjusted pronto. If we have to get live trees to paint over, we'll do it."

Sy's blood curdled in her veins as she recognized the woman's feathery voice. Sandy Petrusky was short and wore the pixie-ragtag style that really only worked well on pregnant people. Her socks were a shade off of each other and she bore the frazzled countenance that went with lack of sleep. Apart from an over-developed, full-figured bosom, Sandy was ordinary.

Sy was insulted. *If Henry was engaged to that person...*

Sandy turned towards the orchestra pit, glancing at her watch. She blanched as she made eye-contact with Sy. She walked like a woman facing the gallows, down the ramp stage-right, dragging each step until she stood before them. "I...I'm Sandy. Thank you for agreeing to see me. I...I feel like such a dope."

Sy gripped her father's hand to the point where she cut off her own blood circulation. "I wouldn't thank me just yet. I haven't decided if I'm going to feed you to the alligators or not."

Sandy blinked, tears oozing mascara across her cheeks. She collapsed in a seat within arm's reach of Brian, like a lamb unaware of slaughter house. "I'm a filthy home-wrecker and now I'm a huge suspect for murder."

Narrowing her eyes, Sy concentrated on piercing through to the woman's soul. Her thoughts were scattered, her emotions raw, and it was hard for Sy to lock down the truth. She cornered a fleeting image. "Are you sure you were engaged? Did you say that just to meet me?"

Sandy rubbed her forehead before nodding. "I'm sorry I lied. But I thought if I could just get you here, I could explain everything and then...I don't know what I thought."

"Wait, what do you mean you lied about the engagement? What on earth for?" Brian bared teeth, snarling.

The lamb quivered. "I told you, I wanted the chance to explain everything and it was stupid but I had to say something. The guy was going to hang up on me. I had to get his attention."

"Well you've got my attention," Brian snapped. "So here's your chance. Let's start with something simple, like what the hell your business with Henry Freitag was."

Sy could've kissed Brian.

"That guy on the phone; he was you?" Sandy's lip trembled and she brushed tears from her eyes. "I-I helped Henry buy the hammock picture. He was so charming and I thought I had finally met someone brilliant and new. If you knew my string of failures, you'd understand."

Chardonnay drifted through Sy's thoughts and she forced herself to breathe. "And? I'm listening."

Sandy hiccupped. Fishing a tissue from her pocket, she caught her dripping nose. "I met up with him every day for that first week. We discussed this show. It's been a dream of mine since the summer I visited my sister in California. We went to this art festival that takes place near the beach and they had something similar, with the paintings and actors and all. I just knew I could sell the idea to the opera house here, but I'd need the funds to get the project underway. A couple of website pleas and begs raised a little, but not near what I needed. And then in walks Henry, and I thought all my dreams had come true."

"He had a gift for inspiring that kind of emotion in people." Bored with the topic of conversation, Sy inspected her fingernails. "Is there any way I can convince you to get to the point?"

"I-*hic*-I um, well then my sister flies out from California to help me you see. And she gets a job at this art gallery, Wilcox and Sherry I think, and she starts introducing me to local artists. Henry throws a party and everyone hands him a check. It was like magic. That's when he bought the *Girl in Hammock* from Billy McK."

"I thought his name is William McKealy."

"After twenty shots of tequila and a random pigeon flies through the open door uninvited, we all call him Billy. He was very reluctant to sell the *Hammock* at first. But Henry convinced him to sell it. My sister said she'd handle the transaction and everything was swimming along beautifully."

Brian's rugged looks softened. "Jasmine Colby was your sister?"

Sandy sobbed and her voice shook. "She's my baby sister, half-sister."

Sy forgot her fingernails and leaned forward, her boredom evaporating. "Did you know Henry was stooping her too?"

"Not until a few days before the murder. I was leaving after spending my day off with him, after he said that he had an appointment and she was arriving with another painting. I figured I'd wait in the parking lot for her to leave and we'd get caught up over dinner or something. Only...she never came down. I waited in that parking garage for hours. And then, at around three-thirty in the morning, she exited the elevator to get in her car. I was furious."

"She didn't know he was stooping you?" Sy asked.

"If she did know, I don't think she cared," Sandy sneered. "My sister and I have never been very close. She had a nasty habit of stealing boyfriends from everyone, not just me, but she'd sell it like she was doing me a favor. 'To protect me' she'd say. To expose the cads for what they really were."

"A real giver." Brian shook his head.

"She was full of shit! She only did it because she could," Sandy wiped her nose again, hiccupping. "She could have anyone she wanted, but she made it a point to ruin my relationships, each time. And stupid me, I'd see her coming and bite on every excuse. But not this time. I didn't answer any of Henry's calls for the whole day. I went back to him the day after that, in the morning, to ask about what happened, to get the truth from him. I thought maybe I could guilt trip him into giving Jasmine up or something. And that's when he dropped the bombshell about being married to you."

Sy felt a burden lift from her shoulders. "That answers one mystery, I guess. It must've been the morning after I caught him in the hot-tub with the wh...with Jasmine."

"He told me I could keep the *Hammock* painting for the play. We exchanged a few choice words but he convinced me that we could keep things civil and be friends. The art project meant everything to me and he was determined to make it up by spending every last penny of his own money if he had to in order to get the thing flying. Then the foreign woman walked in and screamed and I left. I left in good spirits which was the sad part about it. I thought everything was going to be fine."

Sy felt her father tense beside her. "Too bad Henry is already dead. I feed him to alligators."

"When did you learn of Jasmine's demise?" Brian asked.

"I didn't know until the afternoon after it happened, when the police finally got a hold of me. They questioned me down at the station, treated me like some sort of criminal." Sandy shuddered.

"Just out of curiosity, where were you the night they were killed?" Brian, ever the federal agent, asked.

She glanced about, scarlet flaming her cheeks. "I was drunk. For four days I did nothing but sit in the property locker drinking. Henry convinced me everything was going to be fine and I felt so good when I left the condo. Then I got back here and I realized how cheap a person I was, how stupid I had been, and I grabbed someone's hidden stash of alcohol...and...and..."

"No one knew you were here?"

"No, I was behind the roaring twenties in the lock up. It's the furthest away from the doors in the basement, and there's a sofa behind the flats back there only the ghost knows about." She sniffed. "I shook myself out of it and I took a shower in the dressing room before the stage hands got there. Then I checked my cell phone messages and the police wanted to meet with me..."

"What made you want to get a hold of me?" Sy asked. "I wouldn't say that was the wisest thing to do. Maybe I'm the one who killed Henry and your sister."

Sandy froze like a doe caught in the headlight of an oncoming train, her wide eyes locked in a silent scream. "The way the cops drilled me, I figured they had ruled you out as a suspect. I guess I ruled you out as well. Besides, what woman could shoot a gun and kill anyone?"

"I could think of one." Sy folded her arms.

It wasn't a subtle hint. Sandy flinched. "Well, I couldn't. I wouldn't know the first thing about shooting a gun. I wouldn't even know where to find one, let alone load a bullet into it."

Brian's cheek twitched. "Mistresses don't approach grieving widows. What aren't you telling us? What's happened since the police questioned you?"

Her nod was stiff. "Yesterday. Someone broke into the property locker here and the pictures were all thrown around. Nothing was taken. Everything's been accounted for, but I thought, I'd better call you and return the painting to you. I swear that's the only reason. I've got horrible luck with relationships but I'm no thief and I'm certainly no killer."

A moment of silence followed. The next step wasn't clear. Sy worried she needed the men there to prevent her climbing over the rows in an attempt to strangle the mistress. The scared, somewhat mousy woman before her though was just as much a victim, maybe more so. Sandy had lost her financier, her lover, and her sister all in one night. Sy only lost a ten-year investment.

Up on the stage, one of the hands tripped over a power cord and went head first into the easel, crashing the stand and painting loudly against the raised floor. Horrified, Sandy stormed up the ramp to double-up collection efforts, screaming obscenities at the poor man, who gave her the finger when she turned her back. She motioned for Sy to join her, tears falling anew.

"I'm sorry about the picture Simone," Sandy grimaced, "they know better."

"Accidents happen. Is it damaged?" Sy approached the easel which stood once again, displaying the bit of canvas and frame. *Something isn't right.* She gave the picture a thorough examination, but not for damage. She could swear it was missing a dandelion.

"What's wrong?" Sandy asked. "If that blockhead tore the picture..."

Brian and Viktor climbed the ramp as Sy inspected the back of the picture. In the bottom corner, an inept smudge hovered over the artist's signature, as if a marked made in pencil was poorly erased. Returning the canvas securely to the easel, she crossed her arms and glared at the painted strokes of sunshine yellows. "This isn't my painting."

Sandy frowned. "Yes it is. I was there when Henry bought it. *Girl in Hammock* is one of Billy's better pieces."

"No, this isn't my painting. This is a forgery."

CHAPTER XXI

Forged

BRIAN STARED AT THE PAINTING. He knew Sy wouldn't have said something like that out of turn, but if it was a forgery, he had no way of knowing. He'd only seen the original among the photographs in the artist's file.

Sandy looked doubtful. "How can you tell?"

"It's missing a dandelion," Sy said. "Was this the only painting he gave you, or just the one you figured I knew about?"

Brian turned, pissed. He had about enough of Sandy three-times over. She stood silent, chewing on her lip. "Well? Don't leave us in suspense, Ms. Petrusky."

Sandy looked about to bolt. "I-I have...three others."

"Oh, let me guess. *Wind, Red River Valley,* and *The Gray?*" Brian shifted on his feet. How was Sy so calm? "It's not smart to keep information from us you know."

Looking sheepish, Sandy tried to hide behind her hands. "Not the wisest thing I've ever tried to do, I'll admit."

"Art theft is a criminal offense. Do you want to press charges Sy? Just say the word."

"Maybe," Sy circled around Sandy. "Were you afraid I wouldn't loan them to your project? Is that why you didn't volunteer that you had the pictures?"

Sandy revolved on her axis, following her satellite. "Well that. But I wanted to have a moment with my sister, if that makes any sense. I wasn't thinking I was stealing. I wasn't thinking well at all."

"Are the others in the locker too? I'd like to at least see them." Sy stopped circling. "You can keep them for your project if you wish. To be honest with you, I returned home early from Europe in order to help Henry help you, so I suppose it's the least I could do."

A wash of relief and gratitude swept over Sandy's face, melting ten years from her visible age. "I, oh, let me go. I'll get them. I'll be right back." She ran over a stage hand as she disappeared backstage.

Brian shook his head. "You sure you don't want to press charges, Sy?"

"Yeah, the poor lamb has enough on her plate."

Viktor asked her something in Romanian.

"No, Papa, we don't need to torch the opera house either."

"Your family and setting things on fire..." Brian laughed then turned to the painting. There was a ton of dandelions in the grass. "Which dandelion is it missing?"

Sy pointed to the left of a blade of grass near the right tree. "It was something I remember Henry saying about the artist. He has an obsession with the number one-thirty-seven. In this painting there are one-hundred-thirty-seven leaves in the right tree and there are just as many flowers in the original. Here though, there are only one-hundred-thirty-six because that one is missing completely."

"Why would someone knock off a local artist?" Brian scratched his head. He didn't get it. "Is there a demand for art that isn't attached to famous name, like Picasso?"

She shrugged. "Who knows? Art is subjective after all."

Sandy was back with a stage hand in tow, carrying the sum of three paintings between them. Excitement surrounded her as she swapped *Girl in Hammock* with *Wind*. "The leaves in this one are going to be so visually stunning. We've borrowed a wind tunnel from the science center that will allow us to recreate this across the whole stage." Her arm drew an imaginary arch with parade enthusiasm.

Brian recognized the golden leaves from the night before. Up close and personal with the canvas now, he had to admit he was impressed. The painted leaves had detail that mimicked life, so much to the point that they appeared to flutter from a stiff breeze.

He heard Sy snort. "It's stunning, but this one is also a forgery."

"How can you tell if you've never seen the original?" Brian asked in earnest.

"Easy. There are only a-hundred-and-thirty-five leaves."

"Two are missing. There should be a-hundred-thirty-seven." Brian spun towards Sandy. "You said the locker was broken into last night? Nothing was taken, but the pictures were tossed about?"

Sandy looked worried and studied *Wind*, her brow furrowed. She was aging before him. "Well, except now I'm starting to wonder if all the pictures have been replaced by forgeries. You're absolutely right. This one is missing two leaves from the bottom corner."

Brian secured the other paintings from the stage hand who scurried off. He helped Sandy exchange *Wind* for another piece. *Red River Valley* got its title from an old train station by that name which was the subject in the picture. Tinged with deep scarlet and purples as if the platform was hit with the rays of a setting sun, three women huddled on a bench dressed in Victorian-era clothing. A man also in Victorian clothing seemed to compare the time on his pocket watch with the conductor, who was dressed in modern clothing and referring to a wrist watch. The sky was fading to twilight with stars twinkling into existence.

The picture intrigued Brian. There was an overwhelming feeling of time being out of joint. McKealy's other works seemed happier. *Red River Valley* was saturated with regret.

Brian counted. Thirty-two train track boards and a double number of ties rested next to the platform. One stray cat peeked around the corner of the station-building. Two mountain peaks stood in the background. The bricks that made up the station and the wall totaled seventy-five. Brian glanced around to see if the others were also counting.

Sy chuckled low, "Ooh, this one is really clever. There are supposed to be one-hundred-thirty-seven stars I think and if you look at the station board, the train going to Purgatory Falls is listed to be arriving at 01:34."

"Billy is brilliant!" Sandy breathed. "I never paid close attention to this one, but I think you're right. I think there are supposed to be a-hundred-and-thirty-seven stars."

"And there are only hundred." Viktor's deep voice seemed twice as loud on stage. "Let us see gray one."

Brian was eager to please, helping Sandy swap the pictures around again. The puzzle reminded him of the critical thinking training he had in Bureau basic. Picture after picture of almost mirrored images, but one man had a scarf when the other wore a vest, or the shrub was replaced with a tree. Brian loved that kind of detailed work. It made him a good fit with Copyrights.

The Gray leaned safely on the easel. The grizzly scene encompassed scarlet-infused uniforms of confederate soldiers lying in a field. It wasn't as detailed, which seemed out of character with McKealy's other works. A quick count revealed all the soldiers and the sum of their parts were present and accounted for. Set at a waning sun, everything was cast in a reddish hue, so it appeared as if the forest that barricaded the field was on fire.

"This one gives me nightmares." Sandy pointed at the edge of the tree line, "If you look close here, you'll see a rusted tractor."

Sy sighed. "Time's out of sequence again. The artist is a very depressed man."

Apart from the missing detail, Brian couldn't see any-thing wrong until he saw the vacant spot where McKealy's signature should have been. His Bureau training wasn't all for naught. "The forger signed the others, but not this one. Maybe he ran out of time or he plum forgot? This one looks like a rush job entirely. It lacks the level of detail the others have."

"You have connections with art theft yes?" Viktor asked Brian. "What are protocols?"

"I'll contact my office, see what they advise." Brian shrugged. He pulled his cell-phone out, dialed Rosalie's direct line and waited for her to answer. "They may send a team down here."

"Which may scare off killer, yes?"

Sandy looked nervous again. "Does this mean I'm going to go to prison after all, for art theft?"

"You didn't steal anything. My idiot husband just happened to die before you were able to return the paintings to him. A thief stole

172 | S.K. DUNNING

the paintings from the theater." The venom disappeared from Sy's voice. "By the way, I'm truly sorry about Jasmine. Not because she was a victim mind, but because she was your sister."

Sandy sniffed. "Thank you. That means a lot to hear from you."

Brian's call was answered. Rosalie whined in his ear and he pinched the bridge of his nose. "It was late Rosalie. I forgot. I'll send you something later I promise. Just patch me through to Mike Steiner if you would, please?"

Sy giggled. "You should've sent her the sausage."

Viktor paced. "So if art thief and killer are same, why kill owner of art? With owner dead, pictures become evidence, yes? Surrounded by politisti?"

Brian ignored the hold music crackling in his ear. "Affirmative. Well, a strong possibility, certainly."

"I have other artists' works down in the locker," Sandy said. "I wonder if they're forgeries as well, or if the thief only took McKealy's?"

"I go check with you," Viktor offered. His expression was sinister and his intent difficult to read.

Terror settled in Sandy's wide eyes. It was as if she just noticed Viktor's disfigurement.

Sy stepped between them. "No, Papa, don't. She's okay, really."

"It is no trouble, a mea vrabie."

Sy's shoulders trembled, as if she was holding back laughter. "No, I got this one. Honest." She turned to Sandy. "I can go with you to help review them. If something stands out, I promise I'll notice."

Brian watched the girls before turning to Viktor. "What was that all about?"

The old man flashed an evil grin and rubbed his chin as if in thought, "I do not know. I only wanted to have polite conversation with Ms. Petrusky."

"Why do I get the impression that your definition of polite conversation and Sy's definition are conflicted?"

"Perhaps is my English," Viktor shrugged. "I do not speak it so good."

The hold music dropped as the line transferred to Mike, snapping Brian's attention back to his cell phone. "Hey it's…"

"Whatjya do to her, Mate," Mike asked.

"Rosalie? Yeah, I'm starting to feel the wrath."

"Well she bitched and moaned about something. I couldn't figure it out."

"I have a theory about that, but I'll have to tell you later. Listen. The Freitag murder just got too complex for me. How do you want me to handle an art heist? I figure you're the expert."

"Has this got something to do with McKealy?" Static broke up Mike's voice.

Brian moved to get a cleaner connection. "The Picasso-Rembrandt of Chicagoland? That's the one."

"What's missing?"

"*Girl in Hammock, The Gray, Wind,* and *Red River Valley.* Thing is, they've been replaced with forgeries that are nothing short of brilliant, but missing key elements of the paintings. Some things I'm assuming a true art forger wouldn't miss."

"Hmm." Brian could hear the clicking of a pen over the line; Mike's telltale sign of deep thought. "How delicate is your case right now? If I sent a team in, would it blow your cover?"

Brian gave the question serious pause. He hadn't checked in with his own team for a while so he wasn't sure what Jericho would say right now. "Things are a little sticky, but I think the cover is okay. I mean, it's not like the widow doesn't know I'm an FBI agent."

"True enough. Tell me when and where."

AS BRIAN WRAPPED UP HIS CALL with what little information he could, Sy returned with Sandy. Both looked puzzled. Sandy tugged at her wiry hair. "None of the other paintings appear forged. Just the McKealys."

"Well, the art fraud team is going to show up sometime in the next twenty-four," Brian tucked his cell back into its leather pouch. "In the meantime, we need to inform the local LEOs, gather the whole staff together here, and apply the vow of silence. For the moment, we don't want this leaking out. This may impact an ongoing murder investigation."

WITHIN THE HOUR, Detective Shelby arrived with a small plain clothes team and some crime scene investigators. They started the round of questions and fingerprinting. Brian warned Shelby that the FBI team would indeed be coming and possibly take command of the case. "I won't be in charge of this one, Detective. I don't do art."

Shelby's response was gruff, but without malice. "That's okay. Neither do we. This is one case I don't mind handing over. I'd even giftwrap it if I had a bow big enough."

The Sister

I T WAS DINNER TIME WHEN SY, Viktor, and Brian were able to break away from the opera house. Viktor offered to take them out to dinner but Sy reminded him that they were supposed to have Gunny up. As the taxi turned down Brighton Avenue, her cell phone rang. "Gunny," she squealed, "speak of the devil. We're running late but we'll be there soon."

Brian looked out the window, trying not to eavesdrop. Whatever Gunny said however, caused Sy to swear. She wasn't happy.

"Triple crap. Thanks Gunny, we'll be there soon." Breaking away from her call, she leaned forward to address the cabbie. "Change of plans, you're going to drop us off at the parking garage entrance instead."

Concern deepened Viktor's scars. "What is problem?"

"Tina's here and apparently she's brought every paparazzi within a thousand mile radius." Sy dialed the distinct-sounding 911 on her phone. In a voice sounding more stereotypical Asian than her usual European accent, Sy screamed an address at the operator. "There are reporters in the lobby and I think I saw a gun! I'm scared! There was a shooting here last week. I think the killer came back!"

175

She hung up.

Brian looked at her in disbelief. "Did you just file a false report with 911, in front of a federal agent?"

"No, of course I didn't silly," she swatted at him. "Mrs. Yiu, the Chinese lady from the fourth floor called and expressed fear for her life. Oh, don't look at me like that. It's not like she'll answer the door if they knock. She's scared of everything. She'd just stand there screaming at them in Mandarin."

"This will get rid of paparazzi, no?"

She nodded. "The press will cite a million different laws regarding the freedom of press, but the police will have the advantage because they're after an alleged gunman, not because someone is reporting a bunch of idiot trespassers. We'll be able to sneak in through the parking garage and avoid the whole mess."

Brian rubbed his forehead and groaned. "They can track your cell phone you know."

She disagreed, surprising him. "The GPS is broken and it's been programmed to bounce cell towers. They're going to have a really difficult time trying to find a number, let alone trace it."

He held up a hand to silence her, "I really don't want to know. Forget I said anything. Have I ever told you that I think you're certifiably nuts?"

"Numerous times," she giggled, un-affronted.

The taxi drove by the front so they could all get a view of the media circus spilling out into the streets. Just as they turned onto the next street to make their way to the parking entrance, sirens from several squad cars resounded off of the multi-story buildings in the area. Brian chuckled soft and low. Feeling her buzz into his mind, he thought, I'm impressed. You're nuts, but I'm definitely impressed.

You're such a gentleman, she replied.

They piled in the elevator from the garage level. It was a quick ride up to the penthouse. Sy flew into her condo to dial down to the security desk from her land-line. "Gunny? Oh, Jefferson, can you hear me? Send Gunny up with Tina after the camera idiots are gone." She replaced the receiver in its cradle and reached for a decanter on the sideboard. "Whiskey?"

Viktor reached for a glass. "It is Tina. Make it triple."

Sy poured a generous amount for her father and extended near five-fingers of amber liquid to Brian. He accepted. "I take it Tina is a special challenge?"

She tossed back a shot and refilled her glass. "My relationship with my sister-in-law has always been tenuous, even in the best of times. Henry's unfortunate demise can only contribute to its detriment, I'm afraid." A wry grin developed as she brought her whiskey to her lips. "Everything Tina does is for attention. Good, bad, as long as it's not indifferent. Christ himself didn't have near the cross she has to bear daily. Too bad she's famous, because she really couldn't act her way out of a paper sack if she tried."

Brian didn't remember reading about a famous sister in Henry's file. "She's an actress?"

"Hollywood seems to think so. She's been in several films but hasn't had anything but a supporting role until she was cast in The Island of Sharks."

"I saw that one," Brian was confused. "I thought it starred Crystal Teagan."

"It does. Crystal is Tina's middle name and the first house her parents owned was located on Teagan Boulevard."

Brian was uncomfortable. The Island of Sharks was a summer thriller that had the traveling populous scared to venture to the South Pacific islands. Crystal Teagan spent most of the movie naked and screaming, or having sex on the beach with Brad Carmichael, the leading man. "Well, I guess this makes the first time I ever met a girl after I've already seen her naked. Anything else I should be aware of?"

Sy flashed him a sinister grin and warned, "Don't let her intelligence fool you. She really is that shallow."

The aroma of food, a magical concoction of cheese and prosciutto filled the room as Annika brought in a tray of appetizers. "Supper ees almost reedy. Ees Tina Stayyink?"

"Not if I can help it, but I suppose it would be rude to tell her no. Good thing the haz-mat team came to clean up the foyer while were gone, thank you for calling them, Brian. Although, her reaction to the remaining brain matter would have been priceless."

THE ELEVATOR DINGED, indicating the arrival of the security guard and the actress. Annika announced them as she ushered them into the sitting room. Gunny, stoic and imposing, towered Tina. The actress, known as Crystal Teagan, was short, very blond, and the opposite of naked. She looked cross and ignored Brian after introductions were made. *I see how it is,* he thought.

Sy buzzed him. *Just wait. It gets better.*

"Simone," Tina cooed, frosting the space between them. Brian could swear he saw icicles forming in the air. He shivered. She wore her Hollywood pout. "I got here as soon as my schedule allowed. What are we doing about Henry's service?"

Sy's smile was bright and full of teeth. "I thought we could cremate him and then sell little vials of him on the internet for all his fans and mistresses."

"Simone, be serious." She fished a handkerchief from her denim jeans to dab at her watery eyes. "My brother deserves to be honored like a king. He touched the lives of so many."

"Yes, he touched many people." Sy took a long drink from her glass. "He played very well with others."

The actress sniffed and sighed, clutching the handkerchief to her chest in dramatic fashion. "I think we should bury him in Arlington. So many important people are there."

Gunny lost his stoic facade and spit angry fire. "You would dare defile the sanctity of that patch of hallowed ground…"

"As fascinating as that would be," Sy interrupted, curbing rising tensions, "he never served his country and so he wouldn't qualify for Arlington. Anyway, 'where' is moot. He has a plot, Tina, at Graceland. I think it a fitting address enough for his final resting place."

Tina seemed to forget she was crying. "He's going to be buried with Elvis?"

Gunny shook his head and reached for the whiskey decanter. "Graceland is a cemetery here in Chicago. Our most prominent dead citizens are interred there."

"Oh. Well, will it provide enough accommodation for everyone to attend? You do realize there will be hundreds of extremely important people there. The president may even show."

Brian frowned. "As in 'of the United States', that president?"

Tina scowled at him like he was a piece of gum on her shoe. "No, I meant the Screen Actors' Guild."

Sy rolled her eyes, "Truly? I thought we had standards."

The actress dropped her head and shot Sy an evil look from the top of her eyes. "Well, I'm assuming you are going to be attending, so we have to allow for your type."

"Yes, well, we can't all be me, no matter how hard you try, Tina." Sy spoke with equal venom. Rising heat dispelled the cold reception, a history of angry and spiteful words like ghosts swirled in the empty space. Sy returned to the sideboard and unstoppered a decanter. "Would you like a drink, Tina? Cognac perhaps?"

Tina sniffed and tossed back her hair. "Yes, that would be lovely, Simone. The paparazzi were positively cruel and unrelenting this trip. I tried four times to lose them from the time I boarded the plane in Bali."

Sy brought a hand to her heart and gasped, over-exaggerated gestures. "That must have been so horrible for you, trying to lose them on a plane. Now myself, I lost them before I even arrived home."

Annika returned to announce that supper was ready in the dining room. "Danke Annika," Viktor said. "Shall we to the table?"

"I don't eat meat, Annie," Tina said, ignoring Sy's ex-tended drink to pour one of her own. "I hope you remembered."

"Of course," Annika grumbled. "That ees vy I make you chicken."

As the others filed out, Brian grabbed Sy's arm, holding her behind. "Are you okay?" He had only known the actress for a few minutes and he had to fight the urge to punch her. He could only imagine what his crazy, brunette princess had to endure for the last ten years.

He felt a familiar tickle atop his brain-stem. *I'm fine,* Sy's voice broadcasted. *How would you like to play a game?*

Depends, he tried to ignore the buzzing sensation. *Would I get to play whack-a-mole with Tina's head?*

She swapped Tina's ignored glass with Brian's empty. *My father and I are going to keep the conversation foreign. Henry used to get a big kick out of it because Tina would start crying. She doesn't like not being the complete center of everyone's attention, and that used to drive Henry nuts. Gunny knows, we've played this game before in his presence. He knows a few phrases in Korean. What languages do you speak? Spanish right?*

Brian shrugged. *My Pig-Latin is more reliable than my butchered Spanish.*

Well, just make up something if you get stuck then, look at her, and laugh. Trust me; this is going to be very entertaining.

CHAPTER XXIII

Conspiracies & Theories

BRIAN ALMOST FELT SORRY FOR TINA. The conversation at the dinner table blazed about her like wildfire. She picked at the peas on her plate, avoiding the chicken, looking lost. Every attempt she made to return the conversation to English was interrupted with hearty laughter As Annika cleared dinner plates, Tina began to cry.

"Simone, I should lay down after such a long day. I trust my room has been prepared?" Tina pulled a compact from her pocket and checked herself in the mirror.

Sy threw her napkin on the table. "Oh, Tina, I'm so sorry. I had no idea you were planning on staying here. All the rooms are claimed."

Brian thought he saw a smile tug at the corner of Sy's mouth.

Tina turned crimson. "Simone. You knew I'd come. For Henry. Didn't you?"

"Well yes, but I didn't imagine you'd wish to stay *here*, where he *died*. And Papa showed up, and Brian here. And Annika has the housekeeper's suite."

Brian couldn't help himself. "I suppose I could return to the Ritz if I need to...oh, no, I guess I can't really. My equipment is being

183

delivered here tomorrow, and I'm the only one who can sign for it. Homeland Security rules you know. Such a shame."

Tina sniffed. "But the paparazzi! I won't have security. I can't trust anyone else in this pathetic town."

"However did you manage Bali then?" Gunny asked.

"Don't be dumb," Tina blinked. "I stayed with Brad and Angelina."

Sy drummed her fingers on the table. "Maybe you can stay with Tori. Vegans should stick together, shouldn't they? Annika, call Tori for me please and-"

"No, no need. I'll check in at the Ritz under my real name. No one will know the difference." Tina jumped up from the table with a nervous giggle. "As a matter of fact, I should head there now. I'll call you tomorrow and we can discuss Henry's arrangements then."

Brian thought a twister had blown through as fast as Tina gathered up her personal affects and disappeared. He glanced at Sy as the table erupted into laughter. "She doesn't care for Tori I take it?"

"Danke, danke. You're a peach!" Gunny's eyes lit up as Annika deposited a gooey, chocolaty desert in front of him. "No, Tina and Tori actually get along quite famously. Tina had a run in with Tori's dealer though, and if I recall the collector's words accurately as I was escorting him out of the building, Tina is not supposed to show up in Chicago unless she can pay her bill."

"What Tina doesn't know," Sy said between mouthfuls, "is that, against my specific orders by the way, Henry paid her debt in full, with the stipulation no deal would ever be honored again. He wasn't to deal to her at all. Ever. When they insisted on collecting interest, Henry turned me loose on them and they actually gave me change back for the trouble."

Viktor chuckled. "And I lean a little myself, to point dealer goes on holiday and has not been seen back in Chicago."

Brian stared at Viktor's scars. "I meant to ask you; what is it you do for a living?"

Dead-panned, dry-delivered, Viktor replied, "Exactly is most interesting challenge. I am, how you say, consultant? I provide expertise...security...transportation of sensitive property...facilitate business meetings for important people in private sector."

"And above all, provide service with a smile," Sy beamed, pride lighting her blue-brown eyes. "Some of his work is top secret. Some of it isn't, but is handled like it is anyway."

Her father smiled, "So I give you two options to believe, yes? I am criminal or I am law-abiding citizen. Unfortunately, you will have to make choice on your own."

"Oh, Papa, stop. You'll scare him away." Sy tuned to Brian. "He's the good guys, you can trust me."

Gunny returned the topic of conversation to Tina. "Anyway, I'd lay even money that's why Tina is putting up with the paparazzi, though. She thinks if she has witnesses with cameras, she'll be safe."

A LULL IN CONVERSATION stretched across the table as they consumed desert. It was a decadent, pounds-increasing dish. Brian calculated the miles he'd have to run to burn off the calories, and decided to ignore it. He'd worry about his exercise routine when he returned to New York.

A peculiar look fell across Sy's countenance. "This art theft has me stumped. Why swap paintings that are bound to be discovered as forgeries? I'm finding it difficult to believe a forger so detailed down to the brush stroke would simply forget to put a daisy or a star. Is he looking to get caught?"

"Criminals are caught by mistakes," Brian said. "Could be the forger believes he's a better painter. The question truly is if the forgeries and the murders are related."

Viktor leaned his elbows on the table. "The artist, he is alive, yes?"

"Last we checked," Brian frowned. "Why? What are you thinking?"

"It is perhaps nothing. I know story of young man during communist occupation. He was instructed by government to paint some pictures and when he completes commission, the young man is killed in unique accident. This made price of pictures high no?"

Sighing, Sy shook her head. "Can this mystery get any more convoluted? Whatever happened to 'the butler did it'?"

Gunny scooped the last of the chocolate crumbs into his mouth. "You don't have a butler."

"Well, I guess there is that." Crestfallen, Sy pushed her plate away.

Checking his watch, Gunny rose and placed his napkin on the table. "I'd better get on home. The wife will be wondering what's happened to me."

"Give Cheryl our love, Gunny." Sy leapt up to give the man a hug.

"Will do. Let me know when Tina wants another dinner. I still have some moose in the freezer we can force-feed her."

Viktor positioned himself behind Sy. "I will walk with you. We get caught up on old times, no?"

Brian said his goodbyes, accepted a cup of coffee from the housekeeper, and moved back into the sitting room. Sy excused herself to change her clothes. He pulled out his cell phone and stared at it, lost in thought. The day had been a long one and the hour was growing late. The idea McKealy could be next on the killer's list plagued him. He dialed Mike.

"So you think the artist could be in danger?" Mike asked after greetings were exchanged.

"I don't know. Maybe. This whole case was strange right off the bat."

"What'chya mean?"

Brian sipped his coffee, collecting his thoughts. "I mean, why is the Bureau taking this tip of a possible hit-for-hire seriously when it came from a felon some Sandusky police locked up? The man had no relative link to the Freitags at all, so I have to ask, what's his angle?"

There was a pause. "I wouldn't read too much into that. The perp's trying to plea bargain so the prosecution will go easier on him."

"Yeah well it still doesn't make sense. You'd think Weller and Jericho both had more important things to do than assert FBI privilege in cases they obviously don't have any jurisdiction over. I know they knew Simone didn't do it before I booked my flight down here."

"I'm telling you Kirby, you're just spinning your wheels. You know Jericho doesn't do anything without checking with his golf buddies first. Maybe they're leaning on him."

"To what end? And another thing, Jericho hasn't once checked up on me the entire time I've been down here. No one has." The more Brian thought about his situation, the less he liked it. This was one high profile murder case the Bureau could've easily stood by and watched. Let the local force get embarrassed if they pissed off the wrong politician. The phone records came up clean, the bank records were all in order. There was nothing at all to suggest that Sy hired anyone to do the job. That should have been sufficient for them to ignore the whole affair.

The art theft bothered him as well. If Sandy had not already removed the paintings from the premises, would they have been bagged and tagged, or left behind? What if Viktor was right and the perpetrator meant to swap the forgeries in the evidence locker. That would mean they were dealing with a dirty cop. If they were dealing with a dirty cop, could that be the reason more than half of the available surveillance footage of the condo was corrupted?

"Kirby," Mike said, "did you or did you not insist on going out there without a team? Why the hell does this bother you so much? I'd think you'd be having a field day without Jericho breathing down your neck."

"When has that ever stopped Jericho from micromanaging?"

"Touché. All right, I'll tell you what. I'll get a hold of the artist and check on his welfare, and see if I can roust up some protection for him."

"Okay, Mike. Let me know, eh?" Brian said goodbye and hung up. His thoughts were dark and full of trepidation. An art thief was one thing. A dirty cop though, that can of worms would never make it to court without hard-core evidence. Right now, all they had to go on were a string of coincidences.

And the buzzing in his mind was giving him a headache.

"Let's concentrate on one thought at a time," Sy entered the room, carrying a coffee mug of her own, and dressed in sweats and a matching sweatshirt bearing the Swiss Army emblem across the front. Her make-up was removed, her hair brushed and hung loose about her face. She looked tired. Tired and bloody perfect. Henry was an idiot. Sy flashed a weary smile, "I know you're concerned for my welfare but I'll be fine."

"I'm really worried you were also supposed to be home that night," Brian admitted. He knew she could handle herself. He remembered the parrot-tattooed victim lying on the Wint-Mart floor. Still, he felt compelled to keep her safe.

Her smile sobered some. "If I was supposed to be the target, there were a million other ways more convenient that a professional, or even an amateur, would've used. Disabling something on my jet for instance, plunging me and my pilot into the depths of the Atlantic Ocean, leaving the entire world to search for the flight data recorder."

"It's still possible," Brian insisted, feeling sick at the thought of plane sabotage. "We can't rule it out just yet."

"Well, I've ruled out Henry's mistresses," Sy sipped her coffee. "At least the ones I know of. The one, of course, died next to him. The sister, well, I'm pretty sure she was being honest and she's never fired a gun. Shotguns aren't generally a woman's weapon of choice, unless she's been trained to use one."

Brian nodded.

She glanced at him sideways. "That's not all that's bothering you though."

"Affirmative. I'm wondering why I'm here in the first place. I mean, don't get me wrong, this has all been entertaining, but the Bureau could've proved you innocent without intruding into your life."

The elevator dinged outside the condo as Sy replied. "So would they send you here just to spy on me, or are they also keeping you away from the office?"

"Just to spy on you I'm afraid. They didn't really have to ask me twice. I was eager to see you again."

"Really?" Her eyes twinkled and a girlish smile crested her lips.

He felt a blush forming and bit the inside of his cheek to regain his composure. "Well, I thought I might get to drive the Veyron again."

Sy turned to Viktor as he strolled into the room. "You were gone long enough. I'm going to be nosy and ask you what you and Gunny talked about."

"He expressed interest in working for me some time back. I wanted to tell him I had open position." Viktor sat down in the armchair.

"I'm happy for you, Papa, but the place won't be the same without him."

"I tell him he can start work when you move."

Annika appeared with a cup of coffee for Viktor and a cheese and fruit tray which she placed on the coffee table. She disappeared as silently as she had appeared.

Sy tapped her chin. "While the intent is probably to spy on me, let's rule you out first. What case were you working on? Anything top secret?"

Brian snorted, "Hardly. I had a lyric infringement issue that reared its ugly head in Andersonville Tennessee. It was sticky because the copyright was obtained by the man who was allegedly not the author of the work. The investigation is actually tearing the

small town apart. Brothers are fighting brothers and waitresses refuse to say anything."

"I can't imagine anyone trying to sweep that under the table. It's
already too public." She laughed. "You'd think they'd give up spying
on me. I haven't been to Turkey or anywhere else in the Middle
East, or even China in years. I can't possibly be that important."

"And my presence here doesn't explain Henry's death or the
missing artwork." Brian reached for an apple slice, amazed he could
even think about eating after the dinner he just had.

"True."

"So let's start at a logical beginning. Who benefits most from
Henry's death?" Brian figured there could be another suspect among
those who could collect, especially if Sy was supposed to be there
when the killer showed up.

Sy shrugged, "I do, I guess. I get our things, his crap, that damned
Veyron, his seat at Club 33 in Disneyland...I wonder if I get his frequent flier mileage?"

"You have jet, what do you need with miles?" Viktor asked.

"I could donate them to charity." She snagged a piece of Blue Stil-
ton and a pear slice from the fruit tray.

"So if you had been here instead of Jasmine, who would benefit
from your death?" Brian asked.

"Since we have no children, all of my things go to Papa, all of
Henry's things would've gone to his sister. Joint property, with the
exception of a very few pieces, would be liquidated and distributed
to a list of charities. I've lost track of the life insurance policies.
They're in the lock-box still."

"Where's that located?"

"Lloyds of London downtown. Henry would have pulled a policy out for this art project I'm sure, and I think there might still be one in affect for the movie project he had on hold. Three or four of them should be in my name, maybe one in his sister's name. I don't know how many off the top of my head. I'll have to look."

Brian frowned. "I didn't know you could have more than one policy like that."

"It's standard procedure for most producers at the beginning of a project. They get life insurance policies on all their key people. To take a policy out on someone, you only have to prove interest by blood or money, and only at the time of inception."

Viktor shook his head. "I still think key is with criminal investigators of murder."

"I really don't want it to be a dirty cop." Brian said. "Things get sticky."

"Not dirty cop. Perhaps it is crime scene investigator no? They are invisible, underpaid, overworked, and accessible." Viktor leaned forward. "In busy city, many CSI wearing jacket and shoe covers. Police work around them, not necessarily with them. If Secret Service wanted to have double-agent, it would be CSI in this case."

Sy nodded. "They'd know how to clean up after themselves as well. You know Papa, I think you have something there."

Brian's cell phone rang, cutting through the break in conversation as a knife through butter. "Kirby, Copyrights."

"Hey, it's Mike. I just got word. Paramedics were called out to McKealy's home. They found him with his head in his oven."

CHAPTER XXIV

McKealy's House

A CROWD OF ONLOOKERS GATHERED OUTSIDE the artist's home, despite the small hours of the morning. Sy stifled a yawn with her hand and tried to concentrate on the movement of the officials. There was a lot of white noise; so many thoughts being broadcasted at once and none of them cohesive.

Crowds aggravated her condition during stressful events. Amusement parks and movie theaters during the summertime she could handle. Thoughts then were of the happy, family-friendly, G-rated type. Sy did her best to avoid auto racetracks and carnivals. Too many people at those places hoped for something terrible to happen.

The cold air stung her nose, distracting her for a time. The static from the crowd around her was a mixture of hope and curiosity. It wasn't enough to drown out one consciousness, much to Sy's disappointment. The little girl supported in her mother's arms couldn't have been more than four-years old, and all she really wanted to do was go to bed. The lights of the emergency vehicles shone directly into her room through her curtains, however, and she was trying hard not to whine because she didn't want to be in trouble. Her mother, on the other hand, couldn't know this and thought her daughter was too terrified to sleep; and somehow being out in the crowd watching the uniforms do their job would help.

Sy wanted to say something, feeling the little girl's plight. Her whole life, Sy struggled with the emotional wake from her special talents. She closed her eyes and tried to recall the vineyard, to smell the grapes, to watch the bats fly in the setting sun, to no avail. Her mind kept going back to the little girl desperately wanting sleep. Frustrated, Sy exhaled sharply, surprising the people standing next to her. They, of course, thought she was being insensitive to the situation and all turned to shoot her looks.

Sy couldn't take it anymore and walked over to the erected safety barrier. Two crime scene investigators dug through their kits, waiting for word to enter the house. If she could get a conversation started with someone who had a clue as to what was going on, maybe she could shake her mind free of everyone else. She summoned the brightest voice she could muster. "Hello boys."

The investigators looked at each other and then back at her as if they were surprised she'd even speak to them. The more schoolboy-looking of the two smiled and returned her greeting. "Rough night?"

Sy thought of the crowd. "I've seen worse. How are you two holding up?"

"We've seen worse as well. CSI Pitman," the schoolboy introduced himself. "Are you a neighbor? Do you know the victim?"

"Only through my late husband. I've never met Billy but I've seen his work, and he's a brilliant artist." McKealy's works had officially grown on her. She could see the attraction to his pieces.

"I'm sorry for your loss," Pittman said.

"What?"

He looked confused. "Your husband?"

"Oh that. Don't be. My husband was a two-timing jackass." She wanted to ask them if they knew of any crooked crime scene investigators, but couldn't think of a way to ask without being crude.

Brian exited the house and walked across the lawn towards them. "Okay team." He sounded so official. "They think it's safe enough. The windows in the kitchen are open now, but they weren't obviously when the officer kicked in the door. Let the EMTs know if you start feeling light-headed at all."

"Roger that." All business, the investigators walked to the house, donning blue shoe-covers at the door.

Brian stepped over the barricade and escorted Sy through the crowd. She looked back one last time at the little girl and shuddered. *It's not my business, and they wouldn't understand.* She could imagine berating the mother for her mothering skills and the woman's likely reaction. That was sure to go over well.

"We found artist in time," Brian, hushed and furtive, gave her a quick debriefing at the edge of the additional ears at the scene. "Apparently, McKealy was stabilized in the emergency room and he was moved to ICU. The Bureau is keeping him under watch until they determine if it was a suicide attempt."

"They suspect it was a murder attempt?"

Brian nodded, "I don't think it was attempted suicide either. There was an unfinished canvas sitting on an easel in his studio room under the stairs. Most artists don't leave work unfinished by choice."

Her Audi R8 GT was located half a block down. Sy handed Brian the keys. "I don't want to drive anymore."

Concern softened his expression. "The crowd back there, that was hard for you, talent-wise I mean."

Near tears, she nodded. "I'm grateful you understand. My gift is a curse. I don't know what I could've done as a little girl to piss off God, but there are times I wish I could give it back."

"You have this talent because you're probably the one person in this world who wouldn't ever abuse it."

She sniffed. "You wouldn't."

"Like Hell I wouldn't. I'd have Jericho's job, no I'd have the director's job, and I'd have a one-hundred percent conviction rate, holding a record that could never be broken." Brian played with the car keys. "Power does strange things to people. I'm just as weak as the next normal person. I can be corrupted under the right circumstances."

Sy looked back at the dispersing crowd and digested his words. "I suppose you're right. I wouldn't wish this on my worst enemy, let alone my best friend. There's no chance of ever having a normal life, although I think I've come to terms with that as an adult. I mostly wish I had some control over when and where it happens."

Thoughts ebbed away from Sy while the artist's neighbors in the distance returned to their homes. The worst of the white noise had passed and the air was quiet once more. She released a captive breath and recalled her beloved vineyard, full to the brim with sun-ripened fruit.

Her knight-in-something-armor swaggered towards her. "Do you know what I'm thinking now?"

The street light behind him cast a blackened shadow over his features. Her heart lurched into her throat and butterflies settled in her stomach. She tried to access his thoughts, to make the familiar mental connection, but she couldn't. He pulled in close enough she could feel his body heat penetrating the space between them. She fumbled to find an answer, to find words. "No, actually I don't."

His mouth slid into a half-grin. "Good. Nice to know I can still surprise you. Now, how would you like to grab a slice of pie and a cup of coffee?"

The butterflies fled her stomach, leaving it hollow and grumbling. "Can we make it an éclair and coffee? I know a deli on 22nd Street that's open all night."

THE DELI WAS WARM AND BRIGHT, a welcome contrast to the cold, violent world they fled from. Sy ignored the Please wait to be seated sign and dragged Brian to a corner booth.

"Do you mind if I sit with my back to the wall?" He asked before she slid into the desired seat. "It's a law enforcement thing."

"Da, desigur," she replied, switching sides. "I should have thought about that. Papa does the same thing. Henry always wanted his back to the door in case someone could recognize him."

Brian chuckled, settling into the seat. I'm not sure I want to be compared to either man, but I guess your father works."

"Oh, stop. You like Papa, I know you do."

He unrolled the flatware from his napkin. "I plead the Fifth."

The waitress, just out of her teens approached them, wide-eyed and nervous. "Mrs. Freitag, I wasn't, I mean..."

Sy rubbed her forehead. She wasn't in the mood for sympathy or another mistress's confession. She didn't prompt the girl to continue. "It's okay Brenda. Just bring us some coffee and I'll have the gooiest chocolate éclair you have. What would you like, Brian?"

He looked blindsided. "I, uh, what fruit pies do you have?"

Brenda bit her lower lip, "We've got apple left and boysenberry. I think we still have some cherry too, but I'll have to look. Oh, and apricot."

"If you put a slice of cheddar cheese on the apple pie when you heat it up, I'll have a slice of that."

"Uh, okay. Is coffee good for you as well?" Brenda scribbled on her ticket book.

"Please."

Brenda attempted another nervous statement but Sy cut her off with a sharp look and chased her off. Catching the question in Brian's raised eyebrow, Sy waved a dismissive hand. "Brenda's a lovely girl, really, but she tends to be a bit suffocating during a crisis. She should study to be a psychiatrist. She'd fit right in."

"She doesn't look old enough to be working this late." Brian said.

"She's a freshman at Lewis University this year, if you believe it. Her aunt and uncle own the deli, so she's worked summers here for a few years." Sy rubbed her neck, popping tension loose.

The coffee came side-by-side with the pie and éclair. Sy thwarted Brenda's inquiries again and she left them alone. "She reminds me of a cousin of mine," Brian said as he doctored his coffee.

"Her mannerisms or her physique?" Sy stifled a yawn into the back of her hand before sinking her knife and fork into her pastry.

He chewed his pie. "Both actually. Jasona has an easily agitated disposition and she'll believe anything anyone tells her."

"Jasona? That's an unusual name, isn't it?"

He rolled his eyes. "No one could ever accuse Aunt Nini or Uncle Pick of being normal. Of the six children between them, Jasona's the youngest. She's unfortunately got four older brothers: Clover, Worthy, Geordie, Payson, and a sister Yudena. Jasona is about three or four years older than I am. I think."

Sy tried not to laugh. After all, her father called her Simon. "Pick?"

Brian smirked. "Pick's his middle name. Apparently, his two-year-old brother was allowed to name him."

"Dare I ask what his first name is?" She bit her lip, feeling the giggle work its way to her tongue.

"Completely normal name actually. It's Jacob."

"Oh," Sy lost the desire to laugh. She sipped her coffee and day-dreamed for a moment. The chaos of a large family sounded so exotic to her sensibilities. Brian seemed so grounded and accepting of others' faults. She wondered if his family had anything to do with it.

"Euro for your thoughts," Brian set down his coffee and leaned forward on the table, hands folded.

She felt her cheeks flush under his gaze. "I'm a bit jealous."

"Jealous? Of me?"

"Your family."

"Ah, well, I have family in over-abundance. You're welcome to most of them if you really want." He broke into laughter. "I'll have to introduce them to you someday. I bet you could remember all their names."

"Just say when and where," she said. "I'm for the challenge."

"The real test is in the lineage. Figuring out who belongs to who is the difficult part," he said as Brenda refilled their coffee. "I can't even keep them straight most days."

"You're so lucky, you know that?"

200 | S.K. DUNNING

"Ha! Spend an hour with them, and believe me, you'll change your tune." He stirred cream into his coffee. "Henry didn't have much family either, did he?"

"It was just him, his mother, and Tina after the plane crash. His sister Laura was on her way to an Olympic competition somewhere for ice skating, along with their father. The United States lost a lot of talent on that flight."

Sirens blazed as an emergency vehicle roared up the street, pulling Brian's attention to the window-diffused red and blue flashing lights. His somber demeanor touched her heart. "I remember watching the news break, I think. Henry's file mentioned it, briefly. It said something about how their father was Laura's coach or assistant coach. Wasn't he from the West German Hockey team or something?"

"Henry's father was from West Germany, but he skated for the Canadians in his youth." She took the last bite of her éclair and pushed her plate to the edge of the table. "Anyway, Henry's mother never quite coped with the loss and the tragedy left her unhinged for the rest of her life. She was a hard woman to talk to and I, of course, was never good enough for her son. I was just plain foreign trash to her."

"She was just jealous. I bet she knew deep down that he didn't deserve you." He turned away from the light display. "What about your family? Your file didn't mention anything and you only mentioned an uncle."

"He's the only relation I know of. He never married. No children." Sy traced the mouth of her coffee mug, wishing she had something more to share. "Father doesn't speak about it, of his family. I don't know if it's because he defected to Switzerland or if it's due to the nature of his career. Maybe it's both. I tried asking Uncle Juris about it once and he told me to ask my father. I left it alone then."

"And you know nothing of your mother?" he asked. "I imagine you must look like her. I see little resemblance to Viktor."

Sy shrugged, "I suppose you're correct. I've never even see a picture of her. Papa still has so much anger in him, and I think that's why he never tracked her down. He jokes about feeding people to the alligators, but I think if he ever found my mother, it would no longer be a joke."

Brian reviewed the tab and pulled out his wallet to thumb through a few bills. His eyes darkened. "I'm a good agent." His words, his tone were deliberate, calculating. "I don't deviate much from the rules, but I tend to believe more in the spirit of the law than the actual enforcement of it."

He sounded like a novice seeking penance or confessing a grave sin. Sy's heart quickened. "I'm not sure I follow..."

He looked her square in the eyes, his rugged features shadowy and sinister. "I'm not above stretching the scope of my jurisdiction when I feel the cause is justified. If you ask me to, I will do all in my power to track down your mother."

Sy was at a loss. Her knight-in-something-armor offered to sacrifice his security clearance at something as simple as a word from her. Breathing proved difficult and her lip trembled. "To what end?"

"For closure, maybe. Answers...Revenge."

She turned away, no longer able to hold his gaze. Heady, she felt as if she was walking though someone else's dreamscape. It was a tantalizing offer. There was so much she wanted to know, but at what cost? "I wouldn't ask that of you."

He chased her gaze, fishing it up from her coffee mug. "Still, I'm willing. There's nothing-" he cleared his throat, "-there's nothing I wouldn't do-"

"Is this ready?" Brenda interrupted, shattering the spell that gripped them.

Brian glanced up, "I, uh, yeah. No change."

The moment left Sy void of emotion. She wasn't prepared for his oath of fealty. It felt too sudden and she didn't understand why. What was she so scared of? A tear streaked down her cheek. "Stop being so bloody perfect."

"You first."

CHAPTER XXV

Sleepless

THEY STUMBLED INTO HER CONDO at four o'clock, sneaking about in the dark like teenagers past their curfew. Their third winds were finally petering out. The coming day would be a brutal mistress to those who hadn't enough sleep in the night. Sy didn't care though. The deli conversation revealed a new path for her and she was tempted strong to take it.

It wasn't the offer to find her mother. Abusing his position for an investigation over thirty years cold without thought for self or reward could ruin his career. Her heart hurt. She wanted the something to be something more.

Sy sucked in a breath in response to the chill of her sheets as she climbed into bed. She reached out to the cold, unoccupied side of the bed, aware of Henry's absence. Was she on the rebound, seeking a replacement because she didn't want to be alone? Or was it because Henry was the only love interest she had for the last ten years of her existence? Brian Kirby was everything she didn't know she desired in men. He teased her, challenged her, grounded her. She could be fragile around him and he accepted her.

Yet, it troubled her that she constantly compared Brian to Henry, a polar opposite in both physique and temperament. Whatever plague Brian infected her with, it was Henry's dead eyes that haunted her without mercy. She wouldn't be able to move on until she buried his ghost. The question was: would Brian still be there?

She tossed herself away from the memory and onto her side. As exhausted as she was, sleep eluded her. She lay in bed, sifting through incomplete thoughts and complex puzzles. Pushing aside her thoughts of Brian, she tackled her husband's murder. She was certainly more capable of coping with that than her confused emotions.

None of the events in the past week made any sense. There were the forgeries someone was willing to kill to plant, provided the killer and the thief were the same person. If William really did try to commit suicide, why would he leave a painting undone? Was she no longer a threat to the murderer? Was she ever a threat?

Something else occurred to her. Maybe Jasmine was the target. She could've been part of the forgery ring, and slept with Henry as part of the con. Henry knew nothing of art, except that he liked the superiority it gave him when he spoke of some famous pieces. "The key to my job," his memory whispered to her, "is to know just enough to be dangerous, but not enough so the mark feels good about being an expert. It's a delicate dance."

"You exploit people to get what you want," she told him.

"Exploitation is a strong word, don't you think?" he replied, looking smug and confident. "The art of compromise is to let someone else have your way. That's all I do."

Grr! She threw herself on her back and glared at the ceiling. There was something amiss about the whole ordeal. Sy decided to go through it step-by-step, from the time she caught Henry in the hot-tub. She walked through the door. There were rose petals everywhere. She called out for Henry: there was no response. She wondered if their pilot announced her arrival and she frowned because she was hoping to surprise Henry.

Girl in Hammock hung in the hallway, displaying all one-hundred-thirty-seven dandelions. She moved to the bedroom. The sheets were turned down but the bed had not been slept in. She used the bathroom. Why was her curling iron on the counter and not in the drawer like it should've been?

There was blond hair in the iron. Did Sy notice and that's why she took it with her to ask Henry about it? She washed her hands, went back down the hall to the kitchen and heard Jasmine laugh. The French doors to the patio were wide open and she walked out...

Fast forward. She grabbed the keys to the Veyron when she meant to grab the keys to the Audi. She didn't realize that until she got down to the parking basement, but she wasn't going to go back up to exchange the sets.

Not with that whore in the hot-tub.

Wint-Mart bothered her also, but she couldn't get wrapped up in that drama. It didn't really have anything to do with her anymore. Barry had seen to that. She met Brian, her knight-in-something-armor. She drove to Pennsylvania next after a wrong turn and decided to buy an Amish quilt. She couldn't find one she liked. She came home and pulled into her parking space.

What was different about the parking structure?

Her mind reeled. There was a car in space 187b: a blue Toyota Camry, Illinois plates. Normal. Why would that bother her? Space belonged to whom? What car was usually parked in that spot?

No, the blue car was a red herring. That space belonged to the home owner's association and the security personnel could park there. The Camry must belong to Jefferson.

She pushed the up button. She didn't have to wait for the carriage. She started to cry. She could smell something sweet, like the cologne of someone who had been in the box before her. She closed her eyes and thought of Chardonnay.

Sy bolted upright. Someone in the emergency crew that showed up to the murder scene smelled like that. Who was it? She sat in the hallway and the world passed her by. Why the hell couldn't she remember?

She checked the clock beside the bed. The sun would be rising soon. She sighed and reached for her robe. She left the bedroom to sit on the bench in the landing. She tried to pinpoint the smell she remembered, to separate it from the smell of the blood and gunpowder lingering in the space. Officer Giordano interviewed her. Barry showed up. Annika showed up. Sy got to kick Henry. The picture was gone and Barry had to remind her Henry was dead.

I'm just not awake enough for this. She closed the door and headed for the liquor cabinet, pulling out a bottle of whiskey. If it wasn't a perfect day for an Irish coffee, she didn't know what was.

Tina called while the java brewed. "Crap, I'm sorry Simone, for calling so early. I'm still stuck on Bali time I think."

Sy prepped her coffee mug. "You didn't wake me Tina. In fact, I haven't slept yet."

"Oh? I should've insisted you join me at the hotel. It can't be easy sleeping in the same place where he died. I wasn't thinking."

Sy paused. Tina was acting contrary to her nature. "I have to be a big girl someday. I see no reason to delay the inevitable. What were you after?"

"I think we can schedule the services for this Wednesday? That gives us four days to plan-"

"Tina."

"-If you would be a dear and contact this Graceland place and let them know, and then maybe schedule an appointment for this afternoon to go over particulars-"

"Tina."

"-I'd like a carriage hearse and a dove release and Henry's favorite color might have been blue but he looked better in greens. The lining to the rosewood casket should be in a rich green silk-"

"Tina!"

"What Simone?"

"They haven't even released the body yet."

Silence invaded the line. "But they released your condo. You must have just missed the phone call that said to go pick him up."

"They released my condo because the crime scene investigators aren't as backed up as the coroner's office is. They may not have even performed the autopsy yet, or maybe they're waiting for the lab results on his blood and liver tests."

"But the funeral's on Wednesday. You call and tell the coroner that he's got to get a move on."

Sy poured an extra dram of whiskey into the mug before adding the coffee. Tina didn't cause her to drink, but she provided her one hell of an excuse. "Well, looks like Henry and I will be late for his funeral then, because I'm not showing up if he doesn't have to."

"Simone!" Tina's shriek could deafen dogs.

Sy pulled the phone away from her ear until the danger of ear-drum rupture passed. "Oh, dear. You're all flustered. Do you feel better? Let it all out." The distinct sound of the receiver slamming into the cradle echoed as the line disengaged. "Oops, that didn't go well."

"What did not go well?" Viktor entered the kitchen and frowned at the whiskey bottle. "A twelve-year-old? You have such things in your kitchen?"

"Snob. I know what you'd rather have, Papa, but I can put this in coffee and not feel guilty." She waved a doctored coffee beneath his nose. "And you would drink this anyway."

"Da." He accepted the mug with a shrug. "What did not go well?"

"Tina wants to bury Henry to pompous circumstance on Wednesday. They haven't even released him yet, and she's acting as if I should go down there and perform the autopsy myself. As much as I'd like to pull his entrails out through his nose, I'm not exactly qualified to do so."

"It is unfortunate situation, no?" He sat at the island, cupping the mug like a lifeline. "You and Brian had late night. How is artist?"

She sat next to him. "Last we heard he's in stable, but critical condition. I don't think the FBI has had an opportunity to speak to him yet."

"And?"

"And...what, Papa?"

"And what, she says. As if her father is idiot."

Blood rushed hot to her cheeks. "Oh, Brian. We went to the deli for coffee after we left McKealy's home." She caught the look in her father's eyes. "But you already knew that! Who followed us?"

He made a point of examining his fingernails. "I do not know what is your meaning."

She affected his accent, "Do not know what is your meaning, he says. As if his daughter is idiot."

He chuckled, nothing more.

"Gunter and Yousef left their detail after all."

"Do not be cross." He folded his hands. "They not only follow orders, but they volunteer for assignment."

Sy shook her head. "I don't believe it."

"I tell you before; it is father's prerogative, no?"

"No. I meant I don't believe that I completely missed them. I must really be distracted." She splashed another dose of whiskey in her mug and sighed. "What do you think of Brian, Papa, and give your honest opinion?"

"You listened so well the last advice I give, no?"

She pouted. "I know. I'll listen to it this time though, I promise."

He shrugged. "I have him checked out. He is good guy. Not so much as parking ticket in last seven years. He could apply for job protecting United States President based on security clearance."

"But what do you *think*?"

He smiled and leaned to kiss her forehead. "I think you have done much worse, no? Perhaps it is time for you to be happy."

"So you think it's okay if after this is all over with, I pursue this relationship in earnest?" Her heart fluttered at the possibility.

"Plan it right, you will not have to pursue. He chase you, no?" He traded his teasing tone for a more serious one. "Brian Kirby is improvement. And I think he cares for you great deal already. So, unless he does something foolish, I don't feed him to alligators."

She released the breath she didn't know she was holding. "That's what I was after, thank you Papa." She yawned into her coffee cup. "Oh it's going to be a long day, I can tell. I didn't get any sleep. Too many questions and not enough answers."

"Such as?"

"Well, for starters, what kind of cologne does the elevator wear?"

CHAPTER XXVI

Mapping Murder

THE ELEVATOR DINGED AFTER BREAKFAST, and Annika announced Mike Steiner as she led him into the sitting room. "Vood ye like som coffee?"

"Yes…two sugars if you don't mind." Mike shook his head as the housekeeper left. "Is this for real?"

Brian nodded and shook Mike's hand. "I'm already spoiled. It's going to be really hard to return to the office after this excursion, and that's the truth."

Mike sat on the sofa. "Remind me that I want my next wife to be this stinking rich."

"Well, Sy is technically a widow," Brian smirked, returning to the armchair. "You could try making a pass at her. You might get a chance, or you might get fed to the alligators."

"Ha! I don't know if I could handle the excitement. Murder, art theft…"

"I drove a Veyron and an Audi R8 both in the span of a few days. The excitement might be worth it for you."

"Lucky stiff," Mike whistled low. Annika brought him a coffee and a small tray of aebleskivers to place on the coffee table. She retreated before Mike could thank her.

"So do we have word yet on the artist? How's he doing?" Brian asked.

"I spoke to him this morning. He claims he was working on the painting and the next thing he knew, he woke up in city general. What are those things?" Mike pointed at the Danish pancakes.

"Uh, Annika called them aebleskivers. It's a kind of Scandinavian dough-nut. They're addictive, however. I ate twenty of the damned things the first morning I was here."

"Wow, these are better than dough-nuts," Mike said though a mouthful of powdered sugar. "Did the housekeeper make these? Can we make her cook for the FBI?"

Brian laughed, "I don't think anyone can make her do anything she doesn't want to do. Anyone who tries ends up with an ear full of Dutch obscenities."

"Shame. I'd pay good money for these. This is worth the price of admission."

Brian steered the conversation back to the artist. "So McKealy didn't remember anything at all, eh?"

"Not a bleeding thing. He seemed to be incredibly grateful that he wasn't dead, but he claims he didn't see anyone. The doctor said there was a knot on the back of his head that was the size of a large acorn. There's no way this was a suicide attempt."

"Back to square one. I was sort of hoping he caught a glimpse of his attacker." Brian popped an aebleskiver in his mouth and licked the sugar from his fingers.

"Yeah, but get this. There was no sign of forced entry and the suicide note we found seemed to be in the artist's own handwriting."

'Well, we have a very talented art forger. It's not a far stretch to add handwriting to the forgery list."

"We've got the lab looking for prints on the document, but we haven't had any luck. The crime scene was clean also. Almost too clean for my liking."

Sy made an entrance then, in kitten heels and a navy pinstriped pantsuit. A French twist kept her hair out of her face and was laced with a strand of pearls that matched her necklace and simple earrings. She spoke through clenched teeth to someone on her cell phone. "I don't know what I would say to be honest...Well if you think that two-timing, miserable son-of-a-jackal is so brilliant, maybe you should deliver the eulogy." She hung up and looked as if she was about to throw the phone across the room. "I'm not in the mood today."

"Mrs. Freitag, it's good to see you again." Mike rose to shake her hand.

"Thank you for reminding me. I need to get my name changed again. Oh, what a pain! If Henry hadn't already been killed..."

"Was that Tina?" Brian asked.

"For the third time this morning. She had the nerve to suggest I tell the world at his funeral that I found him to be the warmest, most generous man on the face of this earth. She's providing me a script so I don't embarrass myself, she says."

Brian shook his head. "Cheaters deserve what they get. You don't have to sugar coat anything if you don't want to. He obviously had no respect for you."

"What? Tell the world he likes art dealers and hot-tubs? Is it that simple?" A happy dream resonated from the warmth of her smile. "That's sweet, Brian, but not very realistic. I suppose I could find something nice to say about him. The dead can't defend themselves and I shouldn't try to piss off too many people in Hollywood. They occasionally use my services and I don't want to burn bridges."

Mike wiped powdered sugar from his mouth. "What do you do for Hollywood? Just out of curiosity."

"Well, I'm a location scout, which is less impressive than it sounds and a lot more work than it implies. It's not just the look of the location to take into consideration. There's also the need to have the location accessible to a sizable crew, legal ramifications of local authorities, permits available, shoot-friendly weather, those kinds of things can make or break a film shoot. I've been a world traveler as long as I can remember, so it seemed the logical career path for me after I left the military."

Mike whistled, a thin mist of sugar escaping into the air. "I'm in the wrong business I think."

Her cell rang and she groaned as she saw the number. "I can tell I'm not going to get anything accomplished until I bury the bastard." She ignored the call and tossed the phone onto the sideboard. "I wonder if they're going to do the autopsy or if the guest of honor is going to be a no-show at his own funeral?"

"I'm sure they'll get around to it." Brian reached for another aebleskiver. "Famous people tend to get handled first, at least in my experience. I can call the coroner if you like; see what strings need to be pulled."

She shrugged. "I don't care one way or the other. But I have a thought."

"What's that?"

"Is there any way we can convince people that Tina knows who did it, and then set her up as bait? We could catch the killer fast like that."

Brian laughed. He understood her desire; he felt the same way. "Sy, you need to stop wishing people dead. It seems to work."

A sheepish look fell across her face. "No you misunderstand. I don't want her dead. I just want to provide her a situation where she could practice her so-called acting skills."

Viktor slipped into the room, silent as a ghost. His icy stare sent a chill through Brian's spine. Brian wondered if he'd ever feel warmth again.

"Papa?" Sy rose and followed him to the window.

Viktor broke his silence. "Simon, where would you put sniper to target this room?"

That was creepy. Brian exchanged looks with Mike as he shifted in his seat, losing his interest in the aebleskivers on the coffee table.

Simone folded the curtains back and peered out. "I wouldn't. The approach for this window is too exposed. The complex across the street perhaps from the water box on the roof, but even then, it's risky."

"So if target is in this room, how you gain access?"

Viktor's line of questioning unnerved Brian and he tried to catch Sy's attention. She waved him off as she buzzed his mind. *Let us talk it out, Brian. I'll explain everything in a second.* Sy answered her father with a measured tone. "Well, I suppose there are a few ways. My favorite would be to dive off of a helicopter onto the roof in the middle of the night and then slip in through the French doors, but that's mostly because I'm fond of helicopters."

"And you know layout of flat, no?"

"Yes..." A foreboding pallor clouded her countenance and she surveyed the room as if looking at it for the first time. "Yes I'd know where to go because I've been here before. A professional would too."

Viktor rubbed his head, "I think killer isn't as professional as he believe. He relies on his clean-up crew, no?"

Brian's chest tightened. "This is an observation based on personal or business experience?"

Viktor's response was cryptic. "Perhaps both, or perhaps I watch too much television. I think killer is very desperate man. He is good planner, but desperate. It make him sloppy, incompetent."

"Why desperate?" Mike asked, an intent gaze focused on Viktor.

It was cold-war politics; Brian wondered who was spying on whom. The two men were as tigers in the calm before the battle, assessing the other carefully and planning the best angle of attack. Brian half-expected them to start circling each other.

Viktor left Mike's question unanswered, turning instead to Sy. "You remember where they were positioned, no?"

Nodding, Sy walked out of the sitting room into the foyer, father in tow. Brian tapped Mike to follow. Sy pointed to the far wall. "Jasmine was over there. Brian, do you mind?"

"No, of course." Brian moved into position where the carpet had been cut out for forensic evidence.

"And Henry was literally at the door."

"So Henry faced the door or away from door?" Viktor gestured, his hands talking.

"Facing the door, his legs were crumpled underneath him. It looked to me like he answered the door and got a face full of lead. Mike?"

Mike followed Brian's example and stood where Sy indicated.

Brian scanned the room from his new perspective. Something didn't sit right with him about how the victims were arranged. "Sy, you said they were half-dressed? The gunman knocks on the door and surprises them both."

"Except...Mike, you're a hot-blooded male, aren't you?"

Mike coughed, "Um, last I checked."

"If you had a girl in the bedroom and you had weaseled her out of her blouse and you're in trunks and a bathrobe and the doorbell rings, what would you do?"

Brian thought he saw Mike blush in response, "Well, I'd ignore it."

"Exactly. So what if the door rings again and again?" Sy folded her arms.

Mike's eyes drifted towards the ceiling. "Okay, it's annoyed me now. I'm so close to the...er...Promised Land, as it were, and now I'm going to send whomever it is away."

"And what about the girl?"

"I'd've said, 'hold this thought, this won't take long' or something to that nature."

Brian scratched his head, "Henry's already been caught in the hot-tub, and he's expecting Sy to walk through the door any minute...Wouldn't he be saying to get dressed quickly?"

Sy shook her head, "Keys. I have keys. I wouldn't ring the doorbell."

"Can you hear the elevator from the master bedroom?" Brian cast a glance down the hallway.

"Niet. Only from foyer and salon," Viktor replied. "So question is: why is whore half-dressed on back wall and not in bedroom?"

"Maybe she came out when she heard the gunshot?" Mike rocked on his feet.

"Well, except that doesn't make sense." Sy paced. "Shotgun blasts inside of rooms are extremely loud and are unmistakable, even for someone who has never been around firearms. If she was in the bedroom waiting for a quick dismissal, I think instinct would cause her to hide until the danger passed."

"Maybe they were getting things started here in the foyer and they were taken by surprise then?" Brian had little confidence in that explanation, but the case was taking a weird turn. It didn't seem so cut-and-dry anymore.

Viktor tapped his chin where his scars met his throat. "Lift would have dinged, announcing killer's presence before doorbell. Whore would have disappeared to adjust clothing, make-up."

"Especially if Henry thought I might be coming home. If the elevator dinged and I was her, I'd book it to fix myself pronto. And her blouse was not in the room, at all, which means she removed it elsewhere."

Brian assumed the killer took the victims by surprise. Maybe he was already there, but for what aim? He thought back to what he could remember about the pattern of the blood-stains. "I saw some of the aftermath. There was no way the bodies were planted. They fell where they were shot."

"So if he was surprised it wasn't me and the doorbell rang and he opened the door...that doesn't make any sense either." She turned to the door and back again.

"What doesn't?"

"Think about it Brian. If someone you knew was half-dressed when you went to answer a door, wouldn't you give your guest time to leave? I know Henry would. And he'd peer through the peephole to check if he needed to go grab some slacks. He had a public face you know, and never once was he compromised in the tabloids."

"I don't like where this is going," Brian said, bile rising in his throat. "We need the crime scene forensic map. And if the CSI are crooked, we might not be able to trust it if they gave it to us."

Mike shook his head, his face saturated with dark emotions. "We haven't hit a brick wall have we? What about the pictures? Who do you think has those now?"

Sy glanced at her father before turning to Mike. "Look, I don't mean to step on the investigation, being a civilian and all, but is there any way I could convince you to let me speak to the artist?"

He was slow to respond. "You have an airtight alibi for the time during his attack, so I don't see a problem with it myself, as long as we're still in the room. What are you hoping to learn from him?"

"There's something bothering me about his artwork. I can't put my finger on it yet, but..." Sy said. Brian felt the tingle again as she buzzed his thoughts. *I might be able to read him.*

He twitched. *We'll still need tangible evidence you know.*

Yeah, but a hint as to where to look might not be a bad idea, eh?

Viktor returned them to the crime scene conversation. "We need forensic map, no? How do we get copy?"

Remembering a cheerful invite for cold Chinese food and stale coffee, Brian smiled. "I think I know someone who is willing to help."

CHAPTER XXVII

An Ally

MANDY HINES GREETED BRIAN AND SY at the visitors' check-in desk at the station. "I'm sorry we weren't able to give you much notice." Brian attached the pass to the lanyard he hung from his neck.

"Don't be. I like surprises." She led them up the stairwell to the second floor lab, explaining, "I hate waiting for the elevator. Sometimes the bloody thing is stuck on a different floor to unload evidence or cadavers and you could spend your whole break waiting to go up one floor."

"Well I hope we don't end up placing you in a serious bind." Brian held the door open for the ladies as they reached the landing.

"I agree with what you said over the phone." Mandy motioned them toward the outside hallway. "There was something fishy about the way the evidence was collected. It wasn't as methodical as it should have been."

She escorted them to a putty-colored conference room harboring time-abused, low-budget office furniture and a dust-ridden plastic palm tree. Excusing herself for a moment, she let them alone. Brian and Sy didn't have to wait long before she returned to the sterile room, carrying a couple water bottles in addition to the paperwork in hand. She secured the door and closed the blinds before assuming the seat opposite them.

"You worried about prying eyes?" Brian asked, accepting the offered water.

He got a half-shrug in response. Mandy shuffled through her papers with determined movements. "I haven't had my scene-sense go off this bad in a long time. And I'm bummed that you didn't leave me anytime to set up a slide show. I'm good at those."

"It's okay," Sy leaned forward in her seat. "We didn't know we were going to barge in here ourselves until an hour ago."

Mandy flipped over a couple photos for them to see and placed the diagram of Sy's condo in the center of the table. Brian scanned the photos, seeing the crime scene for the first time. Sy appeared focused on the location of items taken from other rooms. "I notice most of the evidence was taken from the foyer. Does it mention where the victim's blouse was found?" Sy asked.

Mandy flipped through her list and then pointed to the outdoor patio on the diagram. "A pile of his clothing was located here near the hot-tub and a woman's blouse was found just outside the French doors."

"So they were outside when they disrobed," Brian shook his head. "That doesn't explain why both vics were found in the foyer."

Mandy paused. "How do you mean?"

Brian mentioned the conversation from earlier with Mike and Viktor. "If they were surprised by a gunman at the door, it wouldn't explain where they were positioned when they were shot."

The tech stared for a moment at the map, her brow knit with concentration. "You're right. When you look at it like that, it doesn't make any sense. Maybe the perp broke in somehow, to burgle the place, and then the vics surprised him?"

Sy examined the diagram again. "I would think there would be more personal items of hers collected as evidence. There's no female-thing listed beyond the blouse? Where was her purse found?"

"What purse?" Mandy looked to her list. "I don't see a purse listed. And that's strange. How does a woman go anywhere without a purse?"

"But," Sy blanched. "A CSI brought out a purse with an ID that said Jasmine Colby and he showed it to Officer Giordano. I remember being confused because the name on the license wasn't Sandy Petrusky. That's how they identified the vic."

Mandy shook her head, "According to this report, the vic wasn't identified until prints when she was delivered to autopsy."

"Do you remember who the CSI was?" Brian asked Sy, feeling a dead weight bottom out in his gut.

Sy bit her lip in a short-lived pout, "I ran out of film for my mental camera. I was paying more attention to Jasmine's license saying she was born in October of '82."

Brian's skin crawled with unease. "Mandy, do you know anyone from the station that lives in the vic's building?"

"No...although, now that you mention it, one of the guys on Bravo Team has an aunt out of town, and he was looking after her place last week. I think she lives over somewhere."

"Was he one of the CSI who responded to the crime scene?" Sy asked.

Mandy's eyes grew wide and frightened as they flickered over one of the documents. "I'll be damned. I've just been suckered."

"What happened?" Brian looked up from the diagram.

Sucking in a breath, Mandy flipped him a report. "He was the one who collected the digital surveillance recording as well. I can't trust anything he brought me."

Sy leaned over, crowding Brian for a look at the paper. "What's his name?"

"Scofield. Daniel fucking Scofield." Mandy's fright was replaced with outward anger.

"That's him! That's the CSI who found the purse!" Sy smacked the table. "Did he ever say who his aunt is?"

"Uh, Karen...no...was it Katie?" Mandy crossed her arms.

Sy tapped her chin. "There's a Katherine Donavon who lives on the eighth floor. She goes by Kitty. I wonder if it's her?"

The taste in Brian's mouth was dark and acidic. The situation seemed dangerous, as if Death waited to ensnare them. He had the desire to run as he turned to Sy, "Do you think you have everything you need?"

Sy grabbed the diagram for one last look and nodded. "I want to go over my condo with a fine tooth comb. If we have someone planting or altering evidence, there's bound to be a trail."

Mandy snatched up the photos and documents, shoving them back into the file. Her hands trembled. "This changes everything folks. I'm not going to be as openly friendly from here on out. I'm looking out for me."

Brian nodded. "Understood. If you need protection, I can set you up with Wit-Sec..."

"No that's not what I mean. I'll raise Holy Hell if it smokes out a snake. Just be there to slap the cuffs on him when it happens. Just-" A noise from outside the conference room caused her to jump, "-just don't be worried about me. I'm going home sick in a minute and I'm going to be out sick for the next three days. After that I'll need a doctor's note."

"You have my card," Brian stood. "You call me if you need to."

She winked at him, "And what about if I don't need to?"

"I, uh," Words lodged in his throat as he detected movement from the corner of his eye. Sy crossed her arms and peered at them with a raised eyebrow. With the threat of a mental trespass looming close, Brian coughed. "Well, in that case, I have to warn you I'm almost twice your age and I wouldn't be much fun because I'm currently pursuing other avenues."

"Too bad," Mandy pouted. "Let me know if the position opens up."

Detective Shelby entered the conference room, "Position?"

Mandy turned without hesitation. "Oh come on, Shelby. He's the first Fed I've come in contact with who isn't a complete jackass. He's been nice enough to answer a few questions. Of course I'm going to try to get a job with the FBI. They pay better and the crimes are more dynamic."

"Ah, well, the front desk said you were here," Shelby said. "Did you find something of interest?"

Sy adjusted her suit jacket after rising from her chair. "No, not really. I'd hoped the crime photos would help, but I couldn't remember anything more than I could that night.

"We were just wrapping up," Brian was relieved that the awkward moment was dispelled. "We still don't know what the link is between the art theft and the murder, if there is one."

Shelby nodded, "I'll walk you out then, and get caught up with Mandy later. Say, do we know how the artist is doing?"

Mandy gave Brian a slight head-shake and Brian understood. Until they knew who was collaborating with Scofield, they couldn't trust anyone. Brian shook his head. "All I know is he's in ICU."

They vacated the conference room, parting ways with Mandy as they boarded the elevator to the lobby. As they turned in their visitor badges, Sy touched Brian's arm. "I smell something familiar. Slightly sweet with a hint of nutmeg. I want the name of that cologne."

Detective Shelby inhaled in a noisy snort. "I don't smell anything."

"Oh well, I guess I'll have to find another gift for Papa's birthday."

They shook hands with the detective, bidding their goodbyes, and left the station. Brian looked to hail a cab but Sy grabbed his arm and tugged him to follow her up the sidewalk. After walking half a block in silence, Brian asked after the fragrance. "I didn't smell anything either. Was that what the elevator was wearing when you came home that night?"

Sy nodded and pointed up the street to a sandwich shop. "It's not the deli, but it's convenient and I'm losing focus. Let's grab a bite to eat and then swing by the Parfumerie and see if I can find the cologne."

Brian checked his wristwatch. "Then we'll need to meet up with Mike at the hospital. He's going to let us talk to the patient at about three."

A QUICK LUNCH WAS ORDERED and made of sandwiches and chips, during which Sy had to answer her cell phone five times. Brian listened to her side of the conversations as she promised Barry she'd make herself available for the Sandusky's prosecutor's office.

She approved the menu Annika called about. She spoke to someone in Romanian and someone else in French. Then she hung up on Tina. "Crap, I should've stopped by the coroner's office and had him speed things along."

"Tina's a bit of a hellcat, isn't she?" Brian started the second half of his corned-beef on rye.

"It's not just her," Sy sighed, inspecting the chip in her fingers as if seeking answers from its cratered surface. "I'm ready for it to be over."

"Stressful, I get it."

She shook her head. "I'm more bored than anything else. I have freedom I didn't know I needed until Henry had the good sense to get himself killed, and I can't do anything with it until this whole mess blows over."

"So I take it you've got plans? You're not going to stick around for a bit?" The dead weight was back in his gut. He wasn't ready to think about her leaving yet.

"I'm going to make sure the arts festival opera gets through production, and then I'm going to sell the condo. After that, I don't know. Maybe take a cruise through the Mediterranean? Why do you ask?"

"Just curious is all. I've never had the type of money you do so I'm trying to figure out..." He stopped short. It wasn't what he meant to say and it came out worse than he meant it. The question he wanted to ask wasn't appropriate either. Henry wasn't even buried yet and he was making a play for his widow.

"Figure out what?" If he had insulted her, she wasn't letting on.

He crumpled his empty chip bag out of frustration. "Never mind, I didn't realize how rude that sounded."

Her eyes narrowed, "Rude? I didn't..."

Her cell phone rang again and Brian was grateful for the inter-ruption. He wanted the whole embarrassing moment to pass into oblivion, never to be remembered in this lifetime.

ANOTHER HALF HOUR found them assaulting their olfactory sens-es at the Parfumerie. It was a high-end retail store, with row after row of locked shelves displaying fragrances behind glass windows and tester vials. Brian flashed his badge and they were directed to the back counter, where the men's fragrances were flogged.

"How may I help, Agent?" said the middle-aged supervisor, Cyn-thia, according to her name badge. She stood ready, with keys in hand.

"This may sound like an odd request, but my witness here re-marked that the suspect had an unusual scent. We thought maybe you could help us pinpoint the brand."

Sy looked pensive. "The best way I can describe it is slightly sweet, with what seems like a hint of nutmeg, and either middle to inexpensive, or the bottle is old and the chemical balance is breaking down."

"Is it popular? Have you smelled it before?" Cynthia asked as she peered at the second shelf of bottles on the wall beside her.

"Another reason I don't think it's very expensive. The circles I travel in don't purchase a small bottle of anything for less than a hundred dollars." Sy's tone was matter-of-fact, not condescending. "I can't say I've smelled it before or since."

"Perhaps something an underpaid technician could purchase on their salary?" Brian asked.

Sy smirked. "Well possibly. But generally when a man wears a fragrance like that, it's because his girlfriend bought it for him. Women change their scents with the seasons; men not as much."

Cynthia agreed. "It's shameful, although most men don't know how to wear their fragrance. They drown in it or rely on the deodorant. But you mentioned the scent itself? The first that pops to mind is Black because you said nutmeg undertone." She reached into her cabinet and pulled out the small tester bottle to spray on the white scent card. "It's not really a vanilla scent, but the lavender undertones with the smoky moss tends to give that impression if worn for a while."

Sy sniffed the air and frowned. "Close. So very close, but still...If the man who wore this had a conflicting chemistry, could that also have something to do with it?"

"For certain. He could eat a lot of dough-nuts and pizza, but that could ruin anyone's pores."

Sy seemed frustrated. Brian wished he was a better help. The showroom blocked his senses to the point he was unable to smell anything beyond the Hayden Rose. His mother used to wear a similar fragrance that came in a spray bottle from a catalog, bearing a name like *If You Like Brand, Then You'll Love Generic...* "How about knock-offs, you know, generic brands set up like the brand named stuff?"

Cynthia choked and sputtered. "That's a long list, Agent. Come to mention it, though, I think the bath store up the street has something close. You know, they have a whole DIY section of fragrances. Perhaps they'll help you get closer to the truth?"

Brian got the impression Cynthia thought little of him and was disinclined to assist them further. Sy didn't seem too bothered by it, so he tried not to let it bother him either.

After getting directions to the bath boutique, they thanked Cynthia for her cooperation and walked a block and a half north at a brisk pace, considering Sy's heels. Brian scanned the crowded sidewalk out of habit, and felt superior when he noticed more than one man examine Sy with a lecherous grin.

They didn't have much time before they needed to get to the hospital. They entered the boutique to the same routine as they had the Parfumerie. Brian flashed his badge and they were ushered quickly to the supervisor. Like Cynthia, this one was less than accommodating and carried an edge of suspicion in her voice as she pointed out the dedicated corner for men's fragrances.

"These are the premixed essential oils and eau de toilettes here, and the lotion testers are next to the sink. We keep the actual product in the back though," the supervisor said.

Sy picked up a bottle and sniffed the cap, setting it down again immediately. "This almond one here is close to what I'm looking for, but still not quite perfect. You say these are premixed? Do you have custom scents?"

The woman nodded. "The raw essential oils are on that display round you passed in the center of the store. You can build your own fragrance which we can then use to make a cologne, aftershave, shampoo, whatever, as long as the ingredients are compatible to the product."

Sy lit up. Brian could tell she had a plan. He followed her to the display round and gawked at the numerous vials. A brochure pocket in the center contained scent cards explaining the three basic parts of a fragrance, namely base, body, and finish. The Science of Scent also had a price list attached that caused Brian to go into sticker shock, but Sy seemed excited at the idea of playing chemist.

"Brian, do me a huge favor?"

"You want me to try the stuff?" Brian looked at the vials with skepticism.

"No, silly. There was a coffee candle at the front of the store. Could you grab it for me?"

"Sure." Brian turned and sorted through the candles until he located one that smelled like the Bureau's coffee. He returned before she finished sifting through vials. "Why the candle?"

"It neutralizes scent overload the way bread cleanses the palette during wine tasting." Sy flashed him a broad smile. "Many of the techniques in wine-making are used in perfume-making. Blending, for example, is as much about the chemical marriage as it is the varietal."

"You lost me at palette," Brian chuckled. "But I think I get the picture."

Each vial had its own glass swizzle stick to aid in the testing. Sy made quick work of the oils, pulling the stick out to sniff, replacing, and at fast-as-lightning speeds. Using the brochure as a checklist, Brian crossed off her no-ways and circled her possibles as she called them out until, fifteen minutes after they had walked in, Sy had a working formula.

Sy gave her order to the supervisor, who frowned at first. "I can't just give this to you, you know, regardless of any official investigation. This is custom work."

"We can get a court order," Brian said, reaching for his phone.

Sy waved him off, "There's no need for a court order. I will buy a cologne, mist spray, lotion, and any other product this can be used in."

Greed reflected in the woman's eyes. "Truly? I can make up thirty-two different products with different sizes starting at trial."

"Two of each, then, please. And have it delivered to this address." Sy pulled a business card from her purse and passed it to the supervisor.

"Oh we don't deliver."

"For me, you will." Sy's voice was strong with a violent undertone. Brian thought she was enjoying this a little too much. "My housekeeper will be expecting you. If the product is compatible to our project, you may be additionally and handsomely rewarded."

CHAPTER XXVIII

Death Sentence

T HE HOSPITAL STAFF EBBED AND FLOWED throughout the sterile
building with a chaotic order. Doctors conferred with other
doctors in hushed conversations and rushed walking as they scurried
through the halls. Nurses ordered about their orderlies, and the ra-
diology techs escorted mobile equipment into the deep carriages of
the service lifts. Sy gripped Brian's arm as they walked through the
lobby. She was pale, and her odd-colored eyes darted back and forth
at the sea of troubled faces. He laid his hand over hers, a sympathetic
gesture, knowing every emotion from those who loitered was assaulting her with a brute force. "I'm here," he whispered. "Lean on
me as much as you need to."

She buried her face in his shoulder and let him guide her to the
elevators.

True to his word, Mike waited for them at the nurse's station
when they arrived at the sixth floor trauma center. He waved them
over as Brian showed his badge to the guards stationed outside the
artist's room. There were several machines monitoring his condition, and Brian was shocked to find him a fragile husk of a man, con-
centration-camp skinny and gray in color. McKealy's condition

didn't make sense for a knock on the head and a nap in the oven. He smelled of death warmed over.

"William, this is Simone Freitag. You agreed to meet with her," Mike introduced them in a tone fit for a library.

William McKealy gave a wan smile. "Ah yes, you will...forgive me for not rising."

His voice was raspy and his breathing labored. Brian recognized the morphine cart attached to the drip bag. The death of his great-aunt Eileen was recalled fresh to his mind. There were so many family members visiting, it made the usually cold hospital room extremely warm. She, like the artist, was on morphine during her final hours.

"I could come back if you would prefer," Sy offered. Her accent was heavy and she gazed intently at the dying man. Brian felt her bristle; something was wrong. There was something about this man Sy didn't like, and she was on a deep-sea-fishing trip in his mind.

"No, no need." He pushed a button and the upper part of his bed lurched forward. "I've wanted to meet you...ever since I met your husband. I'm sorry for your loss."

A chill descended in the long pause that followed. Sy cleared her throat. "I wanted to thank you. Henry bragged about you so profusely, you know. I saw a sense of awakening within him. You are truly a brilliant artist."

"You are too...kind...my dear." His chest heaved be-tween his words, like breathing was a chore he was weary of. "They said...you had some...questions...for me?"

"This art endeavor of my husband's, I assume you knew of it? The Breathing Gallery?"

He nodded, straining the tubes strapped to his nose. "He had...mentioned that when...he purchased...*Girl In...Hammock*. I was very...hesitant to sell...that to him...It is a...special piece...for me. Tequila, however...was a...great motivator."

"All your paintings must hold so dear to your heart. I can tell from the passion so evident in your strokes." Sy asked, "Was the girl, the one in the hammock, was she anyone special?"

McKealy gasped and sighed, giving a feeble shrug. "It is...unimportant...now."

"I am sorry. Loss of a loved one is the hardest event to ever cope with."

She struck a chord. The artist's expression changed. "I have been...selfish. You have...experienced such...a loss recently...yet here am I...brooding about...an event which...happened long ago...and wasn't near as final...You, at least...will have closure...Something I...have never had...something which...I suppose is...of no comfort...to you now."

"I don't suppose it gets any easier, does it?" Tears pooled in Sy's odd-colored eyes, already dark with emotion. "Is that why all your latest works are in those crimson colors? And the, oh how to say, time out-of-joint elements are prevalent?"

The artist closed his eyes. "I feel lost...I've felt lost...for a long time...Ever since...the day she left...I...I am dying...Mrs. Freitag."

Brian's gut was telling him there was something more to it than that. "I am sorry. How long did they give you?"

"Not long...The cancer...is in my pancreas." His eyes opened again, and they flickered brightly with anger. "I am a man...denied vengeance...without hope of seeing justice...done before my...body fails me."

Sy shivered at his words. "What type of justice is it you seek?"

His eyes closed again and he dismissed her. "I no longer...have the stamina...to continue...our conversation...You must...forgive me...We can speak...another time."

"Of course." Sy stepped away from his bed and darted from the room. Brian gave chase. She avoided the elevator, crashing through the stairwell door. Brian heard the pounding of her heels on the metal stairs as he pushed through the door after her. Clang, clang, her determined heels echoed in the narrow stairwell as she descended to the next floor. At the last rung, Brian reached out and grabbed her arm before she escaped to the lobby.

"Whoa, what was that all about? Are you okay?" He pulled her away from the door.

Her half-blue, half-brown eyes flashed with venom so strong, he took a step back. "Not here," Her words were forced through teeth. Mike appeared, leaning on the railing above them. "Just not here," she repeated.

Brian nodded. He didn't understand, but he knew he wouldn't get a thing out of her until she was ready to give it to him. He released his grip, still afraid she'd bolt. She waited with him however, as Mike walked the few steps remaining to the ground floor. "Well, then," Brian coughed, "I guess that means we're done here. Thanks for everything, Mike. I'll call you later if we figure anything out."

Mike looked puzzled. "Sure thing."

The door opened to the lobby, still populated with worried people. Mike turned to wait for the elevator up while Brian followed Sy to the outside world. She acted like a horse with a nearby rattlesnake, with stiff, panicked movements. He stopped her at the curb and looked hard into her wild eyes. "Okay, what's up?"

Sy spoke with a clear, calm voice, despite the anger she was telegraphing. "I'm going to go to the police station. I am going to ask about the coroner and I am going to see if I can get access to the morgue."

"Would you like me to go with you?"

She shook her head. "What I have to do, I should do on my own. There is no need for you to be there."

"I'm not so sure. You're behaving erratically."

She closed her eyes and she muttered something about vines and grapes under her breath. "I promise I won't set anything on fire, or pull anyone's entrails out through their nostrils."

"Did I do something wrong? Are you mad at me?"

Her eyes shot open and she raised an eyebrow. "No, don't worry Brian. I'm not afraid to tell you when you've pissed me off."

"Then tell me what's going on. I can't help you if I don't know."

She glanced back at the hospital doors and dropped her voice into a low whisper. "I can't tell you what I discovered. Not yet. Not here."

"You know you can trust me right?" He felt panic rise within him, fearing he was losing the most important connection of his life. "There isn't anything you couldn't tell me. There isn't anything I wouldn't do."

"I know. I do trust you. More than I've trusted anyone in a long while." She turned and placed a hand on his cheek. "You're a good man, Brian. I-I wish..."

He fought the strong desire to kiss her, but like a magnet, he drew in close. Her hand slipped to the nape of his neck and his hands settled at her waist. In the heat of the moment, the world melted away until all that was left was her. "What do you wish? Sy?"

"I-" Those eyes, mystic and ethereal, searched for something within him. She trembled then, and stepped from his arms. "No, not like this. It's not fair to you."

His heart snapped. He couldn't breathe. "Sy..."

She took another step back. Her voice passed into reality and business. "I, would you do me two, very critical favors?"

A flash of frustration surged. "Fine, what do you need me to do?"

"I need to know the exact relation between that CSI Scofield, Stephen from that art gallery, and McKealy. In fact, see if Sandy can tell you anything more about that night at the party when they went through all those tequila shots. Don't be afraid to bully her; the crying game is probably an act. If I finish up at the morgue, I'll meet you at the opera house."

"Okay," his frustration ebbed from his shoulders. "Consider it done. What else do you need?"

"I need to get into McKealy's home. Can you get me inside?"

"I suppose. Why aren't we asking Mike for that?"

Her lips parted. She showed her fangs and venom colored her words. "Because I don't trust Mike as far as I can throw him. They assigned him to be your handler, Brian. The official informant. He's spying on us. If he were to find out how I know things..."

Brian's cheek twitched. He thought Mike had been a little too smooth and Jericho a little too distant. He didn't like being lied to by his fellow agents, especially not by one he thought was a friend. If Mike was truly his handler, then he should have said something. He was supposed to be someone who had his back. After all the collaboration they did over the past few years, Brian expected disclosure. He glared in anger at the sixth story windows of the hospital and hissed. "Well, that's just peachy."

"And Papa, he doesn't trust him at all. That conversation about the sniper was his way of warning me, you know. Mike is watching you watch me, and not for the reasons you think, but I didn't know for certain until we crossed the threshold of the nurses' station." She met his gaze. "Don't worry, he'd support you in a gunfight, but he'll throw you under a bus if it gets him a rise in the Bureau."

He understood why she spoke of Chardonnay all the time. He was fighting mad. He turned to the curb and whistled for a taxi. As the yellow car pulled over, Sy looked back at the hospital. "Brian?"

He chuckled. The roles had reversed. She was now trying to talk him down from a ledge. He opened the car door for her. "I'm not going to confront him just yet. I still need him. I'm just going to go ask him a few questions."

"Noroc, good luck." She settled into the cab and he closed the door. Brian watched as the car pulled away from the curb, merging into the sea of traffic. He set his jaw and marched back into the hospital and back up to the sixth floor nurses' station.

MIKE SEEMED SURPRISED as Brian rounded the corner of the elevator hall. "I wasn't expecting you back," Mike said. "What was up with the princess?"

Brian masked his anger with a warm smile. "I've no clue. That woman is an utter mystery to me most days."

"I haven't met a single one of them that made any sense," Mike shook his head and laughed. "I suppose she might be worse, eh? What with the money and all, I imagine she's rather high maintenance."

Brian shrugged. "Nah, not really. She's just expensive. Although, I feel I've been chasin' a tornado for a while." He gestured to the artist's room. "So is McKealy asleep?"

"Yeah, I don't think he tried to commit suicide, but if I were in his shoes I would. The doctors have kept him pretty doped up since he's been admitted. They don't think he's going to last long at all. Why do you ask?"

"It's nothing probably, but I'm wondering about the woman he claimed left him. There wasn't any mention of a wife in his file."

The nurses shooed them away from the desk. With a promise to go somewhere else to carry on their conversation, they moved towards the elevators. "No, he never married," Mike confirmed, "but we all know that means nothing in today's day and age."

"I didn't notice if there were any siblings," Brian was fishing and he knew it, but there were so many questions now that didn't seem to have answers. And the small talk was keeping him from kicking the shit out of his coworker.

"Only child. Why the interest?" Mike asked. "Are you working on an angle?"

The elevator dinged and announced the floor they were on and the fact that it was descending. They stepped into the empty carriage and hit the button for the lobby. Still angry, Brian was unsure what he wanted to reveal. "I'm just wondering if he's told anyone about his condition. Could be a reason to stockpile originals. The value of his work is likely to increase tenfold after his death I would think."

"So you think maybe a family member had something to do with it?" Mike pulled a notebook from his back pocket and flipped back a few pages. "He told us earlier today that his intellectual property and creative works in his possession are supposed to go to his old university in trust, whatever else he had leftover, which isn't much, is going to a few charities. He didn't have family left to speak of. Maybe I should have a talk with his old professors or the dean or something."

He returned the notebook to his pocket as the doors opened out into the lobby. They headed for the cafeteria. Brian felt the afternoon need for caffeine and offered to buy Mike a cup of coffee. "Have there been any hits with the local fence network? Is anyone trying to move the man's artwork?"

"Nope, no hits on any multi-work purchases either, except for Henry Freitag." Mike put two sugars in his coffee at the counter while Brian dosed his own coffee with creamer. "We don't know who he purchased the first picture from, maybe the artist himself, for there's no record of it at the gallery. He only offered his work through them."

Brian stirred his java, thinking of a nonchalant way of asking to see the artist's home again. He didn't have a real reason to be there, other than his pocket mind-reader wanted to go. He popped tension loose from his shoulders. "Say you haven't seen my Saint Sebastian anywhere, have you?"

"What in God's name is a Saint Sebastian?" Mike sipped his coffee in a noisy slurp.

"One of the many patron saints of law enforcement. I'm descended from a long line of devout Irish-Catholics, remember? My father gave me the charm when I graduated from boot camp. I swear I had it yesterday."

"I don't remember seeing anything unusual. Where would it be if not in your pocket?"

"Crap," Brian ran a hand through his hair. "You don't think I dropped it at McKealy's house do you? Could they have collected it as evidence?"

"Like I said, I haven't seen anything. I don't see a problem with you going out there to look if you want. The house has been swept anyway. I think the only reason it hasn't been released is because McKealy's upstairs here."

"Thanks, Mike. If my dad ever learned I lost that charm, it'd be the death of me. I bet it slipped from my pocket when I drove her car, so I'll check it first, but if I still don't find it, I'll let you know when I break in."

"Just remember to wear gloves. It's still technically a crime scene." Mike shifted then, as if uncomfortable in his own skin. "Say, what's your take on this Viktor Tomas person?"

Brian frowned into his coffee cup. "Viktor? He's mostly harmless. A big teddy bear with scars. Why do you ask?"

"Nothing strikes you as odd about the man?"

Brian shrugged. "He's fond of alligator causes."

"I think he smuggles guns or tortures spies or something," Mike leaned forward in his seat. "Maybe he's Russian Mafioso and he's negotiated the whole affair?"

Brian shook his head, laughing. "Seriously? I think you need to stop reading those Ian Fleming books. And he's Romanian, not Russian."

"Like there's a difference," he snorted. "You don't see anything weird about his being here?"

"Smack yourself upside the head, would ya? He happens to be a well-connected man, as most wealthy men are, who was able to get away from his business in Greece so he could be with his distraught daughter, who despite the cold facade, happens to be very vulnerable right now. If your daughter's husband had been murdered, wouldn't you try to be there for her?" Sy's words came back to him then. Could the target of Mike's whole investigation truly be Viktor Tomas and not Simone Freitag?

Mike scratched the back of this head. "I suppose. The man gives me the creeps though. I mean, that whole conversation about," he attempted the accent, "'where you put sniper?' nonsense back at the condo. You've got to admit that was weird."

"His question may have been entirely out of place, true, but her answer was colder." Brian took another drink of his coffee. "She served in the Swiss Army, remember? He might have done the same in his youth. After all, he's from an Eastern-bloc country, civil unrest through the eighties...It stands to reason that may have been a daily concern in their lives at one time."

"Wait...You like her, don't you?" Mike's face lit up. "My God, you're smitten with the kitten. I've never seen you like this before."

Brian tossed back the last of his coffee and crumpled the cup. "Nah, Sy reminds me of my kid sister, Lucy, only a little less predictable."

Mike shook his head, not biting the lie, and laughed. "So it's your sister you're in love with? That's sick man."

Brian counted to three in his mind. He was standing at the gate to a French vineyard he'd never seen, and he really wanted to smell the grapes. "Mike, I'm going to get up and leave now. When you get the chance, look yourself in the mirror. I might rearrange your face later, and you'll want to remember a time when your nose was the only feature about it that was broken."

CHAPTER XXIX

Dead & Gone

S Y STRUGGLED TO MAINTAIN HER EMOTIONS and her compo-sure. She was tired of being toyed with, of being conned. What good was it to be a human lie-detector and to have it never work when she needed it to? She spent the entire cab ride in Chardonnay, har-vesting grapes by hand. There was something therapeutic about working her pocket knife through the vines and removing the tiny clusters of champagne grapes at the stem, even if it was only imagi-nary. By the time she reached the station complex, she was calm enough not to kill anyone. At least, she hoped she was.

She paid her fare and tipped the driver generously out of guilt. While she knew there was no way he could have known the stew she was simmering in, she felt she owed him compensation for it anyway. He thanked her profusely and recited his cell number. "Call me anytime, ma'am. I'd be honored to drive you anywhere you want to go."

Greedy bastard, she thought of the driver as a new fare brushed passed her and leapt into his backseat. As the cab cut into traffic, she turned and walked with a steady pace up to the station.

The coroner's office was in the basement of the building and she had to check in at the visitors' desk before she could head down. The deputy working the desk called the morgue on her behalf. A moment later he hung up and signed her in, handing her a badge. He then insisted that he escort her down, and as she was in no mood to argue with him, she let him lead her to the elevator and down into the unpleasant depths of the building.

The deputy was nice enough. His attempts to engage her in polite conversation, however, slipped in and out of her ears without acknowledgment. "I must warn you," he said in the moment she paid attention, "Dr. Davies is a reclusive man who doesn't have much of a bedside manner."

"Ah. No worries, I bet I'm more reclusive."

Dr. Davies was waiting for them in his office. It was a cluttered space, but the clinical, with the various awards and certificates displayed in polished wooden frames from the wall behind his desk. Thick, well-used books lined his bookshelves, focusing on anatomy, disease, and other career specific texts Sy had never seen before. They shook hands and he left her with the impression there was little noteworthy in his ramshackle life. The grip of his hand, while surgeon-soft, lacked the strength that implied a general interest in life.

"I'm sorry for your loss," he said in a rehearsed tone, as if it was his standard remark for these situations. "I was preparing the certificate of death, and the report of my findings. My staff would have contacted you soon to give you the details about when and where you could pick him up."

She took a deep breath of the stale, basement air that smelled of chemicals and lemon-scented air freshener. "I don't suppose you would allow me a moment with him, prior to sending him off to Graceland?"

"He isn't pretty. I don't do the pretty part. That's the job of the mortician," he said. "Even then, there isn't much left to make pretty."

"I saw him not long after his brain evaporated through the gaping hole in his skull. I just thought I could get better closure if I could see him in stages." She mirrored the enthusiasm of the doctor, grateful she didn't have to be perky. He dealt with brutal realities of everyday death, and she appreciated his candor. "Besides, I promised his sister..."

"Fine, we'll bring the vomit bucket anyway." He motioned to the door and then led them out of his office and down the hall. There were a dozen keypads he had to swipe a badge at, which Sy found amusing. The security for the dead seemed to be better than the security they provided for the living. Reaching the last room at the end of the long corridor, he flipped a switch to turn on the florescent lighting, flooding the dark room with an ice-cold brightness. Row upon row of body refrigerator drawers lined the walls, sporting numbered labels that he read as they passed, settling on one just at waist height. He unlocked the drawer with a small key from his keychain and wrenched it free of its casing.

Henry Freitag, gray and placid, was still missing a great chunk of his head. He no longer smelled of the blood and gore she remembered from the foyer. *Frozen hamburger looks better than this.* She examined the Y-shaped stitching across his chest, amused at the realism of the crime shows she watched. There were contusions where she kicked him, differing in size and color from bruising evident on his forearm. Fingers gripped him there before he expired.

"Did he give you much trouble?" she asked. "He never cared much for doctors, unless they were going to prescribe some medication for him."

Dr. Davies raised a graying eyebrow at her, his dark brown eyes showing interest. "I can honestly say that's the first time I've ever heard that question."

"I wish I could say it was the first time I ever asked it. I've had to apologize profusely to the last few specialists he had seen, for his behavior."

"Ah. Well in answer to your question, no he didn't give me much trouble. He died just like his wounds indicate. No hidden poison or pulmonary blockages. He had pizza as his last meal, and he had a great deal of wine in his stomach juices. Nothing out of the ordinary I suppose?" Dr. Davies referred to a clipboard.

"Except for the pizza. He didn't like to eat pizza at home as a rule."

"Maybe he went out then, before he died? Although I hope he didn't drive. Not with that much alcohol in his system."

"No he didn't drink and drive," Sy said. "At least not here in the States. He used to say drinking made driving the Autobahn easier."

The officer whistled beside her. "That's...scary."

Sy squished her nose. "Well, to be honest with you, I think perhaps he told me that just to get my last nerve so to speak. Goad me into nagging him over something. He messed up a good thing, but he just might have saved my life. If I hadn't caught him in the hot-tub, I might've been there instead of his mistress." She sighed and directed her next comment to Henry's corpse. "Henry, you were a complete ass, but I do hope, for your sake, that it's not too warm where you are."

THE OFFICER AND CORONER ALLOWED her an extra moment with the deceased in polite silence. She stared at his lifeless body for a long time, trying to glean an idea of what comprised his last moments on earth. He was with one of the mistresses. What was he doing at the door? Why wasn't he protecting the whore's half-naked body from exposure to unexpected guests? Her thoughts turned then to why she was even there. Was it a sense of obligation that drove her? Did she truly need the closure after all?

Could it even be that simple? Nothing about his corpse suggested life, but she closed her eyes and broadcasted, forgetting any remains of the brain had been removed. There existed now only a void between the surviving walls of his skull. *I met someone when I ran from you. He followed me here when he learned of your demise. He's nothing like you, and you would've hated him. Harsh perhaps, but that's the way things are developing. You abandoned me long before you died, so you don't have a say in this. I'm going to move on, to move past you. You hold no power over me. You never did.*

The officer coughed. He looked embarrassed. "Sorry."

Shaken from the abyss, she smiled at the officer, "No worries. He can't read my mind any more dead than he could when he was vertical. I don't suppose you were able to lift a fingerprint off of his skin there where he was gripped?" She pointed to the bruising on Henry's forearm.

"Unfortunately, no. It's hard enough to get fingerprints off of skin, let alone when it's been soaked in chlorine." The doctor checked his watch with a heavy sigh, indicating his patience for her visit was nearing its end. "Whenever you're ready, I've some documents for you to sign."

She nodded, and let him push the dead back into the wall unit. The tag on the next drawer was labeled Colby, Jasmine under the number. "I don't suppose you'd allow me a peek at Jasmine?"

"Are you her next of kin?" he asked.

"No. I just wanted to spit on her or light her hair on fire. It's a woman-spurned thing."

"As amusing as that would be," he chuckled, "I'm not able to allow that."

Again, she nodded. "You're right of course. It's probably for the best. I guess I'm ready then."

When they were back in his office, she signed the documentation required to forward Henry on to Graceland, and thanked the coroner for doing his work. "I'd tip you if I thought it was appropriate."

"You're an odd duck aren't you?" Dr. Davies grinned like a Cheshire cat.

Sy rolled her eyes. "You have no idea."

The officer escorted her back up, making some comment about the weather being unseasonably cool and dry for a Chicago September. Her cell phone interrupted him, ringing as the elevator doors opened to the lobby. She thanked him for the company and then took a deep breath before answering the call. "Tina, I just left the coroner's office."

"How does he look? Will we be able to have the open casket?" Tina sounded as if she was in the middle of a dance club.

Sy clenched her teeth and thought of Chardonnay. "There isn't enough left of his head for a mortician to make pretty."

"What! I thought you said that you just left the coroner's office. Isn't that his job?"

"No. His job was to gut him. It's the mortician's job to stuff him."

"God, Simone, do you really have to be so crude?"

Sy bit her tongue. Keeping the conversation civil was difficult. She counted to three before responding. "I know. I'm sorry. It's my defense mechanism. If I can laugh at it somehow, I won't cry. But anyway, it looks like we'll be able to have Henry's funeral in Wednesday after all. Well, as long as they have time for it. There could be a run of famous dead people waiting their turn right now. We'll have to see."

She heard Tina accept a drink from someone. "What? Oh, really? Do you think he started a…trend of death?"

"Don't deaths always come in threes?"

There was a long pause. "I thought there was only the one woman found with him. Who was the other one?"

Sy's tongue prepared for a vicious statement until a familiar face entered the building. "Tina, gotta run. Ciao." Hanging up before Tina could say anything, Sy reached out and grabbed the man's arm as he passed her on the way to the elevators. "Scofield, right?"

He had the manner of a nervous rat. "Yes. You're Freitag's widow, right? Simone?"

"In the flesh." Sy giggled to put him at ease and catch him mentally unprotected. "I know this may sound like an odd question, or a really lame pick-up line, but haven't I seen you before? I mean, before Henry kicked the bucket."

"I don't think so." His hands dove into his pockets, hunching his shoulders over. "I would've remembered you."

"You're so sweet!" She cocked her head, flirting. "Now I'm sure we haven't met officially, but I just know I've seen you around. Don't you live in my building?" she asked, stepping casually in front of the elevators to keep him from edging pass.

He chuckled, "No, Ma'am. I can't afford an address like that on my salary."

"Oh? But I thought I smelled your cologne in the elevator before. It's a very unique scent. It's not Black, is it?"

His face froze in the harsh florescent office light. Sy focused on his eyes, pushing into his mind. It reeled with thoughts and events of the last few weeks, the crime scenes he was at, the market he shopped at, the bum on Walker Street he sees every morning on the way to work. "Ah, I, no. It's something my aunt gets for me. She has it made custom."

"I knew it! Ms. Donovan is your aunt, isn't she? That's where I've seen you! Well, I must remember to tell her that she has excellent taste. That scent is positively perfect for you."

"Thank you, that's...very kind of you to say. If you don't mind though, I'm late for debriefing." He side-stepped her and moved towards the elevators.

Sy didn't have much time left. She sifted through the impressions of his thoughts, abstract and rushed, praying that she could find something she could use. He was involved somehow in both the art theft and the murders, but she wasn't sure to what depth. Just as the elevator doors opened, he glanced back at her, assailing her unknowingly with a rash of fresh thoughts, clear and crisp as if he was speaking in her ears.

There was a scuffle on the patio as Henry surprised the partner and Jasmine tried running for the door, coming face to face with the deadly end of Daniel's shotgun. He looked into Jasmine's staring, scared eyes and he watched without remorse as her brain exploded in the foyer.

Sy's stomach wrenched tight and she gave him a cold glare. "Gotchya," she whispered.

SHE LEFT THE STATION with her head held high. As she hailed a cab and settled into the back seat, her anger subsided. Giving instructions for the driver to take her to the opera house, she stared out the window and watched as the outside world blurred by. Daniel pulled the trigger on Jasmine, so there should be some evidence somewhere. She just needed to find the tangible proof now.

Her thoughts raced with the hope it would all soon be over. By Tuesday, perhaps they could close the case. On Wednesday, she could plant her husband and be rid of Tina forever. On Thursday, she could pursue her knight-in-something-armor free of all strings. She blushed and drew a heart in the fog where her breath touched the window and ascribed her initials within. Next to a plus sign, she added BK. And her heart turned a somersault.

Outside the opera house loomed before her as the cab reached her destination. Sobering, she paid her fare and stepped from the car. "And now for act two."

CHAPTER XXX

Dodging Questions

BRIAN KIRBY ARRIVED AT THE ART GALLERY a half-hour after he left the hospital. The door alarm announced his entrance to the historic building and his eyes took a second to adjust to the artificial lighting. White Horse was still the artist of the Month, with a different soapstone sculpture on prominent display next to his easel. A woman seemed gripped by a Bev Doolittle hanging on a freestanding wall in the corner, but other than that, the gallery was empty. A few moments passed before Stephen approached him. The man's appearance had not changed since the last time he had seen him, except his face was twisted in obvious annoyance.

"Sir," the docent hissed, "Ms. Sidle is fully booked. I suggest you make an appointment for next month if your mistress wishes to speak to her again."

Brian withdrew his badge from his back pocket. "Actually," he said, holding the case open for Stephen to examine, "my name is Special Agent Kirby. I need to ask you a few questions."

Stephen looked ill, his eyes darting over to the woman in the corner. She lost interest with her Doolittle and regarded them with a degree of suspicion. "Of course, Agent Kirby, if you would care to step into my office," Stephen said.

"Special Agent," Brian repeated his title for emphasis as he followed the Victorian undertaker into the small front office. Unlike the corporate-looking loft offices, this room was set up to showcase art pieces. Clean lines, neutral tones, and a technical light display seemed best designed for quick sales. "Impressive," he lied.

"Er, thank you, I suppose. How may I be of service, Special Agent," the salesman inquired, taking the seat behind the mahogany desk. "I assume this is about the McKealy artwork again? Your Bureau has already been here asking questions. I've given a statement to them."

Brian noted the smug attitude, so he was going to prod until Stephen let his guard down. Brian put his badge back in his pocket and retrieved his notepad from the other. Sitting down in the client chair, he paused to flip through his blank pages, making a show of searching though non-existent notes. "Yes, I've had the opportunity to review your statement," he lied again. "I was just hoping to fill in the blanks on a separate issue."

"Oh? Well I don't really know anything in addition to what I've already given. Believe me or not, I firmly believe in being open and honest with law enforcement."

Brian raised an eyebrow. "Good. This shouldn't be too painful then. Mr....Kline, was it? What was the exact nature of your relationship with Miss Colby?"

Stephen blinked. Twice. "I'm not sure I understand."

"You were co-workers, was there anything else?"

The salesman shook his head. "I'm twice her age, Special Agent. She and I were strictly business partners."

"Oh? What business?" Brian asked, picking apart the statement.

"Ah, I meant to say business associates," Stephen recanted. "Here, at the gallery, nothing else."

"Hmm, so you had no occasion to interact with her socially, outside of work?"

"None. We travel in different circles. She was a bit common...to be honest with you. Whoring about for a sale." His words dripped with distaste and derision.

Brian scribbled in his notepad. "Did you harbor any resentment towards her? Considering how she got her clients?"

Stephen looked smug again. "No, I've never envied anyone who had to stoop so low. As I said before, she was quite common."

"So when Mrs. Freitag showed up here and questioned Ms. Sidle about the affair between Jasmine and her husband, you weren't surprised?"

"No but you didn't identify yourself as an FBI agent then, did you?"

Brian shrugged. "I was off-duty, assisting a friend. At the time, I was not part of the investigation into this matter. When was the last time you saw Miss Colby?"

Stephen's eyes conferred with the ceiling before responding. "The last day she showed up for work. I forget the exact day, but she was bragging about the sales she made of the McKealy works. She claimed she made something happen, selling art to an idiot at twice the price the pictures were worth."

"And you didn't see her after that?"

"No, and it wasn't until after you left with Mrs. Freitag that we even knew about her unfortunate demise. I assume you've had to take your friend into custody? That must've been difficult for you."

"Why would you assume that?" Brian pretended he didn't notice the sarcasm in Stephen's tone.

The salesman blinked as if blindsided by the comeback. He straightened his back and looked away. "Well, she wasn't exactly happy with the discovery of her husband's whoring behind her back, was she? I mean, who else could it have been? I don't want to tell you how to do your job, but motive. Opportunity. Surely that hasn't escaped your notice."

"I'm glad you wouldn't assume to tell me my job, Mr. Kline. The investigation has already proved her iron-clad alibi, so she was never really as suspect. Now I know you said this already to the LEOs, but just so everybody's on the same page, I need to ask you where you were on the night Miss Colby was killed."

"I don't know. I didn't know I needed to prepare an alibi, so I guess I don't have one." The man had a devilish grin, like he was betting on a fixed fight.

Setting his jaw, Brian leaned forward and stared hard in the man's smug eyes. "Let me remind you of the date, then. It was six nights ago, on September 11th. Now, it's just a guess of mine, but most people these days can remember the 11th, any 11th, even if they're not from New York."

Stephen's face fell and he inhaled deep and slow. "Ah yes, I suppose you're right. I am a reclusive sort of man, Mr. Kirby. I spend most of my time alone in my home, with quiet hobbies. I collect coins and play the piano. While I seldom watch television, I was engrossed in the History Channel that night. There were several shows about the fall of the Towers I found both interesting and disturbing...You don't think I had anything to do with that whore's death, do you?"

Brian forced a chuckle. "Negative. There's no reason for you to be concerned, if what you say is true. You provided us your address, correct? I'll just get that verified and then you'll be in the clear. What about McKealy?"

Stephen's expression was difficult to read, but he stammered as if caught off-guard. "W-what about him?"

"Well, what's your relationship with the artist?"

The pause stretched between them. Stephen seemed to struggle with a decision, squirming in his seat. Through clenched teeth, words hissed slowly. "A cousin, actually. Our mothers were sisters. I suppose you read that in a file somewhere?"

"No, lucky guess actually. There's a strong resemblance between you two, especially around the nose." Brian drew an invisible circle about the center of his face for emphasis, "Do you know about his condition?"

"The cancer? Yes he told me a couple months ago. We've been pushing his artwork ever since, to help him out. Hospital bills and all, first his mother's until she died, and now his own. Tragic really."

"Then I'm assuming you'll take control of his estate, when the day finally comes?" Brian asked. "If I remember correctly, you're the only family he has."

Stephen's dark eyes reflected violence. Brian didn't need Sy there to understand what the man was thinking. He struck a nerve and found a possible motive. The man coiled up as a snake and hissed. "Special Agent, I do not know what you might be implying, but it sounds to me as if you think me a suspect for murder?"

"Why would I think that? Is there something I should know about? You haven't had a falling out with your cousin, have you?" Brian scribbled again in his notepad.

"And if I had?" the snake weaved, ready to strike.

Brian laughed. "Relax. I come from a really large family. There's always someone mad at someone else. That's part of being family I think. Fights are fights. Some might take longer than others to blow over but it all eventually comes out in the wash. I have an aunt that never talks to her half-brother, but she talks about him plenty to anyone who will listen. He treats her the same."

Stephen didn't seem totally convinced, but his fangs disappeared as he answered, his words measured. "Well, Billy hasn't exactly been himself lately, with the illness clouding his judgment. I asked him if he had placed his affairs in order, and he said he had. I found out recently, however, that his idea of order and mine are completely different. That's all."

"So you're not going to be in charge of his estate?" Brian whistled. "That's rough."

"That's not the half of it. He has a living trust or advanced directive, or something legal in place, which is a good thing, don't get me wrong." He replied as if licking a wound that refused to heal. "He's leaving his legacy however, to his Alma Mater. I disagree with that decision, but only because I'm hurt that he thought I didn't like his work. Financially, he has nothing left you know."

"Do you? Like his work?" Brian leaned back and scratched his head. "I don't care much for his earlier paintings, but the few in the red phase I find very intriguing."

Stephen turned his nose up, adopting an air of superiority. "His early works show the naiveté of his youth. Bright yellows and whites, sickeningly happy, really, that is for a struggling artist. Unfortunate it took a diagnosis for him to really come into maturity. Ah well, I suppose there's no point dwelling on it. I have the one he painted just for me, and to be honest, that's the only one I have room for. I would never tell him, but I prefer the impressionists to his half-baked attempts."

"Just one last question I think, and then I'll be out of your hair. Do you know who McKealy was referring to when he told me 'she left me'? He's really bitter about her."

His beady eyes narrowed. "He never had much attachment to any particular female except his mother. But I'd venture to say if it wasn't Aunt Pearl, it was that dancer he supposedly left Lake Forest U to be with. His muse, he said. Bah!"

"Dancer?" Brian smirked. "As in the strip-club variety?"

"Pearl never approved, and she bullied him for it. I didn't like her much myself. She said she became a dancer to put herself through school," he snorted. "As she got older though, that excuse fell by the wayside. She made a ton of money, dumped Billy for a baseball player, dumped the baseball player for a cocaine habit, and the last I knew of her, she got her act cleaned up and is practicing interior design or something equally inferior. Anyway, she was the only woman he ever dated."

"I don't suppose the dancer has a name?"

He drew out his answer. "Not one I recall."

Brian shook his head. "You know the details of her life but you can't recall her name? Come on, you're killing me."

"Memory is a funny thing, Special Agent. I only ever referred to her as Whore, so that's the only name that sticks. But I promise to call you if I remember." He rose from his chair, indicating he was done with the conversation. "If there isn't anything else, I need to get back to the floor. I work on commission here, and you're cutting into my valuable time."

Brian vacated his seat. "Thank you then, for your cooperation. I hope it doesn't prove to be too expensive."

Stephen led him back out into the gallery, "I hope we do not find the occasion to ever meet again. The criminal world is bad for business."

"Oh I do all right." Brian said. "Depends on the business you're in. Oh just one more question, before I go."

"Last one, I trust?" He seemed impatient.

"Affirmative. Where were you last night?"

Stephen stopped. For a moment, a normal human being replaced the Victorian undertaker. "Why? What happened last night?"

"Your cousin was attacked in his home. He's currently in ICU at St. Mary's. You didn't know?"

There was no discernible emotion in the man's countenance. He looked far away, lost in a sea of thoughts. Brian wondered if Stephen, like Sy, had a vineyard in France to disappear to. "No Special Agent Kirby. I haven't been informed. I visited my mother last night before I went home. She broke her hip last month and I check on her every Friday night. She lives in North Shore." He recited his mother's phone number for Brian's convenience.

"And then you were home the whole night?" Brian asked after scribing the number in his notepad.

Stephen nodded but did not offer anything else. He turned to help the woman by the Doolittle, and left Brian to his own devices.

Outside in the crisp evening air, Brian checked his watch for the time and called his office from his cell. "Rosalie, I don't have time for this. Just do your job," he barked out of frustration as she tried to play her usual game. *It's a simple request,* he thought. *Just check out the History Channel airings for 5-11.*

Rosalie dropped her charade and answered with a disappointed, "Yes, sir."

Brian hung up and glanced through the skyscrapers. In the eastern sky, the man on the full moon bore a devilish grin.

Just as he was giving instructions to a taxi cab driver, a text came over from Sy. She was waiting for him at the opera house. It was time to save Sandy Petrusky's life again.

CHAPTER XXXI

Trapped

PATRONS LINED UP AT THE BOX OFFICE of the opera house in the preparation for the evening performance of *The Barber of Seville.* Top billing was going to a person Brian had never heard of, but it did not surprise him. He knew nothing of opera, even less of good opera. His heart tightened as he realized this was the sort of scene that Sy must be used to. These were the sorts of events she attended. The odds, then, for a developing relationship, were not in his favor.

Sy stood with two men near the main entrance. Brian mistook them for federal agents at first glance. Both men wore the tell-tale communication buds in their ear and had the physiques common with ex-military. Their suits, however, were too expensive for government paychecks. The two men were private contractors.

"Speak of the devil," Sy said as he approached them, "here he is now."

"Pleasure to meet you," said the one with short sandy hair with a hint of a Germanic accent. "I am Gunter Kriege and this is my partner Yousef Paquin." The olive-skinned partner nodded once at his name.

"They work for my father," Sy explained.

"Ah of course. Special Agent Brian Kirby, at your disposal." Brian extended his arm for handshakes. "You've been assigned to Sy, I take it?"

"Jawold, Herr Kirby," Gunter replied. "But we volunteered."

"I can't get rid of them and they're not exactly invisible." Sy pouted, her tone resigned. "If my father wants a ridiculous display of power, I suppose I can yield."

Brian grinned. He understood the definition of overprotective very well. Both of his sisters complained of their overbearing father, uncles, and brothers as potential dates were warded off by the droves. "Well, it's nice to meet you. Sy and I need to go inside and ask a few questions. Meet you back here?"

"Jawold," the German saluted.

Sy beamed as they started for the alleyway. "You're a godsend. I was wondering how we were going to handle Sandy with them in tow."

"Well, for the record, I agree with Viktor on this issue. If I had the money and the resources, I'd inconvenience my sisters the same way."

She shot him a look. "You're right about one thing at least. I really need to learn to listen to my father when he gives me his opinion about people."

Brian didn't even pretend to follow. "Who specifically are we speaking of?"

Sy threw her hands up, a gesture of frustration. "The first words Sandy Petrusky said to me over the phone were 'first off, you need to understand that I had no idea Henry was married'. She claimed she didn't know until the Friday morning after I caught him in the hot-tub."

Brian thought back, "Was she lying?"

"Like a snake to a mongoose," she said. "Remember what McKealy said? He wanted to meet me ever since he met my husband."

"Which, if the group had been doing tequila shots like they claimed..."

"Then she definitely knew about our marriage. She's really good, at the lying part I mean. You weave enough lies around your story, and confess to some of them, you just might get away with the core of the tale. She very nearly did."

They neared the side entrance to the theater when they startled a homeless man rummaging in the dumpster in the dark alley. Sy halted, staring at the man intently. "What's up?" Brian whispered.

"This man is really sick." Her lip trembled. "Go grab Gunter and Yousef and call 911."

Brian hesitated. He didn't want to leave her there, alone, even for a moment. *Please, I promise I'll be all right,* her broadcast tickled. He flinched, but proceeded back up the alleyway, dialing emergency on his cell.

"911, please state the nature of your emergency," the operator answered.

"My name is Special Agent Brian Kirby. I need an ambulance to report to the Chicago opera house located on Wacker Avenue." He waved Sy's security detail over to the alley.

"Are you injured, Agent?"

"Negative, Ma'am, there is a transient, white male, late fifties to early sixties." Back with Sy, he mouthed, what's wrong with him?

He's having some sort of fit, like his sugar's dangerously high, she buzzed.

Returning to the operator, he said, "We believe he's experiencing chest pain brought on by some sort of fit, but that's the best we can say. We're not doctors."

"Is someone willing to remain with him and direct the emergency team?"

"Yes, some of my associates are on sight and will be accompanying the team to make arrangements. He's a potential witness to an art theft." It was the look of sheer helplessness across Sy's face that made him determined to get this stranger the best help possible. Sirens echoed through the streets and within moments a stretcher and four EMTs arrived.

"Gunter, please go with them," Sy urged her bodyguard. "I promise I won't leave Brian's side for the rest of the evening. Have the hospital charge the medical account."

Gunter nodded and he and his partner followed the EMTs whisking the transient from the alley. Sy wiped away tears streaking mascara down her cheeks. When they reached the theater's side entry, Brian risked a glance back at the empty alley, remembering comments she made when they first met. How she challenged any one of the hostages to stop and help a homeless man instead of throw a handful of pennies at him. This homeless man hadn't even begged, but Sy knew in an instant that he needed help. She felt his pain, possibly his whole life experiences flashed in her mind. She had no choice but to walk the mile in his moccasins. "I get it now," Brian said. "I'm sorry."

"Sorry for what?" she asked as they stepped through the door and into the dark hallway.

He stopped her and looked as deep as he could into her water-filled eyes. "I don't know how to put it, but I get it."

A smile, sweet and intoxicating, graced her lips. "There's no need-"

"You two shouldn't be back here," a tech said in a mild voice that lacked authoritative concern.

Brian ran a frustrated hand through his hair. He recognized the tech as the one who knocked over *Girl in Hammock*. Flashing his badge, Brian made introductions. "Special Agent Kirby and this is my associate, Ms. Freitag. Is Sandy Petrusky about? We've a few questions for her."

The tech tapped a pencil against his clipboard. "If she's not backstage or in the green room, she keeps to the property locker. I can show you to the green room but I'll need to ask you to stay out of everybody's way as much as possible. We're moving flats back and forth and it could get dangerous."

The green room was not green, much to Brian's surprise. A few makeup touch-up tables stood against the short wall, and a ballet-bar dissected a full-length mirror on the back wall. Performers stretched out at the bar or warmed vocal chords while others negotiated elaborate costumes.

Sy stole an opportunity to touch-up her own makeup at an unused table, earning looks from the performers. She nodded once at her reflection in the mirror and returned to Brian's side. "Let's find the liar."

"Shouldn't we stay here?"

"He didn't say we had to, simply that we should stay out of everyone's way. I want to check out the property locker again. That's the perfect place to confront her anyway."

Leaving the performers to the respective pre-performance rituals, Sy led Brian down the hallway and took the stairs leading down into the basement. She spoke of her run-in with Scofield. "I saw Scofield pull the trigger on Jasmine. I got the impression there was a partner there, and the partner killed Henry, but that's all I got."

"You saw him? Did you happen to see why?" Brian's echo carried in the narrow stairwell.

She shook her head. "I think they truly weren't expecting Henry to be home. The coroner said his last meal consisted of wine and pizza. I know Henry. He's a creature of habit. He disliked eating pizza at home. The boxes don't fit in the rubbish bins and the food itself starts to congeal, with grease oozing unappetizingly to the surface of the cheese. When we'd have a pizza night, we'd bring our own bottle of wine and we'd generally end up at Morelli's. I'm guessing that's where Henry went that night."

The property cage had a keypunch lock, but the gate was open as Brian assumed it usually was during theater hours. The volume of large objects blocked the fluorescent lights in the locker and shadows lurked in corners and under furniture. There appeared to be only one security camera covering the entrance. To the right of the gate stood a table sporting a computer with a scanner, printer, and barcode reader. It was the sort of set-up Brian had seen in libraries, useful for checking items in and out.

Brian followed Sy into the cage, knowing she was headed someplace in particular. "That lends credibility to the theory Henry surprised his killer, not the other way around."

They passed through the Africa scenery, replete with masks, drums, stuffed lions, and more. "So Henry goes for pizza," she said, her steps measured. "It's comfort food and he's officially stressed. Maybe he went alone and Jasmine waited for him in the parking lot at the condo. Or maybe she arrived and he let her in after he got ready to get in the hot-tub. He heads back out for the patio and Jasmine follows. They argue. He tells her to get lost. She tries to seduce him as she had before, not willing to relinquish her cash-cow. After all, she's been selling mediocre work to him at exorbitant prices. Henry's not a morally strong man, maybe she convinces him. Her blouse gets removed at the door to the patio."

French street lamps and signs, three antique bicycles, a backdrop of Paris, and a flower cart lined their path. Sy stopped to frown at a British phone box. "What?" Brian asked.

"The phone box. The shade of red is off."

"You're the only person who would notice."

"You would notice if you had ever seen one. They have laws governing the paint on these things you know."

"Seriously?"

She squished her nose, "You'll believe anything, won't you?"

"Only if it comes from you. And Barry." He shrugged. "And maybe your father."

The art fraud pictures weren't among the portraits in the art section. Sy stopped there anyway and turned. "Now I saw some bruising on Henry's arm right about here-" she demonstrated on Brian, "-and whoever grabbed him did so before he died. The bruising from where I kicked him looked different."

"So let's say he was enjoying the moment and someone snuck up on him and grabbed him...wait. What would make more sense is if she was trying to seduce him and he refused her advances because he was hoping you were coming home. She removes her blouse in desperation and then grabs a hold of him as he turns to walk away."

Sy nodded. "That fits Scofield's scattered broadcast. Near as I can tell he was searching through the back rooms and he heard a voice.

He came out, wondering where his partner was...I don't think it was Sandy, but I think she knows who it was."

From the depths of the locker, they heard the faint noise of the elevator gears in play. Brian and Sy positioned themselves around the shelving to peer towards the entrance. Sandy appeared, dressed in backstage blacks. She punched some keys at the computer and compared the screen to her clipboard before entering the locker. She screeched as she rounded the artwork aisle, her clipboard clattered to the floor. "Holy hell, you scared the shit out of me."

"We had some questions for you and one of the property hands said you might be down here," Brian said. "We didn't mean to startle you."

She stooped to pick up her clipboard. "I only have a few minutes to prep. The opera tonight is fine, but I've got to pull the items we need to review for tomorrow's performance of *Anne Frank*." Her words tumbled out as if there was nothing to keep them contained. She clutched the clipboard tight to her chest and looked back and forth between them with wild eyes.

"Sy, do you want to start?" Brian sensed her twitch like a ram ready to charge.

Sy's eyes narrowed, sharpening her features. "Yes, thank you Brian. Before I ask my questions, I need to warn you that lying to me right now is not beneficial to your health."

Brian added, "Stress caused by lying can lead to several health problems such as tachia-pulminary-defibria and in very severe cases, cardiac arrest."

Sandy blanched. "O-of course. I un-understand completely."

Sy folded her arms and glared. "Where were you the night Jasmine and Henry were shot?"

"I t-told you. I was in the property locker back there, drunk as a lark."

Sy snorted. "Brian, isn't it against the law to lie to a federal officer during an investigation?"

"Obstruction of justice, aiding and abetting, accessory to murder...Shall I continue, Ms. Petrusky?"

Sandy frowned and brushed an invisible spider from her temple. "I'm not lying. I was here for half a week."

Sy stared a while longer. "So you were at my condo, was it to spy on your sister? Did you wonder why she was back when Henry told you it was over? Did you think he was getting rid of you to be with Jasmine?"

Wide-eyed and frightened, Sandy continued to cling to her shaky story. "No, I told you, I had no idea and-"

"We've seen the surveillance footage from the complex, Ms. Petrusky," Brian upped the ante. "We captured an image of someone your height and build. Who do you think it's going to be when we enhance the image?"

Sandy looked like a kicked puppy. All trace of deceit evaporated. Her voice broke, shattering like glass before them. "I-I d-don't know."

Brian shrugged, "Okay, we'll come back to that. Where were you last night when McKealy was attacked in his home?"

A steel, smug resolve stiffened Sandy's shoulders. "I was here. Then I went home. Why are you down here?"

Sy cocked her head. "We were double checking your alibi. You've failed."

Throwing her clipboard down, Sandy bolted for the door. She slammed the gate shut behind her, locking them in as she bounded through the stairwell door and disappeared up the stairs. Brian slammed his palms against the cage. "Fucking shit! Now I have to arrest her. She's just kidnapped a federal officer."

Sy checked her cell, holding it out for signal. "I don't think she believes we won't be found, Brian. She's buying herself time."

"Yeah well, I'm arresting her anyway. What on earth made us go so deep into the locker?"

She flashed a partial smile, trying another position for cell reception. "I wanted to see the art collection again. She claims there was a break in and several items were trashed about, right? That's when we assume the forgeries appeared. We only have her word for it that she obtained those pictures from Henry when she did. Considering her track record for telling us the truth, I wanted to see if her story held water."

Brian kicked the cage before forcing his breath to come under control again. His entire body twitched with rage. "How were you going to check?"

"Well, when I came down here the first time with Sandy, she pulled up the location numbers on the computer, even though she knew right where they were. She had to check them out of the system. I'm thinking it stores some additional information, like who donated it, when it's expected to be returned, so on and so forth."

"You couldn't do the search on the computer?" Brian pointed to the back of the screen.

She huffed, "My thought was to see if the numbers on the other portraits were in some kind of numerical order, and then I could compare dates with those numbers. I didn't say it was a flawless plan, or even a good one. It's just what I had at the time, Mr. Grumpy."

Brian felt her sting and popped tension loose from his neck. He inspected the crisscross pattern the cage had pressed into his palms, focusing on breathing. A vision of a vineyard crept into his thoughts, tempting him to go for a walk through its leafy vines, bringing a chuckle to his lips. "Sorry, I guess I didn't realize how wound up I was." He motioned to the gate. "You've got tiny arms. I don't suppose you could reach through the bars to the keypad?"

She shook her head and thrust her cell back into her purse. "I could, but without an actual pin, we could still be here until they come down to let us out. Let's just use the fire escape."

She pointed up at the red exit sign directing them to the back of the locker. They passed Africa and France again and stopped at the clipboard in the middle of the walkway. As Brian leaned to pick it up, something else caught his attention. Under one of the industrial shelving units, a laminated badge reflected a bit in the dim light. He waved Sy over, who moved to the shelves, lying on her stomach to reach under. Retrieving the badge, she rose and dusted herself off.

Together, they inspected the badge.

Stephen Kline looked back, smug as ever, under big red letters that stated *Volunteer, Property Department, Chicago Opera House.*

CHAPTER XXXII

Secret Room

THE FRENZIED WIND HOWLED between the tall buildings downtown. Sy and Brian emerged from their makeshift prison in the dark of night and the vacant alley. Brian called Detective Shelby and informed him of the incident. "I don't have any solid evidence for a charge other than obstruction at this point," he said, "but that's enough to keep her if you find her."

The night absorbed Sy in its shadowy tendrils. Light, though poor, compressed against the dumpster, the symbol of a lost and dying soul. She tried to shake herself from the homeless man's memories, but they had taken root in her heart. "I hope Gunter isn't having any problems with the hospital. I don't know how much the doctors can help, if at all, but maybe the man won't die alone in the cold."

Tenderness smoothed Brian's voice. "Do you think he has family nearby?"

Sy looked to the stars and allowed her soul to travel the constellations. Images of the man's past flickered like comets in her thoughts and she sifted through the tails for answers. "I don't know if he even knows for sure. He was just in a great deal of pain. You know, he served this country once. Now, he can't even serve himself."

"He's got hope because of you, Sy." Brian, her knight-in-something-armor eased her troubles. "You've returned his dignity, and that's something you should be proud about. I know I'm impressed."

Her heart swelled and she wanted to tuck herself into the safety of his arms. "You're easily impressed then."

He shrugged and ran a hand through his hair. "Well, I'd argue against you but my stomach's rubbing a blister on my backbone. If this turns out to be another long night, we should grab a bite to eat. What'chya think?"

Her stomach agreed with him. "Let's kill two stones with one bird, yes? Do you like pizza?"

THE CAB RIDE TO MORELLI'S LASTED a half-hour longer than it should have. One of the stop lights under the L was off its timer and traffic was a mess because of it. Peanut shells peppered the floor of the pizza joint, crunching under foot as they crossed the threshold. They ordered a medium deep-dish comprised of everything but anchovies, and Sy asked the girl at the register if anyone from the crew of September 11th was working. "I don't know," the girl said. "Tommy, at the bar, he might know something."

Tommy worked as the bartender for as long as Sy could remember. Henry had a fondness for him and gave him generous tips. As Sy and Brian approached the bar, Tommy grinned. "It's been a while, Sy. I'm sorry about Henry. I'm gonna miss him."

"Thanks, but I found out he's a two-timing jackass so I'm not feeling the need for sympathy right now. I appreciate the sentiment however." She perched on one of the barstools and pat the one beside it as an invitation for Brian. "You don't mind that we sit here do you, Tommy? While we wait for our pizza?"

"Of course not. I'll give you a glass on the house if you want, I insist." He popped open a bottle of red wine and began to pour a glass. "What are you having, Friend?"

"I'd love a beer, but I'm kinda on duty." Brian said, sitting on the offered stool.

Tommy hesitated. "You a cop?"

"Kinda. I'm a federal agent."

"No kidding?" Tommy's face lit up like the neon beer advertisements behind his head. "My grandpa was one of them untouchable fellas that brought down Capone. I'll break out the scotch."

Brian laughed. "No, no truly. I'll have a root beer."

"Draft or bottle?"

"Draft since you have it." Brian sounded impressed.

Tommy handed Sy her wineglass and started a frosted mug for Brian. "I'm sorry I didn't tell you about his girls, but since you already know, I guess there's no harm now."

"Henry brought them here?" Sy felt ill, as if the filth of betrayal would never wash off. "How crass can you get?"

"It was a trip, hearing about it on the news. I'd just seen him too, what, that night? It was 9-11 right?" The root beer dispensed, he handed the mug to Brian and wiped down his counter. "He sat here by himself looking all moody. I asked him what was up and he said you were angry with him and he deserved it. So we toasted to the hope of forgiveness and for the souls lost at the towers and he stumbled out of here to call a cab. I don't remember for sure the time. Our power went out briefly near the same time."

Brian wiped a foam mustache from his upper lip. "Was he expecting someone who didn't show, or was he truly here on his own?"

Tommy shook his head, "If he'd been waiting for someone, he didn't tell me, and it didn't keep him from ordering his food."

Some patrons approached the bar, and Tommy excused himself to see to their orders. Sy and Brian picked up their pizza pie and finished what they could of it, ordering some coffee to go after.

THEIR NEXT STOP WAS MCKEALY'S HOME. Brian called Mike and said he still hadn't located his Saint Sebastian, and Sy called her father to let him know they were still out and around. "Sandy's in the wind," she said, almost as an afterthought.

"She won't be in wind for long," her father said. "I've got surprise when you return."

"Is it a pony?" Sy giggled at herself.

"Niet, a mea vrabie. Not this time."

Brian asked the cab-driver if he didn't mind waiting for them. The cabbie expressed a concerned about the crime scene tape across the door. "I'm a federal agent," Brian assured him. "It's okay."

Noting the skeptical look on the driver's face, Sy added, "We also work for Benjamin, and bear his thank you notes."

"I know Mr. Franklin well. I'll wait as long as you want," the cabbie said.

Brian shot her a look as they approached McKealy's house. Sy shrugged. "Sometimes money talks, sometimes it doesn't." She opened her purse and pulled out a pair of latex surgeon's gloves, earning another sharp look. "What, do you want a pair?"

"If you have extra, sure. We should probably step through the side gate and enter through the back, just in case the neighbors are as nosy as they were last night. I also don't want to disturb the crime scene tape."

The back door was locked. Brian poked about in several planters resting on the patio, an effort to find a hidden spare key, while Sy studied the second-story windows. When Brian's search proved fruitless, she directed his attention to the small, middle window open above the patio cover. "If you hoist me up, I think I can get in that way."

He smirked and interlaced his fingers to give her a foothold. His strong arms launched her up to the pitched roof. Momentum propelling her legs over the edge, she scaled the shingles and slipped through the open window, which belonged to a bathroom as she had suspected. The layout of the house was easy enough to navigate and she was down the stairs and unlocking the back door in seconds.

"Look at that," Brian pointed to the top of the refrigerator free of dust. "Don't you think that's a bit excessive and unusual? I've never seen the top of a fridge look that clean."

"Not all artists are slovenly, Brian. I think it's a misnomer. Considering the aggressiveness of his cancer, obsessive cleaning might have been one of the ways McKealy coped with pain." She passed through the kitchen back to the stairs. Is his studio in the basement?"

"Yeah it's this way." He led her to the closet beneath the stairs and opening door, exposed the basement access in the floorboard. They descended into the belly of the house and turned the light on. The easel with the unfinished picture was still there, indicating law enforcement failed to see a reason to remove it.

Sy examined the canvas, biting her lower lip in concentration. Failing to find inspiration, she looked about the room to absorb the detail. The dampness bothered her. Paint would take forever to dry down here, so why in a four bedroom house would he use this for his art studio? Not to mention the light was useless for any artist, with or without stereo blindness, to see and paint shadows with confidence. "This makes even less sense than the forgeries do."

"Good. So we're on the same page." Brian drew her attention to the wall. "Now, when I was down here last, that wall bothered me. Doesn't it look off to you?"

"Old houses settle," she shrugged. "Could be a false wall though."

They inspected the wall intently. It was finished like the rest of the basement, although the paint was more recent, lacking the grayish dust that collected the other walls. Brian tapped the wall, listening for the hollow sound between studs. A section sprang forward at the pressure, revealing a storage space beyond. Excited, they entered the walk-in closet.

Several of McKealy's works were framed and organized on shelves the way the rest of the house had been, to the point of being over-cataloged. A rippled sea of reds and blues spread out before them. And at the end of one of the shelves, a familiar yellow jutted into view.

Lodged between other works, *Girl in Hammock* showed signs of recent disturbance. Sy frowned, confused, as Brian voiced her suspicions. "That one's a forgery too, isn't it?"

She nodded. Flipping the unframed work about to look at the back of the canvas, she discovered a message written in pencil. Phase one of three, no signature, no number. She flipped it back over and investigated the picture again. The dandelions were short a few blooms and the signature was missing.

The ceiling creaked, pulling them from their enigma. Brian put a finger to his lips and Sy removed her heels as she put the painting back. Together, they moved across the floor to the house access and Sy swiped an artist scalpel from the utensils on the easel in passing. If they became trapped for the second time, this prison would prove more formidable. They'd be stuck in here for quite a long time.

The basement door opened and Sy held her breath until a familiar voice drifted down. "Kirby? You in here buddy?"

"Yeah Mike," Brian released a sigh. "Come on down. We've found something you need to see.

Among the paintings in the closet, Mike shook his head. "Are you telling me that the artist forged his own paintings?"

Sy tucked her arms about her midsection in the now crowded space. "No…I think a better explanation is McKealy paints in stages. He's a perfectionist, which might be a way for him to know when the painting is done. Some artists struggle with knowing when to stop."

"So his crazy is a planned crazy?" Mike raised his smart-phone and took some snapshots. "I wonder if he was aware any of them were missing."

"Who else could've known they were back here?" Brian asked. "I mean, false wall and everything."

"Sandy didn't know she was sitting on forgeries," Sy talked through the puzzle. "I'm certain of that now, so she didn't know they were here."

"That Stephen Kline might, be it they're cousins and all." Brian leaned against the door-jamb. "He'd have access to all things William McKealy."

Mike agreed. "That's a good bet. But how does this figure in with everything else?"

Sy yawned. It had been a really long day and her lack of sleep was catching up with her. "Can we work on this tomorrow?" She slipped her heals back on. "I'm losing my ability to focus."

They agreed to split up. Mike wanted to take a few more pictures of the scene and Brian assured him they hadn't disturbed anything except that room. On their way back out, Sy paused at the easel to return the scalpel to the utensil jar. She selected a brick red oil paint tube from the paint tray. The cap was stiff to turn and it took a second attempt with a better grip before it opened. "I don't think McKealy painted anything in a while. These paints are dried out."

"So this unfinished painting..." Mike scratched his head. "Why would he lie about working on this the night he was attacked?"

"You know," Brian said, brushing dust from his sleeve, "if the paintings aren't forged, neither is the suicide note. McKealy intended to kill himself if he couldn't take the pain anymore. His attacker beat him to it."

"He's in a ton of pain, Mike, and has been for a very long while," Sy said, returning the paint tube to the tray. "He must have quit painting months ago because it got to be too much for him. It might also explain why his studio is down here in the damp. He might've moved it from sight so he wouldn't be reminded of his handicap."

Outside, Brian and Sy stripped the latex gloves from their hands and crossed the lawn to the cab. Sy pulled three-hundred dollars from her wallet and handed it to the cabbie in thanks. As they settled in the back seat, she pulled her legs up, tucked into a ball, and laid her head in her knight-in-something-armor's lap. He gave her shoulder a gentle squeeze and pulled loose strands of hair from her face. Comfortable and safe, she drifted off to sleep, smiling

CHAPTER XXXIII

Little Details

BRIAN WOKE AS THE MORNING BROKE through the fog in his head. He felt a presence near his bed and glanced across the room. Sy sat in the armchair, reading a book. She looked dressed for a hiking trip, with jeans and a thin, green and gray plaid flannel shirt. Putting her book down, she crossed the floor to sit on the edge of the bed. "Coffee will be ready soon," she said.

He propped himself up against the headboard, willing the last of the fog from his mind. His heart raced at the prospect of waking to her, sending his blood pumping to his extremities. She was close enough to tackle to the bed. He cleared his throat. "To what do I owe the pleasure? You rather have me at a disadvantage. I'll be a terrible host in this state."

"I wanted to warn you."

"About what?"

"The surprise Papa mentioned to me last night. We remodeled the sitting room, and there's a crowd of people here to help out. I wasn't sure if it would confuse you or not." She pointed to the door. "Annika turned the dining room into a brilliant buffet, but she'll make you an omelet custom if you want one."

"Okay, but that's not all, is it? You've got something else on your mind, don't you?"

Her eyebrow peaked and she dropped her chin low. "Maybe I wanted some quiet time. It's beginning to get chaotic out there."

Brian held her gaze for a long, breathless moment, watching the gold flecks shimmer in her blue-brown eyes. He grabbed her hand and drew her close, yielding to a desire he wasn't sure he was feeling, and wrapped his bare arms around her in a solid hug. She molded comfortably against him, their body heats intertwining. He wanted this, he wanted her, enjoying the pressure against his chest and the sweet scent of apples from her hair. "Me too. I rather like it in here."

He felt her muffled laughter echo through his body. "I like it here too," she whispered. "It's quiet and I couldn't ask for better company, but you know how I get if I don't eat." She broke from his embrace and stood to leave. At the door, she cast a coy glance back at him. "Rain check?"

"Deal."

Pain pinched his heart as the door closed behind her. He smacked the back of his head against the headboard, twice, from frustration. If she had called his bluff and stayed, what would he have done? Was he even bluffing? Didn't the thought of getting tangled in the sheets with her tantalize him as much as holding her pressed against his chest had?

One thing he knew for certain now. The attraction was mutual. It wasn't just a casual flirtation. Now all he had to do was fine tune the timing.

He rose from the bed and dressed quickly. As he wandered down the hall, a myriad of voices twisted around him. Regardless of Sy's warning, the transformed sitting room still took him by surprise.

The furniture was rearranged and the room now housed several computer stations. A large, counter height drafting table stood in the center of the room, and cluttered with pictures and files. A dry-erase board flanked the table's far side.

It was like the war-room back at his New York office when the task force buckled down for a bust. Realizing he gaped like a codfish, he snapped his mouth closed and cleared his throat.

"Hey Fed," Gunny said entering the room. He carried a plate full of aebleskivers and cubed cantaloupe. "Annika's got a buffet going on in the dining room. Help yourself and dig in."

"You don't think this is a little overkill?" Brian asked.

The retired marine laughed, "Of course it is, but when does this family do anything half-assed?"

Brian trudged to the dining room and gaped again. The dining table displayed warming trays and loaded tiers with enough food to feed twenty hungry lumberjacks and their families. He shook his head and resigned, grabbed a plate to help himself. Mandy Hines arrived then, looking like Alice at the Hatter's tea. "No wonder you're pursuing other avenues," she said. "I certainly would if I thought I had a chance. Wow!"

"No lie. There's lobster in that one." He pointed to the end warming tray and repeated for emphasis, "Lobster."

"For breakfast?" She looked about. "If I help you hook up with her, will you adopt me?"

Brian laughed, scooping a helping of mixed fruit onto his plate. "How about I set you up with an interview to join the FBI instead. I think you'd make a good fit for our forensics team."

Mandy started her buffet collection from the back end of the table. "Only if it's in your neck of the woods. I'll move to New York.

Unless, are you moving to Chicago, since you have, uh, extra incentive?"

"I've thought about it. We'll have to see though." Brian poured a cup of coffee from the industrial-sized coffee pot and gathered up his food. He waited for Mandy to complete her own and escorted her back into the sitting room.

Gunny and Viktor hovered about a monitor. "Are you looking at the surveillance footage?" Mandy queried, peering between the men at the screens from her stool at the draft table.

Viktor turned at her voice, "You are CSI yes?"

She nodded, swallowing a mouthful of food. "Mandy Hines, at your service. You must be Sy's dad."

"Da," he answered. Brian could tell he wasn't in much of a mood for idle conversation. "You have seen footage before, yes?"

Mandy abandoned her breakfast and moved closer to the screen. "I've see it yes, but I don't trust it. Why?"

Gunny wagged a finger, "This copy you can trust. I got it from the company direct. We're hoping you'll be able to tell if the copy the cops have is corrupted."

Viktor offered her his seat and she took it. "How far back are you looking?"

"We're currently looking at footage from September 2nd. We're focused on the eighth floor landing hallway and," Gunny indicated the split screen with his index finger, "the parking garage from the same times. Let me know if you see anyone you recognize."

She turned her attention to the monitor while Viktor brought her food and coffee over.

Sy entered, carrying a stack of sketches, which she placed on the draft table. "Papa, why are Gunter and Yousef posted in the landing? No one is going to attack me here with all these witnesses around."

Viktor sighed. "Just indulge an old man. Va rog, pentru mine."

"Nu pot, Papa. They stick out like a sore thumb."

"Annika is happy. She make buffet table. If Gunter and Yousef make her secure, then is worth it no?"

Sy scowled at him. "Fine, but I'm half-tempted to sneak down the fire escape."

The room erupted with investigative minds. Barry arrived to dig into contracts he pulled from public records. Stan Eckhart, introduced to Brian as the money genius for one of Viktor's companies, scoured financial documents looking for discrepancies. Mandy and Gunny worked through the surveillance camera footage for the building. Annika kept the food and coffee warmed and served. Viktor bounced between two computer laptops, speaking to someone on the phone in Romanian. Brian felt right at home.

After the breakfast buffet cleared and the food changed to luncheon fare, Brian received a call from Mike on his cell. "What's up?"

"Just thought you'd want to know. McKealy slipped into a coma about two hours ago. They're not expecting him to come out." Mike sounded exhausted.

"Okay, thanks Mike." Brian looked to Sy for approval. "Hey when you get the chance to clear from there, swing by the Freitag residence with your crew. We may have something for you soon." After hanging up, he thanked Sy.

"No worries. He's your handler. I don't trust him, but we don't want to get caught withholding evidence either." She turned to Barry. "What's the likelihood of getting a search warrant for Kitty's condo downstairs?"

"You are not law enforcement, Sy," he said, still buried in his documents. "We need a judge and something to go on that's more solid than your gut."

Brian asked, "What do you want to search for?"

"The murder weapon," she tapped a pencil on the table while she glared at the diagram of her condo. "Gunny, we need to make sure we keep a close eye on Kitty's condo from the surveillance."

"Already on it," Gunny replied as Mandy typed with roadrunner-speed at her keyboard to adjust the split screens. The thirty-two inch screen now monitored six camera angles.

Sy's phone rang. She groaned and put it on speaker. "Tina, darling, how can I be of assistance? I am in the middle of something so…"

"God, Simone? It sounds like you're at a newspaper stand in Paris. Did you get my email?" Tina's whiny voice leaked into the room with a tinny cast to her tone.

Rolling her eyes, Sy claimed she didn't have a chance to. "I've been kind of busy."

For once, Tina sounded compassionate and understanding. "Look Simone, I think I owe you an apology. I've lost my brother, and he meant the world to me, but you've lost your husband and he must have been your entire universe. I forget, sometimes, that we both love him."

Sy smacked her head, "I'm sorry, Tina girl, I forgot about the life policies. I'll get down to Lloyd's and pull them this afternoon. Wait, it's Sunday. Can you wait until tomorrow morning?"

There was a long pause. "I didn't call about the insurance policy. I just wanted to say I'm sorry for behaving the way I have. We've always been at odds with one another and I don't want Henry's funeral to be the last time we do anything as a family."

Brian looked for the candid camera person hidden somewhere in the room. Sy, too, seemed confused with the behavior of her sister-in-law. Sy pinched the bridge of her nose. "Tina...are you pregnant?"

Viktor stopped mid-bounce and dropped his headset. Gunny muttered something about horse manure being blessed by a dozen popes, and Annika dropped a glass salad plate in the dining room. Barry put down a contract and leaned back in his chair.

Brian choked on his coffee and he realized that if everyone in the room could, they'd all be in France at that precise moment, wandering through a vineyard.

"Yes," Tina said, her voice timid and foreign. "I'm scared Simone. You're smarter at the life thing than I am. What do I do?"

Everyone in the room fixed their gazes on Sy, waiting to exhale. "Well I suppose you're going to be mother. I know nothing of motherhood."

"I'm not fit to be a mother, am I?" Tina wailed. "And I've been drinking all week. What if I've done some permanent damage?"

Sy looked at her father before she answered. "Tina, take a deep breath. It's okay. I won't let you go through this alone. I promise."

Viktor shot her a look.

Tina calmed enough to end the conversation. Hanging up her phone, Sy turned to Barry, "Please set up a contingency plan for the kid. I've a gut feeling that she's going to need all the help she can get."

Barry shook his head. "I'll put a proposal together for approval once the kid is born, but there's not a lot for me to do until then."

She nodded, returning to her documents. "Then unless someone else has an earth-shattering revelation, let us focus on the task at hand, shall we? I need an opportunity to get into Donavon's flat, so make it happen people."

Quiet conversations ebbed back into the room. Brian, recovered from his coughing fit, remembered the product Sy purchased from the bath store. Interrupting her focus, he asked her if she knew if the cologne was delivered.

"I'll check with Annika." Sy rushed from the room.

Mandy slammed her hand down on her desk. "We've got him! We've got them both!"

"Actually, we've got them all," Gunny said, frowning. He pointed to the square showing footage from the lobby. Date stamped for September 11th, the picture showed Jasmine entering the lobby and leaning over the security desk. She distracted Jefferson at his post. In the upper right corner, two boxes showed two men leaving Kitty Donavon's condo, on by the front door, and one by the fire escape off the patio. They were both dressed in black hoodie jackets and jeans, and both carried double-barreled shotguns slung across their shoulders.

When Sy returned with a few of the product bottles, Brian waved her over to the monitor and they watched the silent snub film unfold on screen.

CHAPTER XXXIV

The Briefing

S Y WAS IMPATIENT. She didn't want to wait for the authorities to obtain the search warrant. She wanted to bust down the door to Donavon's flat and tear the place apart. Feeling her blood pressure boil, she paced a rut around the room, trying to focus on Chardonnay and get her emotions under control.

Her knight-in-something-armor assumed command of the investigation from Viktor. After Gunny and Mandy pieced the surveillance footage together, Brian was on his cell phone, coordinating with the local FBI office and their liaison with the Chicago police department. They already had one suspect in the wind; no one wanted to risk spooking another. It wasn't long before joint task teams crowded into Sy's sitting room.

The key players were all present by late afternoon. With Mike and Detective Shelby on board, and the assistant district attorney Paul Caruso conferring with Barry in the corner, Brian called the convention to a form of order. Drawing everyone's attention to the drop down movie screen in the center of the room, Mandy began the digital slide show she had prepped for the event. "You're green," she said, giving Brian the go-ahead.

"Ladies and gentlemen, thank you for joining us this afternoon. While this may seem a little unconventional, the situation demands a level of security that can only be facilitated in a neutral space. As the primary crime scene, this condo serves that purpose well." Brian raised a laser pointer to circle corresponding points. "The facts are these..."

The audience listened with rapt attention, some taking notes as Brian spoke. He began with the party in August. Henry Freitag arranged a fund raiser for the art project. There, Sandy Petrusky introduced her sister Jasmine Colby and the artist William McKealy to the producer. After a round of tequila shots, the four happily negotiated for *Girl in Hammock*, a painting McKealy was reluctant to sell because of a deep, sentimental attachment.

Eventually, McKealy conceded. Jasmine insisted that she handle the transaction. "Our financial consultant has confirmed that whatever the arrangement was, it was not recorded into the gallery books," Brian said as a digital image of a cancelled draft flashed onto the screen. "We do know Henry withdrew a bank draft made out to William McKealy directly for the sum of nine thousand dollars. We also have confirmed three additional purchases for The Gray, Wind, and Red River Valley were handled through the gallery, and personal checks for the amounts of four thousand each were paid to the gallery, and not directly to the artist."

Brian then posed the question: If Jasmine was to handle the first transaction, why didn't it go through the gallery as the other did? Was it because Stephen Kline, the artist's cousin, knew *Girl in Hammock* was never to be sold? McKealy had already cut his cousin out of the inheritance of his estate, the bulk of which is supposed to go to Lake Forest University.

The assistant district attorney, Caruso, asked, "That could definitely be motive there, but for murder? Do we know if Freitag had any connection to Kline?"

Brian shook his head, "We merely suspicion that Freitag met Kline in passing at the gallery, if he met him at all. Kline denied ever actually knowing Freitag. His bitterness appeared to be directed towards his co-worker, and he made disparaging remarks about how Jasmine secured her clientele."

The next series of images to flash up on the screen was the surveillance footage of the condo building. Explaining there were no working security cameras for the penthouse condo, Brian remarked about the day Sy returned home to catch her husband in the hot-tub. Jasmine Colby arrived about three o'clock that Thursday afternoon, September 8th. She parked in a guest space in the garage, and visited Kitty Donavon on the eighth floor.

"Who answered the door, can you tell?" Detective Shelby asked.

"That's a negative, not from this angle," Brian said. "It is our assumption Jasmine was there to visit CSI Scofield, not Ms. Donavon, but that is just pure conjecture at this point. We have not been able to question Ms. Donavon as of yet."

The security footage showed Jasmine Colby ring the doorbell for the Donavon flat and enter a moment later. The footage was then fast-forwarded another hour-and-a-half to when she left. It showed her adjusting her skirt at the elevator and then boarding the carriage. The red laser pointer circled the up indicator. "She disappears here for several hours but Ms. Freitag's statement places Jasmine in the condo." Mandy said. "We don't pick her up again until very early the next morning, long after Ms. Freitag is known to have come and gone."

"And if you look at the shot of Jasmine leaving...there," Brian stated as Mandy paused the playback, "Notice that she appears to be agitated, frustrated, or even scared. She's fumbling as she approaches her car, drops her keys...here and...here." The sedan she got into sat for a few minutes longer before backing out of its space and exiting the garage.

Detective Shelby asked how the footage was obtained. "I don't remember the evidence we collected showing all that."

Mandy replied with a voice full of spite. "Sir, no offense, but that good-for-nothing, son-of-a...CSI Scofield collected this footage from Brinks. The version we received, cataloged, reviewed, and filed, was corrupted. At the time we thought it had something to do with the cameras."

Gunny stood, "For those of you in the room who do not know me, I'm Retired Marine Gunner, Chief Warrant Officer Robert Monroe. I work for the security company as a guard here. I was able to obtain this uncorrupted copy directly from my managing office."

Shelby smirked. "I suppose you didn't tell me because you weren't sure if I was dirty too? I should be annoyed."

Mandy looked sheepish, "Well, when you discover you can't trust one of your coworkers, you tend not to trust any of them."

The assembly moved on, as the footage showed the next few days. CSI Scofield went to his aunt's condo daily, spending long periods of time there. "In and of itself, this is not an issue. Ms. Donavon has been out of town vacationing and Scofield was house-sitting," Brian turned a page in his notes. "Now, we have yet to discover the link between Scofield and the rest of them. Jasmine of course is dead, but both Kline and Petrusky seem to be silent about him. We're hoping Ms. Donavon will be able to shed some light on their relationships."

Sy excused herself from the room. The crowd made it stuffy, despite the central air being on full force cold, but it was their collective thoughts she needed to remove herself from. Out in the foyer, she looked at the holes in the carpet, and the space where the vase had been. As Brian's words drifted from the sitting room, she visualized Henry's final moments again.

Two men exited Donavon's condo, carrying shotguns. The slender, lanky one took the elevator, disappearing after that, and the other went by way of the fire escape. Cameras caught him travel the ladders all the way to the penthouse floor.

Jasmine Colby checked in with Jefferson at the security desk, apparently to ask questions, providing a distraction for the gunmen to burgle the penthouse. She took the elevator to the eighth floor and let herself into Donavon's flat. She was there only a moment before she left again. "What is most curious about this, is if you watch her enter the condo, she has a purse in hand," Sy heard Mandy's voice address the room. "When she left she was not carrying that purse."

That explains why it wasn't listed on the evidence log, Sy thought. Scofield could claim that he didn't remember where he found the handbag. Even crime scene investigators can make a rush error when trying to identify a body, at least that may be what Scofield was relying on a jury to believe. *Very clever.*

Sy watched from the foyer as Brian resumed his presentation. Henry arrived through the lobby door and Jefferson waved to him. They exchanged words, greetings perhaps, or Jefferson told him Jasmine was asking after him, before he boarded the elevator. At the same time, Sandy drove into the parking garage and parked behind her sister's vehicle, pinning it in. There, Sandy waited, presumably to confront her sister about the affair. Within a half hour, the footage caught Scofield coming from the eighth floor, returning to his aunt's condo in a rushed manner, carrying two shotguns. Moments after that, the lanky one exited the elevator in the parking garage.

His appearance caused Sandy some alarm as she stepped from her car to argue with the man. The lanky man shook a finger at her and whatever words were exchanged, Sandy returned to her car and backed away. He then took Jasmine's car and drove out from the parking garage after Sandy.

Brian coughed. "When Mrs. Freitag returned and discovered her husband, she noticed a fragrance lingering in the elevator carriage. She came across the same scent again as the units responded to the 911 report. It has been confirmed that this scent is custom made in a bath boutique and is a gift to Scofield from his aunt." Brian passed a bottle of the fragrance around so everyone could get a whiff. "This is as close as we could get to the actual scent from the same boutique."

Mandy whistled. "That does smell like Daniel, doesn't it Shelby?"

"I can't say that I notice to tell you the truth," Shelby said.

Sy turned away from the sitting room, again feeling anxiety creep beneath her skin. Even her beloved vineyard appeared to be beyond her reach now. The empty spaces in the foyer haunted her. She loved Henry, but why? Was it because she couldn't tap into his psyche? Was part of her grieving due to a fear she would never find another immune to her prying? She and Henry didn't have much in common. They shared a love for movies and wine, and a dislike for Tina and that damned crystal vase. Was there nothing else?

Then there was Brian, her knight-in-something-armor and Henry's polar opposite. Brian took everything in stride with a quiet dignity. She confided her deepest secrets with Brian the moment she met him, something she had never done with her husband. Henry never knew about her talents. He had his secrets and so did she. Secrets aren't the foundation for a successful marriage, Sy thought. She turned to see Brian leave the sitting room.

"A euro for your thoughts," Brian whispered. "Is it sunny in Chardonnay?"

Her senses tingled as if an electric current passed through her soul. "I...I wasn't there this time. Is your presentation over?"

"The assistant D.A. is headed for the judge's office with Shelby and Barry to get a couple search warrants. It's only a matter of time," he said. His look was inquisitive. "Are you okay? You look as though you've seen a ghost."

"I need a stiff shot of bourbon and a day at the spa, but I guess it can wait." She rubbed her neck, wishing tension would pop loose. She waved towards the sitting room. "There's a lot of white noise in there right now."

"Why don't you lie down for a while?" Brian stepped closer, slipping his hands into his pockets. "There's nothing for you to do anyway, and you deserve a break from all this."

She looked away lest she give in to her desire to kiss him. "Oh, Tina'd probably call and wake me up anyway."

Gunny popped his head into the foyer, urgency coloring his words. "We may have a situation."

Brian turned, "What's up?"

"Jefferson called up. CSI Scofield just arrived and is on his way up."

Sy inhaled sharply, "He's coming here?"

Gunny shook his head, "No he's on his way to see Ms. Donavon. But Mandy suspects he's got a friend or two at the courthouse, so he may get tipped off and be in the wind before we're able to deliver the warrant."

Sy bit her lower lip. "I could visit them without raising too much suspicion. I'm a neighbor after all. I could even take the cologne down to them...say that I got some for Papa but he has an allergy to something in it, so I've got to give it away."

Brian shook his head and waved his hand in an emphatic arc. "No, no way. Absolutely not. I don't like it. That's putting you in harm's way. I'll go down and interview them. I can keep them busy for a while. Since Barry's on the warrant, it shouldn't take long."

Her heart flipped. He was trying to protect her. "That's just as risky, Brian." She walked away and retrieved the box of product from the hall closet, calling out to her father. "Papa, I'm going into the alligator pit!"

Viktor stealthed from the sitting room to her side. "And alligator?"

"The alligator is under sedation for the moment, but we don't have much time for the actual procedure." It was a simple code, but one they used when personal risk and unknown danger was involved.

Viktor gave a tight nod and turned to Brian. "You. Go with her." It was a command, not a request.

Sy shook her head. "Papa, I think the ruse will work best if I go in alone."

The glint in his eyes, the set of his jaw...her father only shot that intense look when he was truly scared. "You go with Brian or you go with Gunter. It is not negotiable."

Brian pushed the sleeves of his tee-shirt up. "Don't worry, Sir. I'll make sure she doesn't hurt anyone unnecessarily."

Sy forced a mock laugh. "Very funny."

As they moved for the door, Viktor grabbed Brian's arm. "And Mr. Kirby," he said, his voice echoing in the small space. "I do not need to tell you, I am sure, if she is harmed, I will personally feed you to alligators."

CHAPTER XXXV

Into the Alligator Pit

"OKAY, MUSCLE, JUST PLAY IT COOL AND EASY, EH?" Sy told Brian as she rang the doorbell to Kitty's condo.

"Aye, Captain," Brian saluted while the box of product balanced on the nook in his left arm.

The buzz sounded again as Sy rang the bell a second time. The mid-forties aged woman answered the door. Round in the middle and fond of flamboyant clothing, Kitty was the only woman Sy ever knew who could wear a bright yellow smock and not look jaundiced.

"Simone," Kitty purred, her cigarette-scarred, baritone voice full of grit and brass. "I was just thinking about you. That mess of Henry's...I'm sorry about that. I thought he was no good, you know."

"Thanks. I'm glad to see you're back from vacation. How was Hawaii?"

"It was fantastic, as always. I'm going to move there you know, as soon as my settlement comes through." She nodded towards Brian. "Who's the hunk?"

Brian grinned. "Brian Kirby, but you can call me hunk if you want to. My ego won't mind."

"Well aren't you perfect as a gingerbread man? Hold on to this one honey." She pulled the door open wide. "Come on in, the water's fine."

The condo was clean and free of clutter, but wore neutrals the way its mistress wore neon. "I love your home," Brian said. "Who's your designer?"

"You're a smooth-talker, ain'tchya," a sly grin crossed Kitty's face. "It's all me, you know. I've been a decorator now for a few years. Have a seat. Can I get you some lemonade?"

"Ah, no thank you. I've filled up on coffee and my back teeth will probably start floating soon."

"Sy?"

"None for me either, thank you." Sy took a seat on one of the parson's chairs while Brian took its mate, setting his burden on the floor beside. "So I'll admit to you, I've an ulterior motive for stopping by Kitty."

"Don't you always?" Kitty laughed, collapsing on the sofa opposite. "What is it now? Do you want me to pick another fight with the homeowners' association?"

"No, nothing that crass, really," Sy said. "I ran into Daniel a couple of times because of the investigation into Henry's death and I was intrigued by his cologne."

Kitty's eyebrows peaked. "My Danny-boyo?

"Yeah, so I asked him about it and he told me where you get it from. I thought maybe I could get some for my father for his birthday. Turns out though, he's allergic to something in it."

"You like the cologne, eh? I love the way it smells on Danny. I thought he wore it just to oblige me, but if you like it to, maybe he is wearing it for the ladies." Kitty beamed, bright and pink.

"Anyway, since Papa can't wear it, and Brian here is stuck in his own rut, I thought I'd pass it on to you. I figured it's close enough to what you get so maybe it won't go to waste then," Sy said.

"Well, let me get Danny for you," she said, getting up from the couch and moving towards the back room.

"Oh, he's here today? I'm sorry, we shouldn't have interrupted, then."

"Nonsense, Simone. He can be polite and at least come out to say hello." Kitty disappeared down the hall.

Brian whispered, "Can you tell if she knows anything?"

Sy frowned, feeling awful for trespassing. "No, she hasn't a clue as to what he's been up to. And the way she dotes on him, it's going to kill her to know."

"Have you known her a long time?"

"She's been here as long as I can remember. We're not very close, but every once in a while we'd chat in the lobby and get caught up. And we'd go to bats for each other when we needed to take on the HOA." She glanced towards the hallway as she heard them approach.

Scofield appeared on edge, his face void of color. "Mrs. Freitag, thank you for remembering." He was polite, but guarded.

Kitty rummaged through the box at Brian's feet. "Ooh, look Danny-boyo, there's even shampoo in here."

"Thank you," Scofield repeated.

Sy forced warmth through her tone. "You're quite welcome. So were you here the day that Henry got shot?"

Kitty shook her head. "Sadly no. Perhaps I might've heard something or seen someone. But then you said it was on 9-11, didn't you Danny-boyo?

He nodded, a stiff and blank gesture. He was a board next to his animated aunt as they sat on the couch. "It was a rather grizzly scene. I'm sorry you had to find them like that."

It sounded rehearsed. Sy noticed his dark, puffy eyes for the first time, and his haunted visage. Jasmine's death, his kill, tore him up inside. Sy flashed a smile, "You know the part that frosts my goat about this whole nonsense? I wonder about this tart of his. Henry brought this girl into our home for Christ's sake."

Kitty tugged on her ear and her mouth turned down in a short-lived pout. "I wonder...did they ever I.D. her?"

Daniel twitched like a bolt of electricity traveled through him. "I'm sure Mrs. Freitag doesn't want to keep reliving that night, Aunt Kitty."

His aunt looked disappointed. "I'm sorry if I'm prying. I have such a morbid fascination into the macabre. I'm always begging Danny-boyo to regale me with tales of his crime scenes."

Sy shrugged, dismissing the notion. "Oh, it doesn't bother me one bit. The moment I caught him stooping her, I lost all respect or interest for the man. The dirty, rat-bastard had it coming. What I can't get over is how they met though."

"Did they meet at a strip club?" Kitty asked, her eyes bright with interest. "Henry seemed like the sort that might frequent such a place. I can smell them a mile off."

"Aunt Kitty..." Daniel squirmed.

Kitty shot him a look. "I might be just spruced-up trailer-trash Danny-boyo, but it's not just trash that walks into those places you know." She wagged her finger at Brian. "I'll bet even this Hunk-a-chunk here's even been to one, ain'tchya?"

Brian shook his head. "Negatory, at least as far as my mother knows."

Kitty chortled a throaty laugh. "Yes, yes you I like. But you see, Danny-boyo is afraid I'll admit to you that I was a stripper once. Long, long ago and about sixty pounds away."

Sy winked, "Oh, what does the past matter? I was practically reared in an insane-asylum. The best sorts of linens are the dirty kind, am I right?"

"Absolutely!" Kitty said. "So if they didn't meet at a strip club, do you know where they met?"

"At an art gallery of all places," Sy said. "That tart batted her eye-lashes at Henry and he fell for it. Hook, line, and twelve thousand dollars."

"No!" Kitty raised a hand to her heart. "Really? See, Danny-boyo, that proves it. You don't have to be a stripper to be trash. I wonder if your girl knows the victim."

"I'm sure she doesn't. She wouldn't hang out with that sort." Daniel turned green, his eyes danced in their sockets as if searching for a way out.

His aunt laughed in his face. "Don't give me that line of bullshit. I know you gave her a key to my condo so you could rendezvous in the privacy of someone else's home, without roommates to deal with. If she didn't hang out with that sort of girl, I wouldn't've had to wash the sheets from the back bedroom when I got back from Ha-waii."

"Kitty!" Daniel's skin succumbed to another shade of translucent. "Enough! They don't want to know about my illicit affair, do they? Stop broadcasting all the details."

Sy lowered her eyes and routed the subject back to the case, "Does your girlfriend work for an art gallery, Daniel?"

He looked like a stag in the glow of headlights. Sy could sense Brian tensing across the space between them. They didn't have a clue when the warrant brigade might show. The conversation was moving so fast; their suspect could try to bolt.

Kitty continued while beads of perspiration broke across Daniel's forehead. "Only the second biggest gallery in town worth its salt!" she said, straightening her shoulders. "I introduced them as a matter of fact. I went into Wilcox and Sherry and purchased a couple pieces for a client and Danny-boyo here helped me load the car. The two of them were all doe-y eyed at one another." She turned to him and said in a more serious tone, "And as much as I like her, Honey, you don't want to commit to that light-skirt. I know the games that girl plays. I've played them before, myself."

"Wilcox and Sherry," Sy asked, feigning shock. "They must have known one another for certain then. Henry's whore worked there."

"Now that's a quinky-dink if I ever heard one. Jasmine must have known her then."

Brian leaned forward and gave Daniel a hard stare as if daring him to try something. "The victim's name is Jasmine Colby, Ms. Donavon."

Kitty's face fell. "No! Jasmine was Henry's whore?" She looked to her nephew. Her voice shook. "Danny...boyo...you didn't tell me it was Jasmine they found."

Daniel's thoughts struck out like a jackhammer. *Stupid woman! They know now, because of you!* His mental anguish screamed in blind panic, reliving the whole night as it flashed before him, and Sy. Daniel rose from his seat in a slow, deliberate motion. "No. No I didn't, Aunt Kitty."

"Don't you 'Aunt Kitty' me, boyo!" She sputtered, fury seeping into her eyes with understanding. "What did you do that night, Daniel Scofield? You tell me the truth or so help me, I'll send your body back to Maryland in little plastic bags."

Brian stood and squared off to the CSI, pulling his badge from his back pocket to flash. "Mr. Scofield, I'm going to ask you where you were on Sunday, September 11th, between 5pm and 8pm?"

Daniel quaked where he stood, silent. Kitty raised a hand to her mouth, tears flowing in thick rivers from her eyes. "Danny...boyo...tell them. Tell them you had nothing to do with that girl's death...Tell them!"

Sy drew a slow breath and released it. "He can't, Kitty. If he does, he'll be lying to a federal agent." She got up and backed towards the door, eager to stand out of the way. "He killed her."

"That's not true Kitty!" Daniel found his voice. "I didn't hurt anyone. All I'm guilty of that night is lying to my supervisor about my relationship with her."

"Ms. Donavon," Brian said, "do you own any firearms?"

Kitty's wide eyes reflected fear and anger, but her voice was steady. "I have my late husband's guns. I got them before they had to be registered."

"Are there any shotguns in the collection?" Brian continued, easing his badge back into his pocket.

"Five of them, all different gauges." She pointed towards the hallway. "In the safe in the back bedroom. My husband was fond of duck hunting."

"Have any of them been fired recently?"

She shook her head. "I've never shot them. As far as I know, they're rusted solid back there. Danny can show you. He knows the safe's combination." She folded her arms across her abdomen. "Don't you, Danny-boyo?"

There was a knock at the door. A muffled voice announced it was the Chicago Police. "We're here to serve a warrant."

Sy caught a broadcast. "Brian, watch out!"

Her warning came too late. From the small of his back, Daniel pulled out his stun-gun and jabbed it to Brian's neck, shocking him to the ground. Kitty screamed and tried to help him up, but caught the current second-hand and passed out. Daniel made a wild dash to the patio doors through the kitchen.

Sy probed Brian's mind to check his vitals. He responded quickly, *Go, I'll catch up!*

Sy gave chase, tearing down the fire escape after the murderer. He hit ground and ran down the street ahead of her by only a few strides. Daniel dodged up an alleyway, an attempt to lose her perhaps, but she kept his pace. Their chase moved up one street, through a major artery of traffic, and into the heart of a park. A slow burn leaked into Sy's lungs and legs as she pushed for more speed. She slowed as he disappeared around a cluster of trees, looking for signs of ambush.

She didn't see him round a tree, but she heard him before he fired a stun-gun cartridge. She darted from the path of the probes, spinning about to take him on. Not able to reload, he held the stun-gun at her with the drive-stun-mode visibly arcing, the same mode that debilitated Brian.

Daniel took a swing at her and then another. He only needed to land one good hit. She dodged and parried, sizing up the ability of her enemy. His department's hand-to-hand training was sufficient for an average adversary, but not up to task against the skills of a Swiss Army combat-trained telepath. The scrap only lasted a minute before the palm of her hand connected with his nose in an upward thrust. She felt the two, fragile bones shatter upon impact.

He dropped the stun-gun as his hands flew up to his broken nose and he collapsed to his knees, like the Wint-Mart thug with the parrot tattoo had. Blood spewed through his fingers and onto his clothes in oozy, crimson rivers. Daniel whimpered and she almost felt sorry for him.

Almost.

Sy picked the stun-gun up from the ground and arced it in front of his face. "You attacked a federal agent, you assaulted me, and you made me run, Jackass! You even think about twitching in the wrong direction and I will bring the wrath of God down onto your head."

A cheer rose up around her, surprising her. A crowd gathered, filled with the impression he had tried to mug or rape her and they congratulated her with whistles and whoots. Free to catch her breath, she bent at the waist and puffed, as noisy squad sirens blared nearby, announcing the coming back-up.

As the adrenaline ebbed from her system, Sy glanced up to see Brian jogging towards her. "You okay?" he asked once within earshot.

"I didn't kill him," she said, disappointed, "so you've kept your word. And he didn't hurt me, so Papa doesn't have to feed you to the gators. How are you doing?"

He grinned. "I've got a pounding headache, cotton-mouth, and a fuzzy feeling in my toes, but it's nothing that a scotch won't fix. Mrs. Donavon got a contact shock and complained that her heart skipped a beat, so they're taking her to the hospital to run some tests, just as a precautionary measure."

Sy took another deep breath. In the blink of an eye, the culmination of two weeks came to an end. "This is all rather anti-climactic, don't you think?"

Brian watched the responding officers try to navigate cuffs around a busted nose, and shrugged. "What were you hoping for?"

"An opportunity to burn down another building, I guess."

He laughed and wrapped an arm around her in a solid hug. "Come, I know a great little place that will serve all the aebleskivers you can eat. My treat."

CHAPTER XXXVI

Wrapping Up

S Y TOOK A LONG HARD LOOK AT HERSELF in the bathroom mirror. Mentally and emotionally fatigued, she needed a good cry, a scotch and a foot massage. Her heart still raced from the excitement, and she savored the lingering euphoria left behind by the surge of adrenaline.

Closing her eyes, she heard birds chirp in the heavy, grape-scented air of her beloved vineyard. She stepped out onto the veranda where Jean-Luc uncorked a bottle from their historic cellars to pair with a brandied duck and risotto supper. At the table sat her father, who just put down his viola, Barry, who was still trying to work on his laptop, and her beloved knight-in-something armor, who gazed out over the vineyard with an awed expression.

She opened her eyes and peered deep into her reflection to her own soul. *You'll have to do something about him,* she told herself. *And you'll have to do it soon.*

The remnants of the day gathered in her sitting room, already returned to normal. She joined them with reluctance. It was all over, which meant that soon, Brian would return to New York City, to his life without her. The thought made her ill.

Brian finished a phone call with his office. "Thanks, Jericho," he hung up with a promise to report to work on Thursday. "I have a funeral to attend."

He winked at her. Her heart fluttered. "So, Mike, anybody strike the deal for state's evidence?" Sy sat on the sofa as Annika handed a cup of coffee to her.

Mike devoured aebleskivers by the handful, as if it were his last meal. Pausing to swallow, he replied, powdered sugar vapor rising from his lips. "Kline rolled almost instantly," he said, reaching for another handful of the round pancakes. "His alibi caved as we pointed out that his apartment had an electric outage during the time he was supposed to be home watching television. He admitted that their intent was to rob Henry of the paintings, and it went south when Jasmine called them by their names during the heist."

"I suppose they had to pull the triggers then. Dead men tell no tales, so to speak." Sy sipped her coffee, still too hot to drink without scalding her throat.

Mike continued. "Apparently, the falling out that happened between McKealy and Kline was about more than just a disagreement about affairs being in order. McKealy forced Kline to confess that he paid of the stripper to get her to leave him all those years ago. He changed his will that day."

At the sideboard, Viktor poured a scotch. "Simon, you were in shower when we learn. Sandy Petrusky was apprehended."

"Where'd they find her?"

He swirled the amber liquid in his glass, then poured another measure. "She take ferry to Canada, but was detained at entry. She forget passport."

Sy pinched the bridge of her nose and groaned. "This is going down in history as the month of idiots."

Brian sat down near Sy and tucked his arm behind the sofa's back. "Sandy asked to apologize to Kline when they took her into custody. She attacked William because she thought Kline killed her sister. She put two and two together after they argued in the parking garage, but she didn't know that Scofield was involved. You kill my sister, I kill your cousin..."

Mike washed down another aebleskiver with a noisy drink of water. "Kline dumped Jasmine's car in a ferry long-term parking lot off the lake and took the L home. CSI say they found all the missing paintings in Kline's apartment, plus a few others. He'd been breaking into homes of registered McKealy owners and systematically replacing them with the copies. No one found out about it."

"Except for Jasmine," Brian interjected. "She caught Kline one day going through the galleries records and making notation of the frames that were purchased at the same time. He reluctantly agreed to cut her into his scam and only because she was consistently able to outsell him."

"A tenuous partnership," Sy said.

"And then some," Brian agreed. "She split her commission with him with the idea that she was going to get a decent payout when the McKealys sold posthumously on the black market after he kicked the bucket. Artwork is always worth more when the artist is dead."

Sy chuckled. "And Jasmine flirts with Scofield, finds out he's a CSI...That had to sound like a gold mine to them. Whatever mistakes they made lifting the originals could be cleaned up at the crime scene by Scofield. No one would be any the wiser." She paused to sip her coffee. "And poor Sandy didn't know what they were scheming.

She just wanted the pictures to do her art pageant. I think she truly thought she loved Henry. I can sympathize with that."

"And Kline volunteered often at the opera house," Mike wiped sugar from his chin. "It was a way for him to get into performances for free. So when he found out Henry already gave Sandy the artwork, he thought he caught a break and swapped the pictures out in the property locker, staging the so-called break-in."

Brian snapped his fingers. "Oh, yeah, the homeless man you rescued outside the theater, remember him? He's proved to be a valuable witness. Gunter gave him an impromptu interview after they got the man's blood-sugar under control. He was able to identify Sandy and Stephen both, and place their comings and goings."

Sy chewed her lower lip, "How is he?"

"He'll recover fine. Good news is they've been able to I.D. him and they found a sister living near Springfield. I guess she's on her way to collect him. It's the talk of the hospital, apparently, a true Hollywood ending."

"There's a lesson there somewhere," Mike said, shaking his head. "I don't think I'll ever understand being so mad at anyone leaving me out of their will that I would stoop to that sort of crap. Art theft? Burglary?"

Viktor rubbed his chin in thought, "Greed is powerful motivator, no? When mixed with revenge…you be amazed at what you accomplish."

"Yeah, but…" Mike's voice was sheer disbelief. "Was Scofield driven by greed? I can't imagine he'd risk his career on this scheme for a paycheck that may happen or not."

Sy set her mug down on the coffee table. "I can answer that. When Kitty Donavon brought her nephew with her to Wilcox and

Sherry's, Kline recognized her as McKealy's model, the stripper he dated when he attended Lake Forest."

"Clever, he called her whore so we couldn't trace it back to Kitty," Brian looked at her in askance and she tapped her temple indicating she had gleaned the information during their visit with her. "And Scofield didn't like it?" he asked.

"Not a bit. William met her in one of his art classes. You know, the kind a nude model sits on a stool while a classroom full of twenty-somethings sketch her? As a stripper, she was already used to the exposure," Sy said. "Now, Scofield probably decided that no one should own a painting of his dear auntie without her knowledge or maybe he felt he could get revenge for her broken heart. Stealing the work was his perverse way of protecting her somehow and getting back at the man who exploited her, so to speak."

Brian shrugged, "I guess chivalry isn't dead after all. After Schofield's song and dance, we almost didn't need a search warrant. Mrs. Donavon dug all kinds of things out for us to tag as evidence while waiting for the ambulance. Mandy said they've already found trace evidence on two of the shotguns in her possession and from her laundry basket, they found the clothing our murderers wore that night."

Mike frowned, "They're hoping to find trace off the clothing as well but Ms. Donavon claims she washed the clothes with dandruff shampoo. Apparently, she did that so often for Scofield after he'd been through a gruesome crime scene, she didn't think anything of the blood."

Sy was puzzled. "Why dandruff shampoo?"

To her surprise it was Annika who answered, while she was refilling the aebleskiver bowl. "Meezz Donavon ask me once eef I had seecrit to reemoove blud stains from clothes. I tell her dandruff shampoo best thing for stains." She gathered some empty dishes and exited as quietly as she had appeared.

Gunny, standing at the window, broke his silence. "I hear Ms. Donavon went to the hospital? Do we know how she's doing?"

Brian projected his voice to cross the distance. "They just wanted to keep her for observation. They can't prove stun-guns cause health issues, but they can't disprove it either. After that teen died in Texas, people have been nervous about them."

"Well I bet she's just fit to be tied. She doesn't do hospitals." Gunny glanced at his watch. "I'd better get going. I've got to check in with the wife and let her know I survived another day."

THE HOUR PUSHED PAST MIDNIGHT as he rose to say his goodbyes. Sy gave Gunny a solid hug and encouraged him to take the position working for her father. "I'm moving soon as possible anyway, so there's no real need of you sticking around."

"It all depends on the wife," he said, and followed Annika to the door.

She returned in time to answer the house phone when it rang, interrupting their conference. Annika announced the call was from Tina just as the elevator dinged Gunny's departure.

Sy rolled her eyes and crossed the floor to the phone. "Tina, how are you feeling?"

"Simone...oh crap, I didn't notice the time. I've been avoiding the phone. The press has been calling non-stop since it got out that I'm pregnant."

"It's okay, Tina, I haven't gone to bed yet."

"Do you never sleep? Anyway, you said it was okay for me to go ahead and plan the funeral, right? Well, I met with the director. I'll have to have the bill paid before the ceremony." Tina's voice was timid.

Sy took a deep breath, knowing that the tab was going to be expensive. If she didn't give Tina carte-blanche though, they would have bickered constantly. As much as she didn't want a circus to happen at the burial site, she decided it was worth it for the peace of mind. "Don't stress, Tina. I'll pay it. I'll get the life insurance policies tomorrow from Lloyd's so trust me, it won't bankrupt us."

Tina sounded relieved. "Okay, thanks. I may have gone a little overboard with the doves and the carriage and stuff, but I think he's worth it. He's my big brother, and he's always looked out for me, even when I didn't want him to."

"No worries, Kiddo. I gotta run so stay away from the press and try to relax. We don't want you to stress out and miscarry." She ended the call to dial another. "Barry, check over Henry's plot and service contracts when you get the chance and make sure they're not trying to stiff us. I know Henry paid a ton of money already to the home, so there's a chance they might try to double-dip us." Satisfied with the message, she returned to the sofa.

"Where is Barry?" Brian asked, glancing around. "I thought for sure he'd be here."

"I promised a million dollars to the first person who could lead us to the killer, and that I'd pay the attorney fees as a thank you present. Barry's seeing to my promises right now. Have we heard anything more about McKealy's condition? Has he come out of the coma yet?"

Mike shook his head. "He's still out and the doctors don't think he'll recover."

Sy grimaced. "Shame, really. Sandy's only stake in all this was that pageant. Because she planned her assault on McKealy, though, she'll get murder one if he doesn't come out of it, regardless of the cancer. Kline and Scofield will probably only get a couple points of manslaughter and grand larceny, but will still have less jail time in the long run."

"I wouldn't say that," Brian stifled a yawn into his hand. "If Barry is tending to Kline's defense, he's only going to do it to a certain point. He'll see to it the stiffest sentence possible is applied to their fates I'm sure."

"You're right of course. I don't know why I'm worried," Sy sighed. "Barry's probably the one who encouraged Kline to roll on Scofield to begin with."

THE NIGHT BROKE THEM UP AFTER THAT. Mike took Gunny's example and left for his hotel home. Viktor bid them good night and disappeared down the hall towards the master bedroom. Sy could hear Annika running the dishwasher in the kitchen. Alone in the sitting room with Brian, she felt self-conscious, nervous. "We need to talk, you and I," she told him, leaning back.

"I suppose we do." He sounded unsure of her intent.

She took a moment to collect her thoughts. "I don't know where for sure I'm going to go from here. At first I thought to return to Switzerland, but now, I've no desire to leave."

"What possible reason could there be to keep you from Switzerland, a mea vrabie?" With a twinkle in his eyes, Brian stole the term of endearment from her father.

"I don't want to go...alone."

"Well," he tucked an errant strand of hair behind her ear, a touch that released butterflies in her stomach. "As a gentleman, I cannot allow you to travel on your own. It isn't safe."

"What do you suggest I do then?"

He leaned forward, his fingertips gracing her chin, his forehead touching hers. A heat wave developed in the space between them, driving her heartbeat faster. She tipped her lips closer, ready for the kiss that begged to exist.

His cell phone rang, breaking the spell holding them. Brian held her gaze while the phone nagged him, until he cursed under his breath. "Rotten fucking timing." He glanced at this cell screen, frowning at the display, and answered, "Todd Chambers, how's the investigation going?"

Sy sat back, listening to the hum of the voice coming though his cell phone, amused at the role-reversal. For once, it wasn't her phone interrupting them.

"Something wrong with the case? I'm not assigned to it you know, jurisdiction and all?" Brian stood and paced, a private tour of the sitting room. "Sure, I can come in either Monday or Tuesday next...he did, eh? That makes no sense at all...Yeah, okay, thanks again, Todd."

Brian stood near the window when he ended his call. Sy caught his look from across the room, watched him flip his phone round and round in his hands. The moment before they were interrupted was gone. The surface of her heart cracked.

He cleared his throat, "So the ringleader to the Wint-Mart heist, this Pacelli fellow, says that he's ready to talk, but he won't talk to anyone but me. I guess he said this about two hours ago."

There was something in his voice she couldn't identify. "So what's up?"

"Todd said he just got a call from the prison. They found Pacellli dead in his cell. He was hanging from the ceiling with his bed sheet around his neck."

"Wait, why hang himself if he's ready to talk?" Sy scratched her head.

"Dunno," he shrugged. "I guess they're treating it like a homicide for the time being."

"So what do you want to do?"

He flashed a flirtatious grin, "Well, I may have to go back to Ohio, but I don't want to go alone. If I asked, would you meet me in Sandusky?"

She rocked her head back and laughed, "That depends. Would I get to blow up another Wint-Mart?"

"Only if there's another hostage situation," he said. "And you do the paperwork after."

"Deal." Her impatient cell phone buzzed on the coffee table. Sy glared at it before picking it up. She intended to toss it across the room before she spied the number advertised. Groaning, she sank her head into her hands for a frustrated moment. "I have to take this, Brian, I'm so sorry."

"No worries." He turned to look out the window.

"Hej?" she answered. The woman on the other end was her Denmark contact, referring a potential contract in need of scouting services. Sy hesitated before agreeing to appointment. She would have to leave Wednesday after the funeral service to make Copenhagen in time. Depressed, she ended her call and explained the situation to Brian. "I'm not going to be able to meet you Sandusky."

"Another time then," he sauntered towards the bedrooms, yawning. "It won't be the same without you Sy."

She rose from the couch, resigned to the night. Her eyes felt heavy in their sockets and there was a warm bed down the hall bidding her to go to sleep. Perhaps in the light of day, she would find another opportunity to say what she wanted to say.

She turned off the lights. Darkness flooded the condo and she listened to the silence. Exhaling, she relaxed her mind and stretched her thoughts through the moonless space to connect with her knight-in-something-armor. *Good night, Brian.*

Her heart skipped a beat when she caught his sleepy reply, *Sweet dreams, Sy.*

CHAPTER XXXVII

To Say Goodbye

T HERE WAS AN ENORMOUS CROWD of celebrities gathered for the funeral of Henry Freitag. Brian was bothered by his lack of social status until he saw a movie star adjust her pantyhose behind a tombstone. He chuckled and put his sunglasses on as the sun played peek-a-boo with a lazy cloud. The humid day was mild but a front of high pressure was forming in Chicago-land, and threatened to bring with it an Indian summer. The unprecedented mild weather they'd been blessed with was moving on to seek another venue.

He sat with the family at Sy's instance and Tina's scorn. Barry and Gunny were also in the reserved seats; Barry in his expensive suit while Gunny wore every piece of tin and ribbon he had earned on his Marine uniform. Brian noticed the security must've been handled by Viktor's company, because Gunter and Yousef stood near the podium, ear-buds visible in their ears.

The guest list of the other attendees was the who's who of Hollywood and Cannes. Members of the press kept a less than respectable distance from the proceedings, but didn't harass too many of the mourners during the ceremony.

The preacher was from a local, nondescript church, and provided an equally bland service. Brian had more experience with Catholic affairs, with incense and herbs, and the up and downs of the congregation, but he found he was grateful for the change of pace, considering his only relationship with the deceased was through the woman he developed a crush for. The preacher spoke of love and forgiveness, and of ashes and dust and he ended with the Lord's Prayer. It was short, sweet, and to the point, but also sterile and commercial in delivery. Brian decided faith, like art, was subjective, and just as open to exploitation.

Tina stood as the preacher stepped down, tapped the microphone and looked down at her notes. Long, thick streaks of mascara emerged from under her sunglasses and down her cheeks. For the first time since he met her, Brian felt compassion for the actress. Tina was all alone in the world, shouldering the responsibility of carrying the last of her line. The Hollywood family was a fickle and superficial one, and would not be forgiving if she fell from grace. He hoped motherhood mellowed her out, for the child's sake if not her own.

As Tina stuttered through her initial thank you, Sy stood up and walked over to lend her comfort. Whether she did this on impulse or because she felt obligated, she was there for Tina in her difficult hour.

And Tina could not continue. She turned the microphone over to Sy and collapsed back in her seat, sobbing into a handkerchief.

"Good afternoon, thank you for coming, I... Henry Freitag was a zealot." Sy began with an edge in her voice. Brian twitched, wondering where she was going to go with her impromptu eulogy. She cleared her throat and continued. "Would that we were all so passionate about life, liberty and the pursuit of happiness. Most do not know me by sight, and that was how he protected me, sheltered me. I am Simone Freitag, and it was to my misfortune that I found him in our home, the victim of a burglary gone awry. Henry had his faults, as do we all, but I stand here before you today to publicly affirm that I am infinitely proud of his accomplishments in his career, his unyielding, albeit unconventional support of his family, and his intense passion for life itself. While his years were marred with personal, senseless tragedies, he embraced his losses so he could evolve from them instead of becoming defined by them."

Sy paused and made eye contact with Brian through his sunglasses. Feeling a tickle in the back of his mind, he knew she was seeking his support. He simply thought, *I'm still here,* and he hoped that helped.

She nodded. "Henry often said he was privileged beyond measure, to have been born an American, to have traveled the world, and to have the honor of claiming Chicago as his home. As his wife, I feel privileged beyond measure to say I knew him best, and still he was able to surprise me, inspire me, and support me through his unyielding faith and liberal devotion. He quoted Abraham Lincoln to me once, saying when I die, I would like it said of me by those who know me best that I always plucked a thistle, and planted a rose where I thought a rose might grow. Henry gave me just over ten years of roses, and I would be hard-pressed to find a single bramble among them."

Several people stood up to say similar things after Sy returned to her seat. Brian squeezed her hand for support. *Well, I didn't call him a jackass and I didn't speak ill of his mistresses, so I guess I didn't do too badly, did I?* she broadcasted.

Brian exhaled. *You were far more forgiving than I would have been in your shoes. Your words were absolutely sublime.*

The dull drone went on for an hour while the flowers wilted in their containers. An actress spoke of Henry's dedication to foster 'the craft', a fellow producer spoke of the ultimate loss of talent, and a representative of the opera house spoke of his generous nature. When the last speaker sat down, the preacher offered one last prayer, and Tina signaled for the doves to be released. As they flew off, a dove circled back and bombed the casket. A stream of white poo dripped onto the gilt handles. Brian heard Sy giggle as he struggled with his own inappropriate desire to laugh.

The gathered eventually broke away and some did their best to avoid the photographers and reporters. Tina baled with Tori Tanner and a few of her Hollywood friends. Brian stood for a long time with Sy as she watched the grave-diggers cover the casket with earth.

Viktor asked if she was ready to leave. Nodding, Sy joined them on the slow, measured walk out to the limousine. Reporters tried to harass them as well, but Barry ran interference while Gunter and Yousef cleared a path. Once their group was inside the vehicle, the driver took them down the cemetery path and out onto the main road.

A sign marked the miles to O'Hare International. There wasn't much time left. With the certainty of goodbye looming before him, Brian tapped a heel, unable to sit still as the limousine turned onto the highway. Fate conspired against him from the moment Scofield was arrested, if not before, keeping the opportunity to speak to Sy just beyond his reach. He was about to abandon hope, resign himself to a future without Sy, when she slipped her hand in his and leaned her head against his shoulder. He let go the breath he didn't realize he was holding and wrapped an arm around her.

Viktor broke the long silence. "I am proud of you, a mea vrabie. You were polite and remain composed through whole ceremony."

Brian agreed. "I think you spoke better of Henry than he deserved, certainly."

Sy buried a giggle against his chest. "Not through my own willpower though. I have a secret and I've been dying to tell someone."

Viktor shook his head. "I don't need to hear secret. You pose security threat if you tell secret."

"It's not that sort of secret, Papa, I promise."

"What is it?" Brian shifted to look in her odd-colored eyes. They laughed back like stars.

"Henry wasn't in the box," she blurted.

Brian couldn't help laughing. Barry, however, leaned forward with a serious expression. "Henry wasn't in the box," he repeated.

She nodded, explaining the director took her aside right before the ceremony to confess. "If I had been there with Tina to help make arrangements," Sy wiped tears from her eyes, "it might have turned out better. You see, Henry's original wishes were that he be cremated and then he changed his mind. Well there was a mix-up with the paperwork, probably because Tina staged some sort of over-dramatic fit. The director didn't know what to do."

"Do you want me to pursue this, legally?" Barry asked, indicating he had concerns about the funeral home's conduct.

Sy shot him a look. "No, there's no need, Barry. People make mistakes. I actually prefer it this way anyway. It's something I can tell Tina's grandchildren about in fifty years."

"So who's in the box?" Brian asked.

"No one. They cremated Henry before they caught the mix-up. The director asked me what I wanted to do. I said to fill an urn and hand him off to me later, and load the casket with about a hundred and seventy pounds of broken or unclaimed tombstones." Pride beamed from Sy's smile. "I know that's what Henry would've done if the roles were reversed, or especially if it was his sister being planted."

"So Henry wasn't at his own funeral?" Brian shook his head, laughing anew. "What are the odds?"

"The question now is: do I ever tell Tina?"

Viktor shrugged. "Ignorance is blissful. She has other things to worry about, no?"

THE LIMO PULLED INTO THE PARKING LOT at the private hanger. The driver assisted with doors and luggage, and before long Brian stood at the edge of the tarmac, facing the moment he long feared. Goodbyes made him feel awkward, clumsy, and this one was proving difficult. Viktor clapped a hand on his shoulder, "Brian Kirby, Special Agent. It has been pleasure, no? Do not be stranger."

"Thank you, Viktor," Brian breathed. "I don't intend to be."

"I'll catch up Papa," Sy said, encouraging her father to start for the jet along with Gunter and Yousef, while Barry kept a respectable distance, inspecting his fingernails with the same intensity he displayed over paperwork. Sy cast a furtive glance over her shoulder. "Look, Brian, I know timing hasn't exactly been on our side..."

Brian caught movement beyond the fence. "It's about to get worse," he groaned, pointing to a growing crowd of paparazzi. Airport security rushed to the scene as shouts and camera noises flooded across the divide between them. The longer they stood there watching, the deeper the rows of flashing cameras became. Barry began a slow, measured walk towards the crowd, like a lone firefighter to a wildfire, determined to complete a mission. Brian felt like he was watching a train wreck in slow motion, defenseless against the coming aftermath of a tragedy.

"Mercenaries," Sy spat, following with a stream of Romanian profanities Brian wasn't sure he wanted to understand. "I've been so good about avoiding the tabloids. And now, we're about to be plastered across the front pages."

An idea ghosted his thoughts. "Do you trust me?" Brian asked.

Her eyes narrowed. "Not when you're using that tone of voice. What are you up to?"

"I have some tricks up my sleeve. If this works, you're not the only one who can outwit the press with a phone call." He picked a speed-dial number from his phone. When the line answered, he rattled off his passcode. "Whiskey. Echo. Yankee. Tango. Agent compromised. I repeat, agent compromised." He finished his message with their location.

"That sounded official," she said. "What's that going to accomplish?"

"You'll see. Give it about ten minutes, give or take. Just don't leave my side."

She raised an eyebrow at him before glaring back at the reporters pressed up against the gate. They were like a pack of hungry, angry wolves at the scent of a wounded lamb, their shutters and flashes snapping and snarling at the distance. Sy muttered something about a pinot noir. "Tell me you called in an airstrike or something."

He tossed a shrug about his shoulders. "Or something." He grabbed her arm and spun her around to face him, her back to the circus. "Ignore them. Concentrate on me. On the here and now."

A thin smile framed her response. "I'll give it the old college try."

"Look, I know you haven't known me that long, and I know how inappropriate this is going to sound. After all, we just buried your husband-"

"-Well, technically-"

"-But I think there's something here, between us, and I think it's worth investigating."

Her cheeks turned a bright crimson and her voice hushed with timidity. "You don't think I'm a freak of nature?"

He grinned. "Negative. I think you're certifiably nuts and you have the worst taste in men."

"Oh, so what does that make you?"

"An improvement?" She tried to wrench free, but he held her fast. "Let me finish."

She stopped struggling with a sigh.

"You're nuts. But you're also the best time I've ever had, and I'm not ready to say goodbye just yet."

Screeching tires and sirens wailed over the clamor of the press just as Sy's jet started up its engines. Frenzied camera flashes and the combined commotion of the machines drowned them in ear bending noise as they stood exposed on the tarmac. She turned from him to watch the unfolding scene. The back of his mind buzzed with her voice. *What the hell?*

Agent compromised, he replied. He turned her around again, catching her in his arms, and he kissed her. All noise became background to the wild beating of his heart. She tasted sweet, reminiscent of berries and summer rains. There was power between them, around them, making the whole world disappear. He let her go when time drifted back into shadowy existence.

Wow, she broadcasted, a sheepish grin crossing her lips. *Why did you kiss me?*

I wanted to, he replied. *Do you object?*

No, but... She pointed to the chaos beyond the fence, at the federal agents surrounding the paparazzi. *There's no way this isn't making to the tabloids. What's that racket all about anyway?*

I told you, agent compromised. I'm still technically undercover. The Bureau can't afford to have my face in the tabloids. Right now, all those paparazzi are getting their cameras confiscated in the name of National Security.

The look of adoration in her odd-colored eyes was worth the amount of paperwork he would face and the stern reprimand from Jericho for pulling that card when he didn't really need to. Brian basked in it for a long glorious moment.

She kissed him back. *Just in case.*

I need to go now. The downside to cashing in these chips is I have to have a powwow with a handler.

Wait! She grabbed his arm. *Yes, I think this, whatever this is, is worth investigating, but what if I'm on the rebound. Friendship is more important isn't it?*

You've already got that, Sy. But if you want to give it some time, I'm not going anywhere. Give me a call when you get stateside again, and...we'll see where this goes.

I'm holding you to that Brian. If you don't answer my call, I will personally feed you to the alligators.

Don't burn down anything without me. He turned and walked towards the angry mob.

The sun waned in the western sky as night, eager to claim the world for its own, descended with force upon them. Despite the melancholy ache creeping into his heart as Sy boarded her jet, even the circus of angry camera men and indignant federal agents couldn't shake his positive outlook. Timing couldn't have been worse, but it turned out better than he had hoped.

He took a moment in the midst of the chaos to watch the jet ascend into the twilight. Closing his eyes, he inhaled, imaging a small vineyard in the Chardonnay countryside, where stood his princess waiting for his homecoming.

FINIS

Also By
Shelton Keys Dunning:

PUBLISHED THROUGH OLDEWOLFF PRINTS:

Hagatha Kittridge Must Die

PUBLISHED THROUGH BANNERWING BOOKS:

Short Stories/Flash Fiction

Escape (Precipice 2012 volume 1)
Sticky's Cake (Precipice 2012 volume 1)
The Soldier's Gambit (Precipice 2013 volume 2)

Thank You

There are many authors out there and so many good books to read. I am humbled and grateful that *The Trouble with Henry* has found a place on your bookshelf.

Sincerely,

S.K. Dunning

P.S. – I invite you to stop by and say hi. The more the merrier!
www.sheltonkeysdunning.com
@SheltonKDunning +SheltonKeysDunning
http://skdunning.tumblr.com
http://sheltonkeysdunning.blogspot.com
http://www.flickr.com/photos/skdunning/

COMING SOON

The
Cold Side
of Trouble

Simone Freitag reunites with FBI agent Brian Kirby for another adventure. A body is discovered in a cabin fire just as three teens go missing from a Revolutionary War Reenactment near Brian's hometown of Simplicity Forge. Brian returns to his Smokey Mountain roots when he learns one of those missing teens is his youngest sister, Lucy. But missing teens and murderers have more to fear than the Redcoats and the troubles of an isolated town. A cold–front is coming, and Lucy's kidnapper better pray that Mother Nature finds him before Brian Kirby does.

ABOUT THE AUTHOR

Shelton Keys Dunning has been passionate about reading and
writing since she knew words existed, loving the escape from
reality that both afford. In her spare time, she knits poorly,
takes out-of-focus pictures, runs from spiders, and grows
weeds in the dirt. Her husband laughs at and with her every
chance he gets. Together they live with a tortoise-shell cat
named Whiskey, and dream impossible dreams.